UNKNOWN

HEATHER CRITCHLOW

First published in the United Kingdom in 2025 by

Canelo Crime, an imprint of
Canelo Digital Publishing Limited,
20 Vauxhall Bridge Road,
London SW1V 2SA
United Kingdom

A Penguin Random House Company
The authorised representative in the EEA is Dorling Kindersley Verlag GmbH.
Arnulfstr. 124, 80636 Munich, Germany

Copyright © Heather Critchlow 2025

The moral right of Heather Critchlow to be identified as the creator of this work has been asserted in accordance with the Copyright, Designs and Patents Act, 1988.
All rights reserved. No part of this publication may be reproduced or transmitted in any form or by any means, electronic or mechanical, including photocopy, recording, or any information storage and retrieval system, without permission in writing from the publisher.
No part of this book may be used or reproduced in any manner for the purpose of training artificial intelligence technologies or systems. In accordance with Article 4(3) of the DSM Directive 2019/790, Canelo expressly reserves this work from the text and data mining exception.

A CIP catalogue record for this book is available from the British Library.

Print ISBN 978 1 83598 100 9
Ebook ISBN 978 1 83598 101 6

This book is a work of fiction. Names, characters, businesses, organizations, places and events are either the product of the author's imagination or are used fictitiously. Any resemblance to actual persons, living or dead, events or locales is entirely coincidental.

Cover design by Andrew Smith

Cover images © Shutterstock

Printed and bound in Great Britain by Clays Ltd, Elcograf S.p.A.

Look for more great books at
www.canelo.co | www.dk.com

To Will, Rachel and Adam, for treading the paths of my imagination.

PROLOGUE

Her feet aren't as steady on the path as they used to be. It's strange to fumble once-familiar steps, to look down and see thinned-out ankles and scrawny calves, when inside you are still the girl with the skinny legs and the knitted sweater with the threads unravelling.

Everything else around her is a facsimile of memory – the Highland landscape laid out just as she remembers it. Fifty-one years on, the overwhelming rush of nostalgia is painful. It makes her chest clench and, as she reaches the top of the brae, she has to stop and push her hand hard against herself to keep her heart in her chest, lungs bursting from emotion as well as physical exertion. Her vision sways and then the purple-clad hills come back into focus.

Above her and out of sight lies the lochan: a plate of fresh glass, reflecting a chasm of sky. The thought of it makes her shiver. Beneath its waters lie secrets kept too long. The wind strikes and she staggers a little, planting her feet more securely between the rocks. When she thinks back to that time, it still hurts like a raw wound. In fact, it's worse with an adult's perspective. She aches for the girl she was. It's time to set those secrets free.

Despite the lateness of the hour, it's bright as noon. She had forgotten how the land of her birth keeps the light for longer in the summer, how it barely gets dark at all and the earth seems to glow. At home, night falls like a switch has been flicked.

Since her trip through the village, memories have flooded into her mind and the anger has grown. She was just a child back then. The same age as her granddaughter Leia is now. She was too young to understand, too young to be culpable.

The woman shivers, a full-body movement that goes right through her. There's a creeping feeling at her back and in the shadows of the rocks. It's the ghosts of the past, that's all it is. It's time to throw back the shutters and hold him to account. She thought about going straight to the police station but had an unaccountable urge to see this place again first. To decide if it is real or a figment of nightmare.

Her mind flutters to her daughters. At home, capable, married and running their lives. To her son. Her sandy, sun-tanned grandchildren feel like little drops of memory, quenching her thirst but no longer belonging to her. They'll be having the usual Sunday meal later, the family collected together, loud and raucous and foreign to her. Recently, she's been sitting in the corner, observing instead of partaking. It's been that way since Ian died. Her slide into obsolescence beginning with widowhood.

She hadn't realised until she returned to Scotland, to the scene of her crime, that *this* is home, not there. She's only been borrowing her adopted country and even after all these years, it doesn't fit properly; it's been rubbing a blister on her soul.

Coughing a little and waiting to recover, she steels herself and sets off once more, leaving the well-trodden path and inching upwards, one laboured footstep at a time.

It's weighing her down, all this guilt. She longs to be free of it, to let it go.

A burn cuts a trickling path through the undergrowth to her right, invisible but insistent, spilling from the lochan's chilled waters. Then a rock skitters on the slope above her and she startles, turning to see. The woman shades her eyes with a thin hand, liver-spotted and bony, but she is looking into the sun and she cannot tell if there are sheep above her, or deer, or just the shifting of the rock face as the day cools down.

Finally, she makes it to the shore. Something grips her inside, like a hand. Her legs are unsteady and the water makes her queasy with memory. Rattled, she turns from it and scans the slope above, seeking out her destination.

It takes another hour to ascend the cold valley, dark and untouched now by the sun, eschewed by walkers in favour of the ridge above.

Finally, she finds it. The flat area of grass surrounded by rocks. She collapses onto the green platform with relief, sweat cooling on her as she presses her forehead to the earth. The thing she did that day was the work of a moment, but it cast its ripples through the rest of her life.

It is there, as she lies prone, sucking in air, that he finds her.

She cries out in recognition as he steps over the lip of the rise onto the platform. Of course. A wash of tiredness covers her like a weighted blanket. The demon is here. Now and then merge together. Those eyes. That angular jaw. Not something you'd ever really forget. She staggers to her feet because she's not that girl, not anymore. She turns to face him and her rage rises.

CHAPTER ONE

The glasses sparkle in the light of the chandeliers as the waiter pours foaming champagne into a cluster of flutes crammed onto the round table. Some of the liquid oozes over the top but is immediately soaked up by the thick white tablecloth. Cal barely notices, transfixed by the refracted beauty that glimmers across the stuffed ballroom, overwhelmed by the cacophony of industry small-talk and laughter around him. He tucks a finger into the collar of his shirt, stretching it a little, unused to the constraints of a dinner jacket and bow tie. This is not the natural habitat of the true-crime podcaster.

Shona slips her hand into his beneath the table and squeezes, drawing his attention back from the sight of the Grosvenor Ballroom on Park Lane in full swing. She looks radiant – her shoulder-length blonde hair swept up into an elegant chignon and her shoulders shimmering above a tight black sheath. Outside, a heatwave is assaulting the capital, but in here, underground, it is cooler.

'You're glittering,' he tells her, pressing a finger experimentally to her collarbone. 'Literally.'

She laughs, passing one of the glasses to him, and her earrings dance in the light. 'It's that stuff Chrissie gave me for Christmas. Finally, a chance to use it.' Her face softens at the mention of Cal's daughter, who called from her

Edinburgh uni flat earlier to wish him luck. 'We're going to be finding it everywhere, I'm afraid.'

He kisses her, momentarily forgetting the mixture of nerves and gin and tonic in his stomach. 'Everywhere? Do you promise?'

Shona raises an eyebrow suggestively and then turns to her left, where Cal's producer Sarah is tugging her arm to introduce her to one of the advertisers. As a forensic anthropologist, Shona is a novelty in this room of media darlings and Sarah is delighted to use her to full effect. Unlike Cal, his producer is in her element. Her red dress is low-cut and devastating, judging by the looks of most of the men in the room. She's ignoring every one of them, far more interested in lining up funding for future projects and making business connections. As ever, he's in awe of the younger woman.

He knows Shona doesn't mind lending her expertise, and her distraction gives him another moment to catch his breath. He doesn't fit in here. Definitely doesn't deserve the award for which his *Finding Justice* podcast is nominated.

Another waiter sets a perfectly round beetroot and goat's cheese tart in front of him. He picks up a fork and toys with the lamb's lettuce garnish, unable to eat but trying to force himself. He longs to break free from this place. On the surface, it is glossy, but all he sees is a carefully crafted veneer. Luckily, Cal knows he won't win the award – the list of competitors is intimidating – but he's struggling to dispel a sense of unease. He's the proverbial fish, flopping around on the sumptuous carpet, waiting for someone to put him back in the water and leave him alone.

'Angie texted,' Shona whispers in his ear. He turns, his attention snagged by the mention of the mother of the subject of his last podcast series. 'She says good luck. They're all rooting for you.'

He tries to smile. It doesn't fool Shona.

'What's up?'

'It feels wrong,' he says, gesturing at the excesses around them. 'Indulgent.'

How can he sit here and drink champagne when the families he works with have voids in their lives that can never be filled? It's as if he's profiting from their misfortune. He knows all too well how they feel. He has his own void too.

Shona's fingers close over his. 'I know you're not one for pomp and ceremony, but this is a big deal, Cal. No matter what happens, the nomination is a testament to the sacrifices you've made. It's another sign that people have listened, that these stories matter. No one begrudges you this.' She squeezes his hand again. 'Except maybe you.'

Cal feels a lump in his throat that is little to do with the tartlet he's failing to eat. Her words make logical sense but he feels something building inside him, threatening to burst out.

'Thank you,' he says, forcing himself to push away the past for a moment. 'It's not like I'm going to win, so we can just drink this free champagne and then maybe I can check where the rest of that glitter has got to.'

Shona tosses her head back and laughs – the paleness of her throat gleams in the glow of this night. Cal sips his drink and lets the bubbles fizz down his throat. *It's fine. He's fine.*

For the next hour, he makes polite conversation with the people Sarah has invited to the table – current and potential advertisers – fending off comments about his chances of winning and hoping they're not too disappointed when the announcement is made. The fact that the table is at the back of the room should be enough of a clue.

Eventually, the dessert plates are cleared and the room falls as quiet as a room of over a thousand people can. The host takes the microphone and the lights dim further, throwing the stage and a backdrop of stars into relief. He listens almost absent-mindedly to the first few categories, knowing Best Podcast is one of the last. Shona is right – he doesn't like big events and ceremonies. That's all this simmering feeling is. Introspection always leads him back to the same place.

Margot. Red curls, a strong personality and a fierce love for her younger brother. At nineteen, she was as much a parent to him as his mother and father were. Her absence is a phantom limb. Part of him will always be the nine-year-old he was when they lost her. Or rather, when she was taken from them. He puts his drink down to applaud the Best TV Documentary winner, an old BBC colleague, and feels the hypocrisy of this night pulsing inside him.

How can he sit here and celebrate his successes when the case he cared most about was a complete failure? Jason Barr killed his sister and walked free, and there is nothing Cal can do about it. His fingers curl into fists at the thought of the ex-nightclub bouncer.

He's so tangled in the web of the past, Cal isn't listening to the acceptance speeches and hardly realises they are on to his category. Not that it matters. It's only when he catches the excited glances thrown his way by the others at the table and sees hopeful tension fix on Sarah's face that he remembers where he is and sits up straight, readying a rueful, philosophical expression for the moment the announcement is made.

Everything spins and blurs around him. Too much champagne? He should have paced himself. That's why he's spiralling over Margot, maudlin and regretful when he has promised himself he would relinquish the anger. He tries to tune into the summary of each of the nominated shows. His money's on the history podcast – it has record numbers and is far glossier than all the other offerings.

Then it's happening. His name inexplicably in the mouth of the comedian holding a gold trophy shaped like a microphone. The rush of sound and cheers around him, Shona leaning in to hug him, Sarah leaping to her feet and shrieking in triumph. *What's happening?*

It comes to him like an echo down a long corridor, gradually getting closer, coming into focus. Tears in Shona's eyes. 'You've won, Cal, you've won!'

They're pushing him to his feet and he's reaching for Sarah, beckoning her to come and accept the award, but she's shaking her head, laughing, and he's stumbling across the room alone but surrounded by people. He's acutely aware of the clumsiness of his movements, the applause and the focus, the long time it takes to walk to the stage.

Then he's there, mounting the steps on shaky legs, and the applause dies down. He holds the trophy in his hands and everything stills as he realises he hasn't prepared anything to say. There is no 'just in case' speech in his pocket. His mind is a sheet of blank paper and he needs something, fast. All he feels is despair. He steps up to the lectern, his mouth dry and the award slipping in his sweaty fingers.

'Er… wow. Good evening. Thank you…'

The host is frowning at the delay, his body language twitchy and impatient. It's hot up here under the lights and Cal can't see past the glare to the individuals – the audience an amorphous mass in the darkness. Out there, somewhere, are Shona and Sarah.

He begins by rattling through the personal and professional thank yous, starting with the families of the missing and murdered, and praying he hasn't missed anyone at the production company. The host is shifting forward in anticipation of regaining the microphone when Cal pauses and looks directly at the audience. That wave of tiredness once more sweeps over him. More than that. He's pissed off. He doesn't want this charade anymore. *Enough*.

'Our podcast is called *Finding Justice*,' he says. 'And I've dedicated my life to looking for that very thing. The reality is – it's not always possible to find. All you have to do is look at our politicians and our establishments to see that sometimes there is no justice. That those who trample and hurt other people rise to the top. It's torture, watching perpetrators freed on a technicality or given token jail terms. For the families of the missing and murdered, there is no reprieve. Their grief is a life sentence. Our justice system makes a mockery of their pain.'

The room is utterly still now. He can almost touch the moving beast of silence. Where is he going with this? It's like jumping from a height, the earth billowing up towards him. The host is frozen, a rictus smile on his face, eyes darting in panic.

'I am living a life sentence of my own. My sister Margot was abducted from the side of a country road and killed almost forty years ago. Last year, her murderer was acquitted by a jury of his peers. I cannot keep pretending that when you find the truth, it fixes things. I know the truth and it made no difference.'

He touches the shining trophy with one finger, notices his name engraved on the tiny plaque at its foot. 'Thank you, sincerely, for this honour, but I will not accept this award while Jason Barr walks free.'

There's a moment, a pause and an intake of breath, then the sound explodes around him. Voices, jabbering, shouting, calling his name. Cal is already gone: down the steps, through the fire doors, out into the stifling night, the trophy abandoned on the podium behind him.

CHAPTER TWO

It's early but they aren't the first to park in the car park at the foot of Ben Lawers. As Cal swings his backpack onto his shoulders, he takes in the small red Mini nestled in a shady spot, though there will be no respite from the heat anywhere in a few hours' time. Shona clicks the fob of the car, locking it with their planned route displayed on the dashboard. She sprays her face with suncream and tosses him the can.

Cal looks up at the hill, resplendent in the morning air. 'I hope we have enough water with us.' He looks down at the dog doubtfully, though his backpack is straining at the seams with bottles.

'Just imagine the breeze up there. I can't wait. Rocket will be happier too.'

Hearing his name, the labrador bounces on his paws and flaps his tail.

'We can always cut it short if he struggles.'

In the south, extreme temperatures have been cracking buildings, threatening the vulnerable and desiccating greenery for weeks. There's been talk of a national emergency, forest fires raging in the south-west. Now, the heatwave has travelled north, the sun turning its attention to the verdant Scottish landscape. It's like being in the south of France – out in the garden in T-shirts and shorts, the long nights stifling and close. Cal enjoys warm climates but even he is struggling with the soaring mercury.

It's a relief to have a few days away at Loch Tay to decompress from the shitstorm of the Park Lane awards ceremony. He's already had a threatening letter from Jason Barr's solicitors, reminding him of the man's acquittal – as if he could forget – and Detective Inspector Foulds, who led the investigation into Margot's death, has been tasked with warning him that he's treading a fine line.

'You're a journalist,' she'd thundered down the phone. 'Do I really need to explain slander to you?'

Meanwhile, Sarah's fury is apparently depthless. They've lost advertisers, and the series is hanging by a thread. The worst thing is: he doesn't care.

As they set off up the hill, fourteen miles of stunning loch glittering beneath them, Cal hopes the mountains will give him some calm and headspace. Maybe when he comes back down, he'll know what to do.

'Penny for them,' Shona says, as they pause at the head of the path where it crosses from nature reserve into the mid-level slopes. Cal passes her a water bottle and wipes the sweat from his face. His skin is already pink from heat and exertion, his cap sticking to his head.

'Sarah emailed again last night. She wants a new series fast. She's trying to salvage the unsalvageable.'

'It's not beyond hope, surely?'

A faint breeze stirs the air around them for the slightest second. Cal is afraid to say what he's really thinking. All there is for long moments is the tramp of their feet on the path, loose stones sliding a little, the dog snuffling in the heather.

'I've lost the drive. It just seems so hopeless,' he says eventually, picturing the families of the missing, the way uncertainty eats them from the inside until they're nothing more than shells. 'The thought of doing it all over again… I'm not sure I can face it.'

Shona waits a moment before answering. 'It's a lot – I've seen what it does to you. Total immersion in someone else's loss, adding to your own. You've clearly been struggling.'

'It's that obvious?'

'Well, you did try and torpedo your career pretty publicly last week, so…'

'But if I give it up, then what?'

The idea of being set adrift into a new life terrifies him.

'You'll figure this out. But, Cal… you have to tell Sarah how you're feeling.'

He sighs, swept by fatigue that makes him want to just lie down in the middle of the path and close his eyes.

'I know. I will.'

They tackle the mountain in stages, occasionally catching a glimpse of a lone walker in a green T-shirt as a flash above them – the owner of the red Mini, most likely. Below, cars fill the car park and start to line the verge. Tiny figures string out along the paths beneath them and he is again glad for their early start. Maybe the peace and clarity he needs are just ahead.

Rocket bounds up the steep sections and they summit Ben Lawers via Beinn Ghlas by nine, relieved by the tantalising breezes on the ridge that leads to An Stùc and the next two peaks. As they scramble to the marker on the summit, Cal skirts the peak while Shona takes a direct route a few metres to his left. Intent on placing his feet in the right spots, he startles when he realises the woman in the green T-shirt is sitting on a rock a few metres away, staring out at the view. She is younger than he expected, and perfectly coiffed and made-up, as if she were going to a party, not up a mountain.

'Beautiful day for it,' he says, halting, his breath heaving.

The views are breathtaking: Loch Tay below, a long blue ribbon running from Kenmore to Killin.

The woman doesn't seem to register him for a moment. Then she jerks around, seeming confused, off balance.

'It is,' she says, regaining her composure and turning back to the view, but not before Cal sees that her eyes are red. Her hand shakes as she lifts a shining red water bottle from the rock next to her and slots it into her bag. 'Lovely.'

Cal feels bad for disturbing her peace. He can hear Shona nearby, pulling snacks from their pack and fending off Rocket's insistent labrador nose, so he beats a retreat towards them, grabbing the dog's collar just in time to stop him stealing their lunch.

He clearly stumbled on the woman in a private moment, but he finds the encounter has rattled him. There was something in her eyes – a misery he recognised – and a jitteriness to her movements that is setting off warning flares in his mind. Should he say something? Check on her? It feels wrong to intrude, but wrong not to. Dithering, he reaches for the packet of biscuits Shona has set down on a rock.

'There's a woman there,' he whispers. 'I think she's crying. I might offer her a biscuit.'

The worst she can do is tell him to bugger off. Rocket skitters beside him as he scrambles round, but when he reaches the place where she was sitting, the rock is empty. The woman is gone.

'Did she want one?'

Shona appears behind as Cal scans the ridge ahead.

'She was here but she's vanished. I can't see her.'

'Must be going fast. Maybe we'll see her further along – she might be embarrassed if she was having a private cry.'

—

The rest of the day is more of a struggle. As the sun rises high above them, the land pulses with heat and they take their breaks in whatever shade they can find, pressing themselves to the rocks for brief relief, then forcing themselves into the baking rays. Cal keeps his eyes on the horizon, checking for the woman in the green T-shirt, but he doesn't see her again.

'She must have doubled back and taken another route,' Shona says, pressing her hands to her face, which is pink and streaked with dirt. Below them, the distant loch is mockingly blue. He wishes he could plunge into it.

Their loop takes them all day. Coming down off their fifth Munro, they hit the road above the line of the loch late afternoon and slog along it to the Lochview Hotel. Cal has a blister on his heel and his T-shirt is stuck to his skin. He sinks gratefully onto a wooden bench in the heaving garden.

Content to sit and chat, they stay at the pub all evening; then Cal volunteers to walk up to the car park in the twilight and drive back for Shona and Rocket.

Limbs creaking, he sets off, relishing the aches from a good day's walking, though the blister on his foot is hot and angry. He distracts himself by admiring the fullness of the moon, the way the land is lit by a preternatural glow that he's come to associate with Highland summers. Even so, it's getting hard to see the road. He's so alone out here. A shiver runs down his spine at the open wildness of it all.

For some reason, the woman in the green T-shirt pops back into his mind as he walks. Her sadness made him feel so helpless. Hopefully, she's safely home by now. But when he rounds the bend, what he sees fills him with dread. The car park is almost deserted. Apart from their car, only one other vehicle is left. The red Mini from this morning.

CHAPTER THREE

Cal hesitates, key fob in hand. He doesn't know whose car the Mini is; he's only guessing it belongs to the woman with the haunted eyes. Maybe it belongs to someone else who's wild camping on the hills. He looks doubtfully up at the slopes to the peak. It seems so far now, looming out of the gathering dark. As if their journey up there happened in another lifetime.

He pulls open the car door and light spills out onto the gravel as he lifts his leg to slide in. But something stops him. He looks at the other car again. She seemed so young and lost. What if...? Closing his door, he walks over to the Mini, feeling unaccountably guilty for snooping. There's no note on the dashboard leaving a route or information about when the driver will be back. He peers into the back of the car, sees a few items of clothing scattered on the seats, fast-food takeaway wrappers in the footwell – nothing to tell him who it belongs to or where they've gone. Checking around him, he tries the door. Locked.

He's exhausted and wants to go home, but there's something nagging at him. Shona will probably laugh at him, but she didn't see the woman. Reluctantly, he takes out his phone and dials 101, the police non-emergency number. It's probably nothing but if he calls it in, the Mini can be someone else's problem and he and his overactive imagination can get some sleep.

His garbled explanation of his concerns about the car and the lone woman on the hill sounds strange even to his own tired ears, but the cheerful operator takes his details and asks him to read out the number plate. On hold, he paces the car park, impatient to get back to Shona and regretting his impulse to report an innocuous car. It's the sort of thing his mother would do.

'Mr Lovett?'

The cheerful voice is different. Serious now. Cal stops his pacing.

'Yes?'

'Is there anyone near the vehicle?'

'No, like I said, it's just an empty car – probably nothing, I shouldn't be wasting your time…'

'Can you confirm the location as the Ben Lawers car park next to the Edramucky nature trail?'

'That's right.'

'And you believe you saw the driver of the car on the hill earlier today?'

'Well, I don't know if it was definitely her car… That's just a guess.'

'Can I ask you to describe the woman you saw?'

'Er… she was young, thin, wearing a green T-shirt and black shorts, walking boots. She had brown hair in plaits.' He rakes through his memory for anything else. 'Sorry. I only saw her for a moment.'

But she cuts across him. 'That's very helpful. I'm sorry for the inconvenience, but can I ask that you stay with the vehicle. We have officers on the way to the location now. They shouldn't be long.'

'I don't understand. What's going on?'

It's starting to feel like he's fallen into a trap, stepped into sharp glass that he didn't know was there.

'That vehicle belongs to someone who's been reported missing.'

—

He can see the blue lights of the police car long before it reaches him. The vehicle speeds down the edge of the great loch below, before vanishing behind a fold in the landscape. He can picture it turning right after the hotel, heading up the steep road to the car park. Sure enough, it soon comes into view.

He feels chilled now, tired after a full day in the hills. He's messaged Shona and she's taken a taxi back from the pub with the dog, as there's no telling how long this is going to take. He desperately hopes the woman is okay, cursing himself for not looking harder for her when she seemed to vanish off the peak.

The police car is actually a van. Two officers in bulky vests greet him when they park up. A female officer immediately heads over to the Mini, radioing confirmation of the vehicle and flicking on a torch to look in the windows, while a salt-and-pepper-haired man with a friendly but don't-mess-with-me expression approaches Cal.

'Mr Lovett?'

'Yes,' he says. 'Call me Cal.'

'Thanks for phoning this in, Cal. Hopefully, we won't need to keep you too long.'

'It's no bother,' he says, automatically, bewildered by the efficiency of Police Scotland's response to a suspected missing walker.

'I've listened to your podcast. Are you investigating her case, then? I thought you only did cold cases? Pretty quick off the mark with this one, aye.'

Confusion seeps through Cal's thoughts. Maybe he's not hearing right. 'Sorry?'

The officer gestures at the car. 'Lucie Barnes?'

The name rings a bell on the edge of his mind. Maybe he's just too tired, but Cal can't follow what's going on. He rubs his face to try and regain some alertness.

'I've no idea who she is.'

The man's eyebrows knit together. 'She's a social media influencer who's been missing for a couple of days. We've had a welfare alert out for her and it's gone a bit mental online. She has a lot of followers.'

'I've been trying to stay off socials.' Cal can't bear to watch the clip of his implosion at the awards ceremony one more time. There are even memes of him strutting off the stage. He swallows at the thought.

'Ah, I'm the same.'

The officer opens his phone and scrolls through some images, holding the screen so Cal can see. 'Can I just check if this is the woman you saw today?'

This picture is of a smiling woman with shining hair piled on top of her head. She's posing on a beach, the turquoise water indecently blue behind her. The perfectly made-up face and pout are familiar from this morning, though her eyes are clear instead of red-rimmed.

'That's her, yes.'

'How did she seem?'

'I think she was upset. It looked like she'd been crying.'

'Right.' The officer signals to his colleague and she reaches into the van for a map, spreading it out on the bonnet.

'Can I ask you to point out exactly where you saw her?'

The torch-wielding officer trains her beam on the paper. Cal leans forward and finds the path up to the summit of Beinn Ghlas.

'Here.' He presses his finger on the map, tracing a line to the Ben Lawers peak. 'Like I said, I don't know where she went after that. We didn't see her again. I looked out for her, as I was worried.'

'Nowhere on the ridge?'

'No.'

'And what did she have with her? Do you remember?'

'Just a small pack. I didn't even see a coat or a jumper.'

'So not planning to wild camp, by the sounds of it.'

'I don't think so.'

Cal feels the threat of the slopes behind him. It's hard to imagine night up on the hill alone, lost or injured in an unforgiving landscape of steep drops and treacherous rocks. He pictures the woman looking out over the loch, remembers how drawn she seemed.

'Thank you. You've been very helpful. I'll just take your details and then you can be on your way.'

'Are you going to look for her?'

'Mountain rescue teams are on their way. We'll wait for their assessment.'

Cal unlocks his car and turns on the engine, cranking up the air conditioning as it's still warm inside. As he puts it into gear, the officers step back to give him space. He turns onto the road, the red Mini in his rear-view mirror, slipping from view.

—

It's only ten minutes along the road, but by the time he turns into the small holiday park where he and Shona are staying, Cal's eyes are heavy and his throat hurts. He pulls the car into the parking place beside their wooden cabin with views of the loch below, and turns off the engine.

He's filled with fatigue so great it's almost tempting to stay put. But then his eye catches movement at the door of their cabin, a shape emerging and barrelling towards him. His initial reaction – still wired from the events in the car park and the strangeness of the evening – is one of fear.

Quickly, he grabs for the door handle, ready to propel himself out. Then he realises who he's seeing and cries out in recognition, desperate to leave the seat for a different reason.

'Surprise!'

In a few long strides, Cal crosses the grass to his daughter and seizes her in a tight hug.

'What are you doing here?' He draws back, suddenly concerned. 'Is everything okay?'

Chrissie laughs as Rocket bounces between them, overjoyed to have his favourite humans in one place.

'Yes, Dad. I'm fine.'

'But the art elective?'

She shrugs and he's sure her face darkens for a moment but it's hard to be certain in the low light outside the lodge.

'It wasn't for me. No big deal.'

His daughter is generally an open book, not to mention studious and serious about her art. It's not like her to skim over something like this or to show up unannounced. But Cal is too weary to probe so he follows her into the kitchen, where Shona is pouring cold white wine into mismatched glasses. She looks up when they enter the room.

'You're back. What happened?'

'That woman we saw on the walk today has been reported missing,' he says. 'The mountain rescue are going out for her. A Lucie Barnes.'

'You saw Lucie Barnes?!' Chrissie stares at him. 'Today?'

'Yes, how do you know who she is?'

'She's famous for being a travel influencer. She and her boyfriend. It's been all over the internet that she's vanished. It looks like the boyfriend did something to her. There's a video doing the rounds of him gripping her wrist really tightly, and loads of people think he's really controlling.'

'Well. As of this morning, that's not true.'

His daughter's eyes shine with interest. 'So where did she go?'

'That's just the thing. She vanished. One minute she was there, the next gone.'

Shona sets down the bottle. Her face is grave. 'It's steep terrain out there… She needs to be careful.'

Cal thinks of the hulking line of hills above them, studded with rocks and steep drops. He pictures the woman's thin wrists and the air of misery that surrounded her. They were so close. He knew something was wrong and he let her slip away.

CHAPTER FOUR

MORNA, 1952

The rain hammers into her face as she walks back through the village from her work at the guest house – too tired and soaked to run, hands chafed and red with the scrubbing, buried deep in her pockets to keep as much warmth as possible. The falls are full and roaring, sweeping branches and debris downstream, making Morna shudder at the river's power as she crosses the bridge. If you jumped in there, you'd never come out.

At least she had been warm for a few hours: at Mrs Baird's guest house the fires are lit all the time and the heat clings to the building even during a cold day. It fascinates her when she catches sight of them, these families with their rounded cheeks, here for their holidays to see the falls and walk on the hills. She's now into her sixteenth year, and yet Morna has never had a holiday, suspects she never will. She can't imagine her life ever changing.

In her pocket, she clutches the few coins, wishing her da would be out when she gets back but knowing he'll be waiting for her. He needs her money for drink. The weather urges her on but the knowledge slows her, a no-win situation if ever there was one.

Their cottage is the last in the line, the gate off its hinges and the grass three feet tall out the front, once-white bricks stained by the weather and neglect. It didn't use to be like that. When her ma was alive, she played out front, she thinks. Vague memories of peg dolls they used to make clothes for with wee scraps flitter into her head but she shakes herself to push away the memories. No good comes from wallowing. Water slides down her neck.

'Far you been?'

She's barely inside when he's upon her, grasping her wrist, his other hand held out for the coins, the need for spirits in his eyes like fire. Morna cries out and only sees his face contort further. Her eyes fix on the drinkers' purple of his nose, the bumpy skin making him a repulsive creature from a fairytale or a nightmare. Old pictures show a different man, one she doesn't remember, one that might as well never have existed.

'Here,' she cries, pulling the coins from her pocket, offering them on a shaking hand.

He shoves her anyway and her body slams against the wall. Coins spill to the filthy floor, spinning in circles. As she rights herself, he curses and backhands her, sending Morna falling away from him. Her hand flies to her cheek, pressing the red-hot smarting feeling; her eyes fill with tears. Dropping to her knees, Morna gathers the coins, pressing them into his hand as he growls and swears above her, unsteady on his feet. She hates him.

Then he's gone. The door swinging, rain spilling over the step, driven in by the wind that blew her home. Morna groans and slumps from her knees back to the floor, feeling the cold seep into her bones. She's too tired to even close the door. After long minutes she forces herself back to sitting, wincing at the slight cut on her cheek where his ring caught her skin. Da hasn't had work in a long time. Blacksmiths aren't in the demand they used to be and since the horse kicked him in the head all those years ago, he's been different. Worse than he was before, when Ma was alive. People see it. Folk in the village cross the street now to avoid him, especially when he talks to himself, shaking his head so his shaggy uncut hair flies out in great tangles. No one sees her.

Morna eases herself to her feet, crossing to the open doorway and thudding the door closed. Immediately, it is quiet, save for the tap dripping. She unfurls her other fist, clutching the one coin she managed to pick off the floor. There's another in her pocket and that's all there will be until next week. It's not enough for food, never mind saving the fare and lodging money for a move to Glasgow with her friend Betty. A dream. She crosses the room to the cupboard and opens the door. All that's left for tonight is a husk of loaf, mould speckling its flank. Every week she tries to go hungry, save the coins, but always she gives in. She is weak. It feels like there is no escape in her life, no kindness, and there never will be.

—

She's been in bed for an hour or two when she hears the door to the cottage crash open below and the light go on, spilling through the cracks in the boards, illuminating her tiny room. He isn't alone; he's brought a pal from the inn and her heart thunders inside her as she listens, trying to work out who it is, for some of the men look at her with acquisitive eyes and have wandering hands.

They are as loud as if they were in the room with her, their voices bursting up through the cracks as she shivers beneath the covers in her nightie and thick socks, hot water bottle clutched to her chest. They've a different kind of bottle to keep them busy at least.

Sleep must come, because when she wakes, it is dark and still. The kind of stillness that means there's a presence. Her heart thumps in her ears so she can't hear properly, panic rising. Someone is in the room with her. No. She must be imagining it, frozen like an animal in the road. Then a footstep, staggering closer in the darkness. Terror shoots through Morna. She should get up and run but she can't, pinned by fear to the bed. She lies perfectly still, waiting, for once praying that her da will wake and come looking for his friend.

But then there is a noise below, the sound of glass breaking and her father cursing at the mess he's made. The footsteps shift towards the door, moving with drunken stealth, the air clearing around her. Morna's chest hurts. When the intruder has creaked down the staircase, she slips from the bed and lifts a chair across the room, wedging it tight beneath the handle. None of them have ever come up the stairs before. She thought she was safe here. Her hands are shaking and her bladder bursting, but she won't move the chair until morning. She won't sleep.

CHAPTER FIVE

When he checks the news on his phone the next morning, the story is on the front page of the BBC website. *Influencer missing at Loch Tay. Police issue appeal to hillwalkers.* Cal sits up in bed and slides from beneath the covers, padding to the hallway and closing the door softly so as not to disturb Shona. His hips scream with the movement and his feet ache from their exertions the previous day.

Rocket clearly feels the same. The dog's tail thumps when he sees Cal but he doesn't move from his bed, laying his head back on his paws and closing his eyes. Cal tousles his fur, scratching his ears in the place Rocket loves.

'You stay there, boy.'

He makes a cafetière of coffee and opens the doors onto the wooden deck with the view of the loch below. It's already stiflingly warm in the cabin and the weather is predicted to hit high thirties today – unheard of in this part of the world. The little holiday park is still quiet – a collection of around twenty simple wooden cabins overlooking Loch Tay.

Sitting in a patio chair on the deck, Cal scrolls the story about the hiker. Lucie, a twenty-six-year-old travel blogger, left the home she shared with boyfriend and fellow blogger Tyson four days ago and was reported missing by her sister. Police are concerned for her welfare and have appealed for anyone who has seen her to get in touch. Lucie's car was found abandoned at the Ben Lawers car park. Mountain rescue are now searching for her with drones and dogs. Bare facts.

He pours a cup of coffee and opens Instagram, searching for Lucie's account. The images are all glossy and stunning – Lucie perched on the edge of a waterfall, lying on the beach, making friends with cats in a Japanese town devoted to them. She always looks smiling, pouting, perfect. The comments section of her latest post – a stylised image of a dying pot plant – is filled with rumour and interpretation. There is speculation about her state of mind, possible depression and Tyson's behaviour, which many of Lucie's fans clearly see as controlling. He studies her smiling face, flushed cheek pressed against Tyson's on a night out, his hand awkwardly holding her wrist by her side. Can you read anything more into her expression or is it just an awkward camera shot? People are speculating in their droves.

Cal twists to look up at the hills above them, wishing he could go back in time and talk to Lucie. With this level of scrutiny, how does anyone live a normal life? He resolutely ignores the notifications that have popped up for his own account, trying to focus on his breathing and the water before him. He's supposed to be relaxing and planning his future, but now his fingers keep twitching towards his phone, refreshing Lucie's feed.

Only Chrissie emerging from the cabin barefoot and tousled, rubbing her face, forces him to stop. She yawns, gesturing at the coffee pot on the table. 'Morning, Dad. Is that still hot?'

'Sit,' he says, pushing back his chair. 'I'll make another.'

She looks exhausted. It's so unlike Chrissie not to spill her thoughts the moment she sees him. Sensing now is not the time to raise the subject, he resolves to give her space and instead sets croissants on a plate and fetches the jar of strawberry jam from the fridge while the kettle boils. The food prompts Rocket to make the arduous twenty-foot journey to the deck, where he flumps beneath the table, ready to hoover up crumbs that come his way.

Chrissie scratches the dog's belly with her feet. 'Any news on Lucie?'

'No, still missing.'

He can feel his daughter's eyes on him, assessing and astute as ever.

'She'll turn up, Dad.'

'I hope so.'

'What's the plan for today?'

He grasps the change in subject.

'Well, we're low on food so I was thinking we could go into the village for a big breakfast and mooch around the shops. When Shona wakes up.'

'Shona's awake,' a voice from the inside calls. 'Needs food.'

Chrissie grins as she appears in the doorway. 'Sounds like a plan.'

—

They drive down into the village and park on the main street. The sun is baking the pavements and the air seems to shimmer with heat. Rocket stayed at the cabin, sleeping, and Cal's glad they didn't bring him. You could fry their breakfast eggs on the tarmac, and his paws would be scorched.

'This heat is so weird,' Chrissie murmurs, shading her eyes. 'Can you order a bacon roll and an iced coffee for me? I'm going to see if I can get some flip-flops and a hat.'

'See if you can find any handheld fans,' Shona calls after her. Chrissie raises a thumb in response.

The cafe is full but a couple of older men squeeze up on a long table in the shade to make room for them.

'Thanks,' Cal says, relieved. 'Is it always this busy?'

One of the men shakes his head, emptying a sachet of sugar into his cup. He's wearing a sleeveless vest that shows off his pale scrawny arms and grins mischievously.

'It's the twitstagrammers.'

'It's the weather,' his slightly more dressed companion disagrees, flapping the neck of his polo shirt.

'I saw a camera crew doon here the morn. Folk are rubbernecking,' the first man says.

Cal can see how they relish bickering with each other.

'You mean Lucie?' he interjects.

'Aye. Apparently, she left her car in the car park at Ben Lawers and took off up the hill. She'll nay be doing so well in this heat. They'll be wanting to find her.'

A waitress takes their order and Cal scans the street for Chrissie, saying nothing.

He pictures the conditions on the mountain. It was hard going in yesterday's heat but today is even worse. If Lucie's lying injured, she may not be able to raise the alarm. Or, if the stories are true, maybe she's picked a quiet place to end her life. Despite the sweat on his face, he shivers.

'Aye. They'll no want it happening again.'

Cal's mind jerks back to the present, pulled by the string of their words.

'*Again?* What do you mean, again?'

The man wearing a vest folds his arms, clearly delighted to have an audience. Chrissie slips through the tables and sinks onto the edge of the bench next to Cal, a bag full of shopping in her hand.

'Jane. Hillside Jane, they called her. Some walker found the body but she'd been out there a while. Picked to bits by crows, like. Just bones left. Billy here was on the mountain rescue team back then as a volunteer. Never found out who she was, did they?'

Billy shakes his head. 'Unrecognisable.' He sucks his teeth. 'Bad business.'

'Really?' Shona's eyebrows knit together as she accepts her coffee from the waitress. Cal suppresses a smirk. *Any mention of bones and she's all over it.*

'No DNA? No missing-person match?'

The man in the vest shrugs. 'This was twenty year back.'

'So what happened to her, then?' Cal leans in.

'She's buried in the churchyard at the other end of the loch,' Billy says.

The sky is cloudless, but Cal feels a shadow passing over them.

'I guess maybe people forget the hills are dangerous,' he says. 'They're so beautiful. It's sad to think someone could have an accident and lie there that long.'

'Jane wasn't an accident, though.'

Chrissie is watching the men carefully.

'What do you mean?' she asks.

'Oh.' Billy sighs, easing off the bench and putting a hand to his back. 'It may or may not be true. But there's some that say Jane was murdered.'

CHAPTER SIX

They drive with the windows open and the hot wind streaming in, tangling Chrissie's hair. Cal glances at her in the rear-view mirror. She's quieter than usual, staring out at the glimpses of loch flashing through the trees to their right, laden with thought. Her hand rests on the dog's back and the old hound leans into her, panting. It's taking everything he has not to demand access to her inner thoughts. When she's ready, she'll speak.

His mind returns repeatedly to Lucie, alone somewhere in the hills. Behind them, a helicopter is taking laps of the mountain. Cal can see the speck of it in his mirror.

'Do you think there's anything we can do to help?'

Shona shakes her head. 'The police and mountain rescue will be co-ordinating. They'll have a lot of local volunteers who know the hills here – I suspect they won't want other people blundering in and getting stuck.'

He sighs. 'True. It just feels wrong, sitting and watching.'

'They should find her today.'

Gradually, they drop closer to the water and its presence makes his whole body thirst. At the village at the head of the loch, they cross a bridge over the river in front of the church, pale and magnificent on its rise. The loch behind is almost five hundred feet deep in places.

'I want to swim in it,' Chrissie breathes as the beach comes into view. 'Now.'

'We're almost there.' He laughs.

They park next to the small beach, which is filled with families cooling off in the water. As soon as they leave the car, Chrissie sprints to the water's edge and wades straight in, the dog at her heels. Cal has a flashback to other holidays when she was smaller, holding on to his hand for protection as she dipped her toes in the waves. The memories make his eyes smart.

Shona follows them onto the sand but Cal pauses a moment, transfixed by the view of the church. That must be where Jane is buried. While they paddle and splash, his eye is drawn repeatedly to the spire.

Shona catches him looking.

'Want to go and have a look?'

'Is it that obvious?'

Leaving Chrissie and the dog to the water, they towel off and follow the road back round on foot, past the gated entrance to a castle and a small shop. The street is quiet, vibrating with heat. Passing a war memorial cross, they enter the churchyard under the lych-gate, both instinctively coming to a halt and breathing in the change in atmosphere.

There's a strange feeling in the walled graveyard, which is cooler, almost dank. Around them, the stones are crammed into the space. The inscriptions on some are clear but, further back, the older graves are weathered and eroded so they can't read the details. Moss covers them, dried and flaking in the heat.

They move from stone to stone, reading the inscriptions. Cal feels sticky and watched; the place is too still. It takes them so long that he thinks they'll have to give up, but eventually they locate the grave, close to the wall. The stone is simple.

'Jane' 2004. May she rest in peace.

'There she is,' Shona says, crouching and touching the inscription.

The wording is elegant yet sparse. Cal takes out his phone and snaps some pictures, then he remembers this isn't an investigation; it isn't his case. Old habits die hard. The grave is immaculate, perfectly weeded and tended. It feels poignant, standing where Jane's remains are resting while Lucie is missing in the same hills.

'Can I help you?'

Cal spins round to see an older man approaching, his face flushed by the heat, heavy grey eyebrows over deep brown eyes and thinning hair. He's taller than Cal by a good few inches and his short sleeves reveal pale arms. 'Or are you simply taking refuge from the heat? It's intolerable out there.'

Cal smiles. 'A bit of both, to be honest. We heard the story about Jane and wanted to see where she was buried.'

The man's expression sobers and he moves closer, his eyes on the stone.

'A sad story.'

'She was found on the hill?' Shona asks.

'That's right. Twenty years ago now. By the time she was spotted, her remains had been exposed to the elements for some time and it wasn't possible to identify her. No one ever came forward and the police eventually released the body. We volunteered to bury her here and maintain her grave.'

He crouches and pulls out an invisible weed.

'It's a beautiful spot,' Shona murmurs.

'It is, aye.'

'And you work in the graveyard?' Cal asks.

'You could say that, but I work inside the church too. I'm the minister.'

The man chuckles.

'I'm sorry,' Cal says. 'We didn't realise.'

'Not at all.' The man gestures at his shorts and T-shirt. 'You can't really tell from this get-up.' He stretches out a hand. 'Tavish Dewar.'

'There was no DNA match, then?' Shona asks when they've shaken hands. The minister's grip is strangely cool. Otherworldly, Cal finds himself thinking. The heat is messing with his brain.

Tavish shakes his head slowly. 'No.'

'And they haven't revisited the case more recently? With some of the newer scientific techniques, perhaps? Isotope testing?'

The minister studies her, the surprise showing on his face.

'Sorry.' She laughs. 'Professional interest. I'm a forensic anthropologist. Cal here is a true-crime podcaster. We're supposed to be on holiday, mind.'

He spins round to look at Cal. 'Are you going to look into Jane's case?' There's a spark in his eyes, an interest Cal didn't plan to ignite. A strange fear lurches inside him, his memory flashing to the awards night.

'Oh,' he says. 'No, I'm sorry if we gave you that impression.'

'We saw the missing hiker when we were walking yesterday... It's been on our minds,' Shona explains. 'When we passed your church, we thought of Jane.'

The minister's animation subsides and his eyes swivel to the hills. 'Such an innocent view, but so dangerous. Usually, it's the snow and ice that people aren't prepared for. I don't remember a summer this warm.'

'How long have you been the minister here?'

'Actually, only a little longer than Jane's been here,' Tavish says. 'But my father held the post before me so I've known this village since I was a child.'

'Really? A family calling.'

Tavish laughs. 'Something like that. I took over when he retired, though he's still with us. He's not so well these days but he'll be ninety-eight this year.'

'A good age.'

'It is. His lucid days are fewer and further between but he's well looked after by the nursing home. This heat is a nightmare for them, mind.'

'It must be.'

They stand in silence for a moment. It's peaceful in the graveyard; the sounds of children splashing in the water drift on the soupy air, somehow feeling further away than they are. A place where time seems to slow.

'How did Jane die?' Shona asks. 'The men we spoke to said there's a theory she was murdered.'

Tavish rubs his chin with his hand, leaving a streak of soil on his skin.

'That wasn't the official finding. Unexplained, I believe. These hills may look pretty, but they're lethal if you don't know what you're doing. The mists come down and, well, you're in trouble. It doesn't take much to lose the path.'

Cal feels Shona shiver beside him.

As Tavish turns away, he feels the urge to call out one more question.

'Is that what *you* think happened?'

The minister turns back, a deep sadness in his eyes as he looks again at the immaculate grave.

'I think the most obvious explanation is probably the most likely. These mountains don't give second chances.'

Cal can't help but apply the words to Lucie. By the sound of the distant rotors, he concludes they're still up there, looking for her.

CHAPTER SEVEN

MORNA, 1952

Morna's on her way home from the shop, wondering where she can hide some of the food so her da won't find it, and maybe she can eke it out for the week. Sometimes she filches scraps from Mrs Baird's kitchen, salivating at the smells of food the guests inhale, the pieces they discard without thinking. It keeps her going. Her father always seems to manage the coins for a pie or a piece of fish at the inn. He never thinks of providing for her, not anymore. She's her own provider now.

Ahead of her, children spill from the school yard, voices ringing like bells as they run, laugh, grab each other's bags and tease. She watches the older girls, a pair of them arm in arm, heads bent towards each other in secret consultation, and her chest aches. She left last year, at fifteen, misses the routine and the quiet of it, but there's no point in wishing. Tucking her head down, she counts steps, trying to blot out the memories.

Almost past the gate, she doesn't hear her name called at first, looking up in confusion when the voice filters into her mind. Mr Bainzie, the young schoolmaster, is watching her, a look of concern on his face. Down from Aberdeen, he always wears a tweed suit, and his shoes shine on principle. He once told the class that he polished them every evening, and the difference between his life and hers floored her.

'How are you, Morna?'

She nods, trying to smile and turn her face from him all at once, ashamed for him to see the bruised side of it.

'Have you time for a cup of tea?'

She looks one way up the street, then the other. But it isn't really a question – he's already turned to go inside. As though she were still his pupil, Morna follows him in. The smell of the building takes her back, filling her heart with nostalgia. Things were never good at home, but here she was left in peace for a few hours a day. The Leaving Certificate wasn't the freedom for her that it was for others, though. Chained to her father's house. She's thought about leaving him, fantasised about it, but where would she go? It's a dream, that's all. She has nothing. No money for the bus or the train, no one to help her escape.

'Do you see Betty these days?'

She startles. They were thick as thieves back then. But Betty took the chance to go, moving to Glasgow and taking a job in a shop, like so many of the girls have done. Betty's mother used to tell her all about it; Betty wrote sometimes, and they had all these plans for Morna to save up and join her, but the longer things have gone on, the more contact has faded away.

Morna shrugs. 'Not so much.' She wonders if he can see how much it hurts.

Their lives are different. They live in different worlds. Betty's news – of dance halls, curling her hair in the toilets on a Friday night, stepping out with a young man – wasn't something she could compete with. She's drawn away and been drawn away from. The worse her father gets, the more the people in the village keep clear too. Morna doesn't blame them.

Mr Bainzie leads her into the kitchen without comment, lighting the gas stove and putting a kettle on the ring. He takes a tin of biscuits from the cupboard and sets them on a small table, indicating that she should sit. It occurs to her that they aren't so different in age – but it feels like a wide gulf. He's newly married, with a baby at home and a smiling wife.

'They're going stale – eat as many as you're able. You'll be doing me a favour.'

Morna blushes at the lie.

She isn't used to having a man serve her. She watches, uneasy, as the teacher pours the hot water into the pot, takes a half-empty pint of milk from the windowsill. It's warm inside, though the school is echoey and strange without children. Her eyelids feel heavy after the previous night's lack of sleep, the horror of the man in her room still fresh. She tucks her head down and swallows the urge to cry.

'Sugar?'

Morna nods. Mr Bainzie stirs in a heaped spoonful and sets the tea in front of her.

'Now, then,' he says.

CHAPTER EIGHT

Chrissie carries two glasses of gin and tonic out to the deck, condensation running down the sides. They have been banished from the kitchen by Shona, who is grilling fish and chopping salad and has told them to *get out of her road*. Cal takes his glass gratefully, sipping the cool liquid, closing his eyes at the feel of the ice cubes on his lips, the chill in his throat. It's eight in the evening but the heat is palpable, wrapping itself around them and squeezing.

He's thinking about Lucie, alone in the hills with no such respite from the scorching weather. When they drove back along the loch to the cabins after the afternoon on the beach, they passed a police car stationed at the base of the road to the Ben Lawers car park, a sweating officer in short sleeves handing out fliers adorned with her smiling picture. But there is talk of having to stand down the search team when darkness falls.

Cal keeps picturing her sitting on the rock, looking out into the distance. The way she rubbed her face when he approached. The way she vanished.

The image of the grave from today, another missing woman, lurks in the back of his thoughts as well. He googled the case earlier, unable to resist further investigation. The Scottish mountains claim around twenty lives every year, but the victims are overwhelmingly male. Some of them are never found.

Jane, on the other hand, suffered catastrophic head injuries on the hill but has never been identified. Her DNA wasn't in the police system, and no one knew who she was, even when an artist produced a sketch of how she may have looked before the elements ravaged her features. All efforts to identify her failed and then time moved on, leaving her behind.

'You're quiet.'

He looks up to find Chrissie studying him.

'Sorry, you're right, I was miles away.'

'You couldn't know how bad Lucie was,' she says. 'When you saw her.'

She knows, of course she does. And she's right. He has been torturing himself, because bystanders do spot people in distress, do help them. It happens all the time. Did he think he had some kind of attuned sense? The honest answer is yes. But it's arrogant to assume he can see everything.

Chrissie looks pale, he thinks. Not her usual effervescent self, though she's putting on a good show. He opens his mouth to ask why, but she gets in there first.

'What happened last week, Dad? At the awards.'

'I honestly don't know, love. I just saw red, I guess. You know I hate those things.'

'You still think about Jason Barr a lot.'

He slugs back the gin, feeling his muscles tense at the mention of the name.

'Always.'

Chrissie's green eyes are still fixed on him. He takes a breath. Now is his moment.

'And what about you? You haven't said much about the elective and why you gave it up. Are you okay?'

Her eyes cloud and she drops her gaze to her glass, rolling the tiny remnants of ice around it.

'Yes,' she says. 'I'm fine. Totally.'

At that moment, Shona calls from inside that the meal is ready. Chrissie is on her feet and gone before he can stop her.

—

Later, Cal and Shona lie side by side in bed under a thin sheet, too hot to sleep entangled as they usually do. The air is like treacle – even with all the windows open in the cabin, not a hint of breeze stirs the curtains. It's quiet now. The helicopters have stopped their search for the night.

Gradually, Cal listens to Shona drifting into sleep but he can't do the same. He keeps picking up his phone and scrolling through the articles he can find about Lucie and about Jane, the two of them conflated in his mind. The articles put Jane in her sixties or seventies. What was she doing up the hill alone? How can no one have come forward to identify her?

His mind twists back and forth, between the two women, and then to Sarah and the producer's expectation that he will start another case. He's tired, burned out. What could he do or be in another world? Something far from death and sadness.

He must slip into a doze, because the buzzing comes to him as if in a dream and it takes a moment for him to realise it's his phone. He hasn't plugged it in, just let it fall onto the mattress after his late-night scrolling, and so it's vibrating right next to his head.

Cal sits up, not wanting to disturb Shona, and snatches up the handset. Number withheld. His stomach plunges.

Half-asleep, he swings his legs over the side of the bed and pads to the hallway, drawing the bedroom door closed behind him as he accepts the call.

'Hello?' he whispers, his ear pressed to the static.

Silence. No. Not silence. There is soft breathing at the end of the line.

But he knows, of course he knows.

'I know it's you, Naomi.'

'I need to speak to you.'

Her words are like sharp wires in his fingernails. She kept calling him after the trial last year. The wife of his sister's killer. Naomi Barr. *Hang up, Cal, just hang up.*

'I don't want to talk to you.'

'I don't have anyone else.'

Cal waits on the precipice.

'What do you want?'

'He talks in his sleep. It's making me crazy. He said Allegra again.'

Cal swallows bile. Allegra Carlo was killed more than thirty years ago, in fields miles from Jason Barr's home and regular haunts. When Naomi mentioned her before, it almost sent him mad. He fell down a rabbit hole of research and panic for nothing. A man is in prison for the murder of Allegra and her children. He confessed. He did it. It wasn't Barr.

Their calls became another strand of torture – a sick and twisted connection that endured between him and Jason Barr against his will. Naomi's regrets at the man she chose are nothing to do with him. He can't be the scapegoat. He thought she'd stopped. He thought it was over.

'He didn't kill Allegra, Naomi. I looked into it.'

'But he's getting worse. He says other names too.'

Cal's chest tightens. He can't go there. Not after what happened at the awards. He's on edge as it is.

'There are people you can call if you need help,' he says. 'I'm not the right person.'

'They won't understand,' she whispers.

'*I* don't understand.'

And he doesn't. Not why she married him, why she loves him, why she stays. He knows what the man she is married to is capable of. That she's living with a monster, breathing his air, sharing his bed.

It has also occurred to him that maybe Naomi Barr is toying with him when she makes these calls, doing it on her husband's instruction. It's not impossible. At the trial last year, she wore a replica of his murdered sister Margot's necklace, her fingers caressing the golden swallow as Jason Barr took the stand.

Is that movement in the background? That muffled sound. Is Barr listening in to this call? Is he laughing at him?

After the verdict, Cal took to walking the streets, finding himself drawn to the house where Barr now lives: a mansion-style home containing a charmed existence for the devil himself. He spent those nights torturing himself, unable to move forward and to forgive himself the missed shot at justice. His skin prickles with heat at the memory of Barr standing at the window, watching him right back.

He's on a final warning with the police after those walks. He cannot afford to give in to obsession anymore; he is moving on from that, leaving it behind. Anger swells inside.

'You can't call me,' he hisses.

'What would Margot want you to do—'

Cal ends the call, flinging the phone onto the sofa like a burning coal.

Outside, the world is clothed in silver light, the loch glittering in the cold brutality.

The need to hurt Jason Barr crawls through his veins like poison.

CHAPTER NINE

In the morning Cal wakes late, the disturbed night a distant dream. Shona doesn't know about Naomi and it needs to stay that way. He cannot go back to those obsessions. Margot wouldn't want him to, he's sure. He tried and failed to get justice but at least she was found and had a proper memorial. She was remembered. Not like Hillside Jane, buried in an anonymous grave.

He's only just showered and dressed when his laptop announces a video call. In the fog of tiredness he had forgotten he was due to speak with his producer, Sarah. Cal's stomach drops. Even before his emotional implosion at the awards ceremony, Sarah's patience had been wearing thinner than ever. Now it's non-existent. He has to tell her what he's thinking.

Shona, Chrissie and Rocket have gone for a walk. There is no reason to reject the call. Taking a deep breath, he presses the button to join and sees she's calling from a busy production office, the background hum a contrast to the rural quiet at his end. Her black bob has been shaved on one side since they last spoke and as she tucks the longer side behind her ear, he catches the flash of statement jewellery on her wrist.

'Nice hair.'

'Thanks,' she says crisply, but he notices there are shadows beneath her eyes that aren't usually there.

He waits for the acerbic comments that usually flow in her affectionate but brutal tones. Nothing.

'Are you okay?'

She sighs and looks behind her before answering.

'Not really. It's a bit stressful. They're making some redundancies.'

Cal stills. 'You're not going, are you?'

Sarah loves her job. She lives for it.

'Not sure yet.' She shrugs. 'It would really help to have your next podcast plan in place, though. We're out of time.'

Cal's face sears with heat and dread, his resolve draining away. Hazel eyes pin him in place, now laser-focused on the matter in hand. How can he tell Sarah he's quitting now? Once upon a time, he found her intimidating and annoying, yes, but he has grown to see her brand of no-nonsense as a refreshing dose of humility for his soul. He doesn't want her to lose her career over him.

'Come on, Cal. You must have something.'

Before he knows what's happening, he's talking, bull-shitting.

'Well, I've got some leads, some initial options to follow…'

His mouth is dry and he reaches for his glass of water, playing for time.

'That's what you said last month. You need to just choose something, Cal. Please.'

'I know. I'm sorry. You're absolutely right.' He can't do this. Can he? Cal finds the words spilling from his lips, regardless.

'Have you heard of Hillside Jane?'

A minion passes behind her, briefly blotting out the light.

'It doesn't ring any bells.'

'Twenty years ago, the decomposed body of a woman was found on a hill next to Loch Tay. No one's ever been able to identify her. She wasn't reported missing, her DNA hasn't come up on police databases, they can't track where she came from, nothing. It's a total mystery. Cause of death was unexplained but I spoke to some local people who said she was murdered. Her skull had been fractured.'

'Suspects?'

'She doesn't even have a name. Police investigated for a long time but got nowhere. Eventually the Procurator Fiscal released the body for burial. Now Lucie Barnes has gone missing in the same area.'

'The Instagrammer?'

'Yes. Hopefully, she'll turn up soon.' Cal crosses his fingers. 'But the attention her case is receiving might trigger memories for Jane.'

He knows he's clutching at the slenderest straws. *Shut up, Cal, shut up.*

Sarah's face twists in desperation.

'How would you go about it?'

'Well... I guess we try and jog memories.' Sarah makes a face. 'Shona was also talking about some testing that could be done on hair and bone samples.'

'You could do a joint investigation!'

Her eyes flash and Cal realises he's starting a chain reaction that's already out of his control.

'Er... I'm not sure.'

'Honestly, this is a lifesaver. All I need to do is get a couple of advertisers interested and this could work.'

He drops his gaze to the keyboard. There's no way he can back out, is there? Sarah has supported him through so much. And anyway, is jacking the whole thing in a mistake? The decision is seismic. Is he ready to make that call?

Sarah narrows her eyes, but then there's a commotion in the office and she signals to someone off camera that she's coming. 'Send through the details. Thank you, Cal. Thank you.'

Sarah never thanks him. He stares at the empty box on the screen where her face was and groans.

CHAPTER TEN

As they drive away from Loch Tay the next day, Cal is dismayed to see the helicopter is back, scanning the hills. In this heat, Lucie can't have long left if she's out in the open. Today everything feels insurmountable, a feeling not helped by the bad night's sleep. Naomi called again in the early hours, insistent that he do something to help. When she hung up, he lay awake, staring at the ceiling, his mind jumping from one problem to the next. It was light when he finally dozed off.

The journey to Perth takes less than an hour and a half, the road running along the side of Loch Earn and through normally lush countryside that is currently wilting. Sarah has worked fast, using Shona's name to get them a meeting with Police Scotland representatives to discuss collaboration. They park with an hour to spare, buy iced coffees and take the dog for a walk in the North Inch park, alongside a wide stretch of the River Tay where he can cool off. Cal envies him.

They leave Rocket and Chrissie in the shade of a tree and take the baking streets out of the centre. Perth police station is a squat, grey cube of a building perched at the side of a roundabout. He and Shona wait for twenty minutes, until the officers are ready to meet. Sweat beads on his forehead as they sit in the reception.

Eventually, DS Matthews leads them to an interview room, accompanied by a young red-faced DC who looks like he's only just out of school. He has angry pimples on his chin and his Adam's apple bobs as he swallows nervously. Matthews just looks harassed; strands of her brown hair have escaped her tight bun and she huffs them away from her forehead.

'Sorry to keep you waiting,' she says, pulling back a chair and gesturing for them to do the same. 'The heat is causing all sorts of madness at the moment.'

'Thank you for seeing us.'

Cal introduces Shona and is relieved to see that her reputation precedes her – she's greeted with more warmth and less suspicion than he is. The officers listen as Cal runs through his interest in the case, as well as his history of podcasting and the awards the series has won. If he can't get them on side, he's going to have very little to go on.

'I listened to the last series. I couldn't believe it when you found the body there after all that time...' the young DC says, excitedly, sitting back chastised when Matthews gives him a look. Cal's willing to bet she's not a fan.

'Look, the case is a conundrum and any publicity that might jog memories or bring information to the surface is welcome,' Matthews says tightly. 'If you're going to do an appeal then the SIO will give his blessing. But you'd need to keep us informed every step of the way.'

'Of course,' Cal says. 'And if anyone from Police Scotland would like to be interviewed about the case, we'd be happy to have you on.'

The young officer looks excitedly at Matthews but she squashes him with a withering glance.

'We'll let you know.'

She slides a folder across the table. 'I can't let this leave here, but given your credentials,' she looks at Shona, 'if you'd like to take a look at the post-mortem and crime scene photos, I'd be interested in your views.'

'I wondered why the case wasn't categorically ruled murder,' Shona says. 'Local people we spoke to seemed to believe it wasn't accidental, but it's categorised as unexplained rather than suspicious.' She flips open the file. 'Who did the post-mortem...? Ah. Hunt.'

She and Matthews exchange a meaningful glance.

'Hunt by name...'

Shona smirks.

Cal and the young officer watch the two women, mystified. He's just relieved that Matthews is opening up. Shona spreads the photographs in front of them and Cal grimaces at the decay and damage the elements and animal activity wreaked on Jane. The remains are barely recognisable as human.

'Female, older, possibly sixties,' Shona reads. 'No birthmarks, tattoos or identifying features. She had older, healed fractures, though.'

She looks up at Matthews, who shakes her head.

'No match to any medical records we could find. Everything that could be done to establish identity was, but it all came to nothing.'

'Harris lines,' Shona says, thoughtfully, reading the report.

'What are they?' Cal can't help asking.

'Growth arrest lines that form in the bones of children or adolescents. She could have been malnourished as a child,' Shona says. 'If she was neglected or abused and the fractures were never treated, they wouldn't be on file. This one in her arm had healed badly.'

'Exactly,' Matthews says. 'And the fact that the body lay out there for a year meant any evidence there might have been was washed away or compromised. The team interviewed as many local people as possible by the looks of it, put out regular appeals, but nothing.'

'It suggests she didn't have any connection to the area,' Shona says. 'But then...'

'What was she doing up there?'

Cal is amazed at how Matthews has thawed as she chats with Shona.

'How would you feel about the podcast paying for some new tests on the samples taken from the remains?'

'We have a DNA profile that has been run through the police database and logged in case of a future match.'

'That can only check close familial matches,' Shona says gently. 'Parents, siblings, children. And only in the UK. We'd like to see if we could submit Jane's samples to databases that can track much more distant relationships, in the hope of narrowing things down. Finding the haystack before looking for the needle, so to speak.'

After a moment, Shona adds, 'There are other tests that might help too... Isotope testing of hair or teeth can help identify where a person grew up, and where they were living in the final months of their life. That way, we could pinpoint a country or area, which might make it easier to target our genetic and family history searches.'

Cal crosses his fingers.

Matthews grits her teeth.

'I'd love you to do that,' she says. 'But it won't be possible.'

'Why not?' He can't help but butt in, crestfallen.

The DS sighs, her frustration breaking through.

'Some idiot destroyed them.'

CHAPTER ELEVEN

EPISODE ONE: OFF THE BEATEN TRACK

A keen walker, ex-schoolteacher Alastair Bainzie spent all his spare time up in the hills above Loch Tay when he retired. The Ben Lawers range of seven Munros sits above the vast stretch of water, and Alastair and his dog, Luna, would look down on it when they were on their daily hikes, the villages and people like toys below.

Since the death of his wife, Beth, Alastair has lived in a residential home not far from the village. His three children live in the area and see him regularly. He's a favourite of the staff in the home. When we visit, he's sitting outside in the shade, a blanket over his knees even though Scotland is sweating under extreme temperatures. In pictures, he is wiry and straight-backed; now Alastair has a thick mop of grey hair, and his limbs are thin and wasted. His eyes return to the mountain peaks constantly, magnetically drawn to their majesty.

'Can you tell me what happened that day in 2004?'

'Luna and I set off in the morning to do the loop, but the clouds had come in and conditions were ropy. I wasn't worried, as we knew the paths so well, but decided not to finish the last few peaks. We dropped into the valley to the lochan at the bottom to walk out that way.'

'And what happened then?'

'*The dog dashed off the path. Didn't come back. It wasn't like her. I had to follow, as I thought she'd gone after a rabbit and fallen into a hole, got stuck somewhere. But she was in the mists on the side of the hill, just waiting and whimpering. I followed her bark to a pile of boulders. When you squeezed around them, there was a flat area of ground you'd never know was there. I didn't realise what she'd found until I was right on top of it...*'

'*That must have been harrowing.*'

'*Aye, the jacket was still holding up, but the rest of her... had been badly damaged. Luna wouldn't go near. When I reached the spot, she shot behind me. Tail between her legs. She knew. Then I saw the woman's head... I could see the skull through the hair and... I'm sorry.*'

'*It's okay. It sounds awful. If it hadn't been for Luna, it sounds like you wouldn't have found the body?*'

'*Not in a million years. She was a good dog.*'

'*What did you do?*'

'*I stumbled back to the sheep path I'd been on. Used to keep a flask in my bag for the peaks — a tot of whisky at the top, you know? I took that out and drank half of it.*'

Alastair is shaking his head while he speaks. There's a tremor in his hands — it's hard to tell if this is the memory or old age.

'*Then I came to myself and carried on down the hill until I met the stream off the lochan, followed it to raise the alarm.*'

'*Did you call anyone from up there?*'

'*I didn't have a mobile phone then — not that there would have been any signal anyway. If you go up there, you'll see it's an eerie place, so quiet in the shelter of the peaks, a bit of a bleak dead end. By the time I got down, I almost thought I'd imagined it. But the dog wasn't right. She was shaking.*'

'*Who did you tell?*'

'*I knew the mountain rescue team a bit — I used to volunteer with them when they needed to do big searches, so I went and *found Jim Donovan, the man in charge of it. He notified his police contacts and I led a group of them back up that same day.'*

'You must have been fit to do that in your seventies.'

'Aye, I was. Back then. It was strange, though – the mists came in so close you could hardly see. They muffled all sound. By the time I came back down, it was turning dark. I felt like someone was watching me the whole time. But every time I turned round, there was no one there.'

The following day, scenes of crime officers attended the site, then mountain rescue workers lifted the woman from the smooth grassy platform high above the shores of Lochan Nan Cat. They carried her back down the mountain and she was taken to Glasgow for a post-mortem. The skull fractures were severe enough to have been the cause of death. However, with Jane having lain out in the elements for around a year, and in the absence of other forensic evidence, the pathologist refused to rule out accident or suicide. Officially, cause of death remains unexplained.

That's not the only mystery in this case. No one knew who this woman was. She died without a shred of identification on her and, to this day, we have no idea what she was doing on the hillside.

After searching in vain for some connection to the local area, then the wider Highlands, then Scotland, then the rest of the UK, the police broadened their search further. But, despite international appeals, no one has ever come forward to claim her body.

In a world with competing demands on police time, and with no one to advocate for her, Hillside Jane, as locals called her, has faded from view. A year later, her body was released to the authorities and she is buried in a small churchyard in the village at the head of the loch, still waiting for someone to claim her.

Alastair is haunted by the lack of closure. He had no idea when he found her bones that the woman would take hold of his thoughts in the way she has.

'I dream about her sometimes.' He's looking up at those hills again, as he speaks. 'It feels like she's trying to tell me something. She wants us to listen.'

This is Finding Justice, *and I am your host, Cal Lovett.*

CHAPTER TWELVE

MORNA, 1952

The church is a place of respite and tranquillity, its strong walls keeping out her troubles. This is a place where she does not have to be on edge. From the quiet of a pew at the back, away from others, Morna watches the minister as he sermonises, his voice lifting up to the rafters and crashing back to her.

She hears the grumbles of the congregation sometimes – that this new minister talks too much, lectures too long – but she prays only for it to continue so she can stay in her seat, quiet and warm and safe. Her eyes sometimes close against her will, eyelids pinned by exhaustion. She always jerks them open guiltily, afraid she will be cast out of one of the few remaining places of calm.

Only, one day she is too tired to fight it. The sleep is a sickness that forces her under. Her da had friends over the evening before and even though she took herself away out of sight, she lay awake afraid, listening to their roaring tide of conversation. Once or twice, she heard her name on the lips of the man with the hungry eyes and she knows, deep down in her gut, that his interest is too great, that a reckoning is coming.

When she heard the footstep on the lower stair, she had sprung from the bed, throwing back the covers and grabbing her dressing gown, tying it tight before darting through frigid air to the top of the stairs. Her movement startled him, put him off balance. She could feel her heart's fear strong in her chest, this brazen high-risk strategy her only chance to avoid what she knows inside is coming.

The man halted, reeking and drunken, unsteady on his feet even as his slow mind tried the calculation.

'Da!' she called to her father, seeking protection from a man who was a poor promise of defence, but all she had. 'Da!'

'Whaaa?'

She heard him rouse at the fireside, the clatter of the bottle hitting the floor, the cursing that followed. Her father would not know what had woken him, but it was enough. The man at the foot of the stairs touched his cap and retreated, the movement more of a promise than a farewell. How long can she thwart him? For the rest of the night she had sat shivering, legs hugged tight to her chest and her back against the headboard, long after the men had left and her father had staggered up the stairs to bed, his snores rattling through the wall.

The minister's hand on her arm wakes her and she cries out in the empty church, tears springing to her eyes automatically. It's just as her father says. She is useless. But he doesn't shout, instead holding out his hands to quiet her as you would a wild creature.

'I'm sorry,' she stammers.

The look he gives her isn't quite kindness, but it's not cruelty either. His hair and beard are dark and unruly, and he is handsome in the way that the crags of the hills are handsome. Later, when she remembers this moment, she will think, *I was not the wild one.*

'You didn't like my sermon?'

'No, it's not that...'

He barks a laugh and turns away from her. There is no doubt in his own mind that he is compelling.

'I understand. I see you watching. You are one of the few who listens fully.'

'It won't happen again,' she stammers. 'Please.'

'For centuries people have taken shelter in God's house,' he says, walking down the aisle, away from her. 'All are welcome here. Sinners most of all.'

Morna's chest tightens and she bites her lip to stop disobedient tears spilling free.

'Thank you,' she whispers. But the minister is gone.

CHAPTER THIRTEEN

Somehow Shona manages to use the news of the destroyed samples to leverage copies of the file from the police. Today, they're going to find the spot on the hillside where Jane was found, far off the beaten track.

They set off early and drive to the ingress point for the walk, leaving Rocket with the holiday park owner, who adores the greedy labrador. It's not the same route they took to the peaks but Cal is still on edge, looking at every verge and lay-by for signs of Lucie.

The news has reached a fever pitch. Her boyfriend Tyson has been taken in for questioning; the police force local to her home have referred themselves to the watchdog over 'previous contact', and there is talk of pulling back the search and sending divers up to the Lawers Dam after a member of the public claimed to have seen a lone woman there at dusk the day she went missing.

They park at a small lay-by north of the Lochview Hotel, cross the road and take an overgrown track up a steep bank that looks like a dead end. Instead, it turns into an even steeper path through woodland. As the others take the lead, Cal hangs back, snapping pictures and trying to imagine Jane walking this route all those years ago.

If she was an outsider, how did she know it was here? Once she left the road, she would have been invisible. As they walk, he battles disappointment over the lost samples. Truth told, he was pinning his hopes on some scientific help – without that, the task of discovering Jane's identity seems almost impossible. They'll have to hope that someone remembers something and responds to the appeal they've put out with the first episode. It's a shot in the dark.

After about half an hour, they emerge from the trees, stopping frequently to admire the view behind and sip from their water bottles. Cal scans the horizon, Lucie ever present in his thoughts, his eyes always open for the woman who has been swallowed by the vastness of the landscape.

'At least there's a breeze up here,' Chrissie says, wiping the sweat from her forehead and passing the bottle to Cal. 'What was it like when she was found?'

'According to the notes, it was wet and misty,' Shona says. 'Nothing like this. They think she lay out here for at least a year, though, so her body was battered by all the seasons.'

'By the time she was found, it was hard to get people to remember seeing a lone female walker. Thousands of people pass through the villages every year,' Cal says.

Forced to stop to catch their breath, he turns and looks back the way they've come. Loch Tay seems even more dramatic from here – from a height you can appreciate the length of it, a split seam in the cloth of the landscape. He's still breathing heavily when they move on, falling into step with Shona behind Chrissie, struggling with the incline but determined not to be left behind.

It takes several hours to reach the spot. They lapse in and out of talking as their boots hit the uneven path in a trudging rhythm. Cal records some thoughts as they go, awed by the isolation.

'We'll reach Lochan Nan Cat first, though her body was actually found on the hillside above,' Shona tells them, refolding the map.

They break from the track at a small dam and follow the river upwards, the ground springy beneath their feet. Frequently, they lose sight of the path, which is not well trodden, but then traces of it reappear and they regain it. Cal starts to think they will never reach the horizon, but eventually they crest a rise and find themselves in a sheltered horseshoe-shaped valley below the peaks. Ahead of them lies a body of water shaped like an hourglass, still and watchful. The lochan.

It's bigger than Cal imagined. Beyond it, what looks like a sheer wall of rock rises to the ridge above. Cal can see the top of Ben Lawers in the bright blue sky.

All three of them halt and stare at the water. It's a strange place. Cal feels almost held by it, transfixed.

Chrissie is reading from a walking guidebook she took from the cabin. 'Some say the water is haunted or cursed,' she tells them.

Shona chuckles but Cal feels less confident. The place is truly desolate.

'Jane must have been fit,' he muses as they stare at the water, and he stretches to loosen the ache in his legs. 'To make it all the way up here, given her age.'

'True. They estimate she was at least in her sixties,' Shona says. 'Maybe older.'

Her voice drifts into the air, the sky cloudless above. Nothing seems to move on the landscape around them.

'What was she doing here?' Chrissie's voice is small. 'It's so remote. We haven't even seen other walkers.' She turns her face up to the ridge line, where tiny specks in brightly coloured jackets are moving like ants towards the peak.

'I wish we knew,' Cal says. 'This isn't somewhere you stumble on by accident. Her journey seems so specific.'

'Maybe she knew this place. Maybe it meant something to her,' Chrissie says.

'She was found up there,' Shona says, studying the map and pointing to the steep slope above them that is littered with boulders. 'Looks like a bit of a slog, I'm afraid.'

They turn along the curve of the lochan, reaching the point where the banks almost meet in the middle of the hourglass. Then Shona strikes a path away to the left, following the faintest of tracks up the side of the hill.

Eventually, with Cal wheezing for air, she stops.

'Here,' Chrissie says, her hands lifting her pack away from her back to dry the sweat. She points to a small cairn of stones. 'Could this be it?'

'It must be.'

They pick their way across the uneven hillside. Cal slips a little in the deep heather and his ankle strikes a rock. He winces, feeling a sharp pain and the promise of a later bruise. Chrissie leads them to a high pile of boulders. Checking the police file for confirmation, they follow her through a tight fissure and emerge on a small grassy platform to a hidden resting spot.

'Wow.' Shona turns in a circle, taking in the space. Cal can see her professional abilities swinging into focus, assessing the terrain. The platform is sheltered and private.

'It would be hard to find unguided,' he says.

Shona is pacing the platform, craning her neck and peering up at the hill.

While Chrissie passes round a water bottle, Shona sets her pack on the ground and takes the crime scene pictures out, spreading them in front of her. They no longer have to imagine Jane lying on her back, face to the sky, ravaged by animals and battered by the weather: she's there in front of them.

Cal starts to take pictures of the location, narrating their movements for the podcast recording.

'I don't understand,' he says. 'How you would fall and hit your head here. It's so sheltered.'

'I don't think you would,' Shona says. 'Look.' She points to the wall of rock that overhangs the platform. 'If you fell from above, you'd miss the platform entirely.' She looks over the lip. 'Falling from here would make more sense, as you'd strike those boulders, but then she'd have been found at the bottom and she'd probably have more injuries.'

'Could she have crawled back?' Chrissie suggests.

'Maybe, but why? She'd have been knocked unconscious. And even if she did wake, she'd go downhill for help, surely?'

'Unless she was confused?' Cal says.

'True.' Shona frowns at the scene. 'I just don't think she'd make it all the way back up here with injuries that severe. I think I'd struggle even now.'

'So what does that mean?'

'I honestly don't know.'

'Could a rock have fallen on her from above?'

'It's not impossible but with that overhang, anything that fell would most likely overshoot. She had more than one head injury but there's no sign of a rockfall, now or in the pictures.'

'So why didn't Hunt rule out an accidental fall, then? It makes no sense.'

Shona scoffs. 'I'm willing to bet Hunt didn't come up here. He will have done the report from his desk – typical of him, and one of the reasons he was retired earlier than he would have liked.'

Cal and Chrissie perch at the edge of the platform and look down at the rock-strewn hillside below as Shona paces behind them, unloading a tape measure from her pack and muttering to herself.

'It's dried out,' Chrissie says, looking at the lochan. 'In the guidebook it's bigger. The heatwave has depleted it.'

She points to the fallow beach-like circle around the water where it has shrunk, leaving the ground exposed.

'It'll fill back up when the rains start again,' Cal says. 'Is it deep?'

'According to the book, it is. More than a ten-storey building, they think. I might go back down and walk around the edge.'

Her boundless energy makes Cal feel wistful for his youth.

He settles onto a bigger boulder, feeling the blessed relief in his knees, and pulls a sweater from his bag, amazed at the novelty of being chilled in this heatwave. In this shaded spot it's many degrees cooler than in the sun. Even on a warm day, it's exposed here. When the sun went down and the stars came out, it would have been freezing. Was Jane still alive then? Did she die fast or did she feel death coming for her?

'I think I'm done,' Shona says a little while later.

'And?'

Shona sighs. 'It's impossible to say for sure but, looking at the position of the body and being here now, it seems very odd to me.'

He wraps his arms around her and kisses her. 'Is that your professional conclusion, then? Odd?'

She laughs. 'That's the best you're going to get.'

'We can't rule out foul play, then.'

'If she was found with those injuries down there,' Shona gestures to the village at the end of Loch Tay, 'I wouldn't hesitate to say it was murder. So it shouldn't be any different here, really.'

While Shona repacks her bag, he looks for Chrissie and finds her far below: her tiny figure is stepping from rock to rock, almost at the water's edge.

It's rare to have this little to go on. In all his other cases, the victim's life has been the key to unlocking the mystery. Jane had nothing on her. No bag, no wallet or other identifying information. There is no CCTV from back then, no way to follow her trail, just scattered bones and sinew.

He isn't sure what alerts him to the fact that something is happening below. Maybe it's a sort of parental sixth sense, unchanged from when Chrissie was an unruly toddler with corkscrew curls and a talent for trouble. He sees her crouching at the shoreline, interested in something, and jerks out of his reverie, slipping his microphone into his pocket.

'Something's wrong,' Cal says. 'She's found something.'

Shona crosses the platform to his side, sliding her arms into the straps of her rucksack.

Chrissie is calling to them now, cupping her hands around her mouth, but she's too far away for them to hear the words. They start ploughing their way back to the pathway, single file, eyes on their feet so they don't fall.

When they reach the edge of the lochan, they jog along the shore, feet moving over cracked mud. Chrissie is now crouching in the dirt by the water's edge, removing her shoes and socks. The earth around them is parched and splitting; no streams course into the lochan to swell it.

'What is it?'

She holds out a shiny red bottle, dented but gleaming. 'This was in the water.'

Cal feels a rush of blood to the head. He recognises the bottle immediately.

'And there's something else there too. The light's reflecting off the water and I can't quite see it.'

'Where?' Shona is stripping off her boots as well, following Chrissie in. Cal carries the bottle to the dry beach behind them, turning it over in his hands. Apart from a few dents, it is in good condition. It hasn't been in the water long. He scans the area, frantic now. *Where is she?*

'Look. Can you see?' Chrissie is knee-deep in the water, wincing at the stones beneath her feet and calling to Shona. She points at an item in the lochan, barely a shimmer, a mirage that fades in and out of view.

'Oh. Yes, wait.' Shona bends forward. 'Can you get it?'

'What is it?' Cal watches as Chrissie plunges a hand into the water, up to her elbow in the chill.

When it emerges, she's holding something blue and shiny. It takes only a second to register what they're seeing.

A mobile phone.

CHAPTER FOURTEEN

The phone is dead. Smashed and waterlogged, it looks like it's fallen a long way. They need to alert the police and mountain rescue, who have been focusing on the ridge above and the other side of the hill in their search for the missing woman. Cal looks up to the line of Munros. It seems so unlikely that Lucie could have walked down this way, but Alastair had spoken of a way down off the ridge this side.

They pace the area, trying to find a phone signal with no success. To get any mobile reception, they will have to hike back to the small dam they passed on the way up the hill.

Chrissie's face is pale with realisation. 'Do you think Lucie went into the water? Is she dead?'

Cal and Shona exchange glances.

'It seems so shallow,' Cal reassures her. 'I don't think you'd go under here.' Though that's exactly what he's worried has happened.

'But if you wade out further there's a lip and it drops away. See where the water changes colour? I couldn't see the bottom.' Chrissie's voice trembles. 'The guidebook said it's deep, remember?'

Cal gives her a tight hug.

'The phone and bottle may be nothing to do with Lucie,' he says lightly. 'But we have to call it in to the police to be safe. They can decide how relevant it is.'

'We should leave someone here to mark the spot,' Shona says. 'I don't mind staying put while you two go.'

'No,' Cal says. 'You both go. I'm fine to wait.'

The idea of being here on his own makes goosebumps rise on his arms, but Cal likes the idea of leaving Shona here even less.

They take a moment to split water and supplies between them, while Shona pulls plastic evidence bags from her rucksack to seal the bottle and phone.

'I suppose I shouldn't be surprised you have those,' he says, rolling his eyes. 'Ham sandwich, KitKat, body bag...'

'You never know,' she says.

But their attempt at a joke is too close to the bone and Chrissie doesn't smile.

—

Cal watches Chrissie and Shona pick their way down the edge of the stream, following the trickling water in the direction of the track below. When they are no longer in sight, he scans the unmoving surface of the lochan, half-expecting to see Lucie floating there. An involuntary shudder passes through him.

He has no idea how long it will be until the mountain rescue team arrive or Shona comes back for him, so Cal decides to sweep the area for more clues. He looks at the water with distaste, resolving to search the shallows only when he's exhausted the land-based options. Alone in this eerie place, he welcomes the thoughts of Margot that spring into his mind. He's never told a living soul, not even Shona, but when he's on his own, he occasionally talks to his sister, always has done.

For the next twenty minutes he holds an imaginary conversation with her, exploring in increasing circles from the place they found the items. He pictures Margot beside him – as she was then, forever nineteen. Together they work their way along the shore and out into the tussocks of grass, the peaty mounds and the boulder fields on the slopes. At first glance it looks straightforward, but the landscape is deceptive, and Cal finds himself falling into crevices and holes, scraping his hands on the rocks. Lucie could be anywhere.

The heat bleaches the landscape, bouncing off the water and into his eyes. At one point, he thinks a sound reaches his ears. He holds still, hearing only the thundering of his own blood. A heron sits silently at the end of the lochan, watching as he holds his breath. Nothing, just his imagination. He should go back now. This is far enough. But Margot beckons him on. *Just one more hillock.*

Then he hears it again, for sure this time. Margot dissolves.

'Lucie?' He calls her name and it bounces off the walls of the valley back to him, echoing over and over. 'Lucieee!'

Cal waits, then moves forward and calls again, listening. This time, he is sure he hears a groan. Galvanised, he springs forward through the turf, moving further from the lochan, over the peaty rise covered with boulders.

There, half-under a cluster of rocks, pressed into a sliver of shade, he finds her.

The green T-shirt is filthy, her hair is matted and spread across her face, her arms are scratched, the skin torn. Cal halts, aghast at the blistering sunburn on her exposed legs, at the size of the ankle and foot stretched out in front of her, bootless, distended. Looking down on the sight of a corpse, he feels the urge to vomit. But then the corpse moves.

Crying out, he plunges into the hollow, calling her name.

Lucie shifts slightly and groans, but her eyes remain closed. Frantic, Cal automatically fumbles for his mobile, cursing at the lack of signal in this forsaken place.

Grabbing his water bottle, he eases in next to her, afraid to move her.

'Lucie, can you hear me? Help is on the way. My name's Cal, I'm going to stay with you.'

With one hand under her neck, he gently lifts her head and tilts his water bottle to her parched lips, which are as cracked as the earth by the shore. She whimpers and slumps back, exhausted. She needs help quickly but no one will be able to see them – he can't even see the lochan from here. No wonder she hasn't been found.

Scrambling out from under the rocks, Cal grabs his bag and shakes free the contents, then climbs onto the boulder pile and props the bag on the top. It's not much but maybe its garish orange tone will act as a beacon to the rescuers. Back down next to Lucie, he shakes out his waterproof and hangs it from the rock with his sweatshirt, trying to increase the shade puddle over her. Then he navigates around Lucie's swollen ankle, sliding in beside her and tilting her head for more water.

It feels like days he lies there, tipping sips of water into her mouth, praying that she can hold on. He talks nonsense to her, tells her over and over that she's safe and he's got her, unsure if she can even hear him, the words as much for his own reassurance as hers. Gradually, Lucie seems to regain some awareness, so he keeps feeding her tiny sips of water, occasionally crawling out of the swelter of his makeshift shelter to look for the rescue party.

As she becomes conscious, Lucie cries with pain and her whimpers tear at his heart. She must have been fetching water from the lochan, but why did she drop her phone and bottle in and leave them? How did she manage to crawl this far? He can only imagine that she fell on her way off the ridge and heatstroke then addled her brain, frying her body and mind in the punishing sun. At night it must have been cold and terrifying in this bleak place. How has she survived?

'Lucie,' he says when she cries out. 'I've got some paracetamol. I'm going to crumble them into some water and I need you to drink them, okay? It won't taste nice.'

He doesn't know if she understands but he takes the lid of his flask and dissolves the paracetamol in a couple of mouthfuls of water. She grimaces and gags as he painstakingly feeds her the concoction but he is heartened by the fact that she doesn't fight him, that she must understand what he's doing.

Task complete, she slips into sleep and nothing he does can bring her back to the surface. Afraid she is slipping away, Cal leaves the den to look for the mountain rescue team, returning to the rise closer to the lochan to check for them. Nothing moves in front of him, and he wants to cry and shout with despair. Should he walk out and come back for her?

But then Margot appears in his mind again, a memory of light and comfort, and he chokes down the panic. No. He won't leave her. He can't. He stays.

When he returns, Lucie seems to be resting more easily, her breathing less ragged. The water and painkillers must be doing their job. Alerted to his presence, she moans and whispers a stream of words. It is more than she's said before. He leans close to hear.

'In the water. It's in the water. It's in the water.'

Maybe she's talking about her phone.

'It's okay, Lucie. Help is coming, I promise.'

Her eyes jerk open, searching for him, fear riven in her gaze. Her hand grips his arm, hard. It's almost like she's having a seizure.

'There's someone in the water.'

Cal shivers. Her words are a reminder of the fate they assumed had befallen her. But as they lie there, waiting for interminable minutes and hours, she says it over and over again. 'In the water. In the water. In the water.'

The mantra crawls inside his mind and takes on a life of its own. Beaten by the heat, he half-slips into a doze beside her, holding her hand, and it's all he hears, moving into his mind like a sound wave. It's so strong that when the shouts of the rescue team reach his ears, he doesn't immediately understand. But then he's up and out of the hollow, calling, screaming, waving and stumbling.

It's a blur. Faces, water bottles, arms touching him, lifting Lucie, strapping her leg even though she screams. The crackle of the radio, the dog barking, Shona beside him, her cool hands on his skin. Tears tracing lines in the dust on his cheeks.

He hears words spoken as if in a dream.

Helicopter. Airlift. Now.

But the words in his mind keep revolving.

In the water. In the water. In the water.

CHAPTER FIFTEEN

MORNA, 1952

He watches her when he gives his sermons now. Morna feels that he addresses only her, safe at the back of the church in her pew. At the end of the services she lingers, gathering the hymn books and delaying the moment when she will have to leave.

'I feel there is something you need my advice on,' he says. 'But you are afraid to speak.'

Morna looks up at him in wonder, but this close, she cannot bring her eyes to his face, only his chest, broad in front of her. She nods.

He touches his finger to her chin and tilts it so he can look into her eyes. Morna feels her whole body turn crimson.

'Whatever you say to your minister is in confidence.'

'My father, he...' She swallows. 'He drinks.'

The minister nods. 'I had heard.'

'It makes me frightened. He has friends who come back to our house, who...'

The minister's eyes darken and she is afraid. 'Have they touched you?'

Morna cannot speak. She shakes her head no.

'But you are afraid they might?'

She nods.

He studies her for a moment. She cannot look away. His eyes are the darkest brown she's ever seen: deep and impenetrable.

'Let me think about it,' he says. 'Would you like to take a walk with me?'

The question startles her and she flushes.

'A walk?'

'Yes. Into the hills. How about Saturday? I'll meet you on the path by the old castle. I will think about this problem you have.'

She nods, knocked off-centre but entranced. How will she get permission for this? Her father will see it as a gallivanting waste of time. He saw her coming out of the school once, after Mr Bainzie made her a cup of tea so she could dry off after a rainstorm, and his fury was terrifying.

So, on the day, she just avoids the asking, slipping away early to meet her saviour in the shadow of the ruin. There he is, standing over the beheading pit, gazing into its depths. He doesn't look up. Not even when she approaches him and announces herself. He stands as if in prayer and she feels foolish.

After a moment, he tilts his head to her. 'They used to hang people from the tree over there. Did you know that?'

She swallows and nods, because all the local children know the ghost stories from this site, know that old Malc has seen lights floating here in the darkness, though most say he'd had too much to drink in the inn that night. But he isn't looking at the tree and neither is she. Transfixed by those eyes.

They walk along the shore until they reach a path up and to the left into the hills, one she's never tried before. It twists along a tiny burn, which they have to cross several times as the path changes its mind about which side it wants to follow. Eventually, they leave the woodland and climb up, further than she'd usually go, the village concealed in the turn of the land below them, the hills dark and forbidding above.

The clouds have moved closer together, filled with angry rain, and it seems obvious that they should turn back, but he doesn't, striding with long legs and all the faith he has in himself, while her limbs tremble and burn with the exertion.

When it begins to rain, he pulls her into the shelter of some rocks, and it seems to her that this is ordained. As she shivers, it is natural – not wrong – to accept the arm around her. Though now they are this close, she cannot help but notice how handsome he is. He knows what is right, though, doesn't he?

When his lips touch hers, she feels confusion but she also thrills with warmth and attention, like a creature starved of light and sustenance. There is no choice. She would not feel she could refuse him even if she wanted to.

'We can't tell them.' He draws his mouth from hers and inclines his head towards the village. 'They wouldn't understand, would they?'

She thinks of her father, of his moods and tempers, the cold in her house and the reek of the bottle. He would skin her if he could see her now. She shakes her head.

'This will be our secret.' He holds her face in warm hands and she wants to cry. 'Ours alone.'

This time, he only kisses her. The next time they meet, he lays her down on a bed of grass and pulls the clothes from her piece by piece so she barely notices, until she is shivering under the steel sky. He trails a finger from the dip in her throat to the place between her legs and she feels no shame because she is chosen. She arcs towards him, almost regretting it, afraid he will think her brazen.

'Next time,' he says, standing and walking, leaving her to scrabble for her clothes and chase after his long stride. Wondering all the long way down the hill if she has done something wrong.

'You did well,' he says as they part, and the relief pours over her like the waterfalls that tumble from the mountain.

And so she goes back again and again, drawn to him, not choosing, just following. Sometimes, they walk and talk. Or, rather, they walk and he talks – lessons, observations, guidance. At these times, she waits, crestfallen, for a touch that doesn't come, rejected. 'Don't sulk,' he says when he sees her face. And she knows she has failed to be what he needs.

So when he does lay himself on top of her, she accepts the comfort with gasping gratitude. The oddness of it, the thrust and sharp pain, she absorbs it all, silently. Starved of attention and affection. He is the answer. She keeps the secret, revels in the knowledge that while the others all listen to him, parts of him are hers alone.

CHAPTER SIXTEEN

Cal wakes in a bright environment and at first he thinks he is still on the hill, but as he stretches and opens his eyes, he feels the cooler air, hears the beep and quiet bustle of a ward, sees the clean, white sheet covering him.

'Dad? Shona – he's moving.'

He turns his head and his daughter is there beside him, her skin pink from their long day in the sun, her eyes huge with tears that spill down to her smile when she sees he is awake. Cal feels like he's had the best sleep of his life, a dreamless rejuvenating unconsciousness. Then he finds himself pressed into a double embrace, both Shona and Chrissie crying and laughing together.

'Lucie?' He croaks the word, remembering the woman crammed into a tiny hollow, trying desperately to escape the harshness of the environment.

Shona's face comes into view above him.

'She's alive. They had her on a drip before the helicopter landed. Do you remember walking down to the dam? The team carrying her? You went in the helicopter.'

Cal shakes his head slowly. 'Sort of, but not really.'

'You were pretty out of it. You had heatstroke too. The mountain rescue team went up to meet you and told us to go down the hill. I should have gone with them.' She wrings her hands. 'They couldn't see you so they came back but we knew you had to be there, so we went out again. That's why it took so long.'

He closes his eyes for a moment. The wait had felt interminable. It makes sense now.

'I tried to leave my rucksack where you would see it.'

'You needed a drip to rehydrate too,' Shona says, smoothing his hair from his forehead. 'Then the doctors said it was just exhaustion and you should sleep.'

'So you did,' Chrissie says, laughing through her tears. 'All night and then some.'

'What time is it?'

'Almost eleven in the morning.'

Cal feels bewildered – and starving. His stomach rumbles.

'And what about Lucie? Her ankle looked completely busted.'

'She was lucky you found her. The doctors said she wouldn't have had long. That water and paracetamol you gave her kept her going. She has some cracked ribs as well as the broken ankle, severe heatstroke, sunburn and dehydration. She's come round, apparently, but hasn't been able to tell anyone what happened yet.'

Cal shuffles up to a seated position. He feels sick when he thinks about the woman lying out there alone and waiting to die.

'When can I get out of here?'

'They want to observe you for a few hours and then you'll be free to go.'

—

Over the next few hours, Cal starts to get drips of information, from the staff, the police officer who comes to take a statement and the rampant news stories online. From them he learns that Lucie's parents have rushed to her bedside and Tyson has been declared no longer a person of interest. Lucie fell coming down off the ridge, smashing her ankle and her phone. After waiting for someone to come, she crawled down to the lochan in search of water.

Scanning the gossip sites, he wonders how she will ever go back to a normal life. Every detail of her existence has been picked over, her relationship dissected. And yet it's still impossible to tell from the outside what drove her to flee her home and head into the hills. The comments are filled with criticism about her preparedness and the resources needed to find her, as well as views on her appearance, her accent, her intelligence. It's brutal. All he keeps flashing back to is how broken and vulnerable she was, on the edge of death in the hills.

He turns off the phone; his mind is teeming with thoughts, leaping from one mystery to the next. That must have been how Jane met her end, alone and exposed to the environment. He hopes it was quick, that she didn't know what was happening to her. Even in this pristine hospital, he finds himself afraid of that lochan in the hills.

Seeing Jane's final resting place confounded him – it's so remote and yet specific. But with no samples to work with and no revelation from the scene, how can he possibly make progress on her case? He's picked a hopeless option. Maybe it was self-sabotage, a way to torpedo his career without having to admit that he's done.

Later in the afternoon, Cal is allowed out of bed to take a shower, and everything he does feels like a treat. He relishes towelling himself dry, pulling on clean shorts and T-shirt, even groaning at the post-walk aches. Smoothing Shona's moisturiser on his burned nose, he stares into the mirror and winces at his reflection. He looks like Rudolph.

He's about to leave the hospital with Shona to go back to Loch Tay when a doctor sticks her head around the door.

'How are you feeling?'

'Great,' he says. 'It's been the full spa treatment here.'

She laughs. 'Are you up to visiting Lucie before you leave? She's asking for you.'

It's a shock to see the usually groomed Instagrammer. Her skin is burned, her legs so bad that the sheet is held off the skin, her ankle raised up too. There's a drip in her arm, a tube to her nose and she's holding a morphine clicker.

When they see him, Lucie's parents immediately leap to their feet. Cal is propelled back a step by the force of her mother's embrace. They thank him over and over until he feels battered by the praise, and the doctor suggests they wait outside for a moment.

As he takes the seat next to Lucie, her eyes follow him, and what looks like a smile twists the corners of her mouth up ever so slightly. Everything about her looks sore and dried out.

'Thank you,' she whispers.

He pulls the chair in and leans close to her, and for a moment it's like when they were in the hills, an intimate proximity. For a second, Cal feels like he knows her better than anyone in his life – that no one else can fully understand what it was like out there. He feels as protective of her as he does of Chrissie.

'You don't have to thank me. I'm just so glad you're okay.'

'I'm sorry.' A tear rolls down her cheek and he can see the anguish on her face.

'You don't have to be sorry. There is nothing to be sorry for.'

'I had to get away,' she says. 'From Tyson. From everything.'

'You're safe now.'

'No one will believe me,' she says. Her eyes bore into his. Her voice is a husk.

'I believe you. Controlling men are so clever. People that matter will believe you.' He thinks of Jason Barr, of Naomi. Of how the biggest barrier to leaving is inside the victim. Control they have barely noticed wrapping its tentacles around them.

But Lucie is shaking her head back and forth, distressed at his lack of understanding.

'No,' she says. 'What I saw in the water. No one believes what I saw. They say I was delirious. That I'm making it up. They're not listening.'

Cal's mouth is suddenly dry. He remembers her mantra. *In the water. In the water. In the water.* He remembers the way she was huddled beneath the rocks, like she was trying to escape.

'The lochan,' he whispers.

She nods, the movement obviously painful.

'There were bones. After the fall coming down from the ridge, I lay there all day and realised no one was coming. My phone wouldn't work. That night, I started to crawl down to the lochan for water but just couldn't get there. I was so desperate. I thought I was going to die.'

She sucks in air, tears squeezing from her eyes. Cal takes her hand.

'Then when the sun came up, there it was, the water, and I thought it was going to be okay. But no one came and it was so hot. They say it was four nights. It felt like forever. On the last day, I crawled into the water to cool down...' Her eyes are wide and terrified. 'There were bones.'

Cal feels pinned by her gaze.

'Bones?'

She nods. 'I panicked. Dropped my things and my ankle was screaming agony. I couldn't get out of the water, it felt like it was pulling me in... I had to get away.'

Cal watches the memories cross her face, sees the terror she felt amid the scorching sun and the hopelessness of being trapped without a way to call for help. He can see she thought she was going to die.

'You're safe,' he says. 'There's no need to worry now.'

Gradually, her breathing calms.

'Do you believe me?'

And even though it makes no sense at all, even though she was delirious with pain and sunstroke, he does.

CHAPTER SEVENTEEN

They walk Rocket slowly down to the village, past the craggy spectre of Finlarig Castle, which is briefly visible in the trees before vanishing from view. The media circus has packed up and left, moving focus to the hospital where Lucie is being treated, but the place is still rammed with people – many in walking clothes, the tap of their walking poles playing percussion on narrow pavements.

'We're earlier than we said we'd be. Shall I call Chrissie to find out where she is?' Shona asks.

Cal takes out his phone.

'No need… I can tell you exactly where she is.'

He opens Find My Phone and clicks on her device. 'This way.'

Shona shakes her head. 'So weird.'

Cal grins when he sees Chrissie waiting on the bridge overlooking the Falls of Dochart. She casts a picturesque figure, lost in thought, her eyes on the water. The falls are apparently much reduced from their usual volume, given the weather, but they're still impressive, thundering in the background, foaming and bubbling.

He touches her shoulder and she springs back, startled. The dog barks once in surprise.

'Dad! You made me jump! You're early. How did you know I was here?'

'He stalked you,' Shona says.

Cal holds up the handset and Chrissie rolls her eyes.

'I'm not a teenager anymore, Dad. Invasion of privacy.' She laughs, throwing her arms around him for a hug. 'Actually, I still have you on my phone, so we're even.'

They walk to the other side of the bridge in the direction of the inn. There is so much to say, and yet everything feels overwhelming and it is difficult to know where to start. Miraculously, they manage to find a table and they order and sip their drinks, the foaming water a soothing background noise. Cal soaks in the atmosphere, feeling every moment as precious.

'Lucie told me she saw something in the lochan,' he says when they've ordered food and more drinks. 'That's why she dropped her phone and bottle, why she tried to get away.'

'What did she see?' Chrissie tilts her head, curious.

Cal glances at Shona.

'She says she saw bones.'

'What?!' His daughter slops her wine on the table.

'I know. It's crazy, right?'

'She had quite a tumble,' Shona says. 'And she was delirious. She almost died.'

'That's why the doctors and police don't believe her.'

Shona studies him, taking in his expression.

'But you do.'

'I don't know. She was muttering about the water when she was there. I know it's so unlikely, but I can't shake the thought. What if the receding water has revealed something that's usually hidden? What if it's related to Jane?'

'Wouldn't we have seen it?' Chrissie leans forward. 'When we found the phone?'

'I didn't really look for anything else,' Shona admits.

'You don't want to go back up there, do you, Dad?'

Chrissie shivers at the memory of the place and he can't blame her. It's so different to other places he's visited in the hills; a depth of bleakness lies over it.

'Not particularly.'

At that moment, the server appears bearing huge plates of food, breaking the intensity of the discussion. Cal reaches for his plate of fish and chips, suddenly ravenous. The conversation turns to cutlery and ketchup but his thoughts keep drifting up into the hills.

Now that he's seen where Jane lay all that time, he so desperately wants to give her a name, a history. But they've got nothing to go on. Only this slightest notion, the conviction of a woman half out of her mind with pain and sunstroke.

—

They sit until the dusk is sinking down over them, a seeping of indigo that comes with a hint of blessed coolness, deciding that they'll have one more drink and then wind their way back. Chrissie goes to the bar.

'They ID'd me,' she says when she comes back with the drinks a few minutes later.

Cal and Shona giggle at her expression.

'It's not funny! But I also got talking to one of the bar staff about things – Sean. He says one of the regulars has always claimed Jane came into the hotel bar and that he met her.'

Cal stops laughing.

'Really? Who?'

'Not sure, but Sean says he'll ask them to speak to us.'

They've almost finished their drinks when the barman approaches and starts piling glasses onto a tray. The man has dark eyes and a mop of brown curls, his shirt sleeves rolled to display a line of Japanese characters tattooed on the underside of his tanned arm. He's smiling but clearly pushed for time – the garden is still rammed, with drinkers also lining the low wall overlooking the falls.

'I've spoken to Pat and Walt for you,' he says when Chrissie's introduced him. 'They've had a few, though… and I don't know how seriously you can take them even when they're sober. You could always wait another night and catch them earlier on. They're in here all the time.'

Chrissie looks at Cal for a decision. He can see she's impatient to find out more and he's reluctant to let even a whisper of a lead slide away.

'Go!' Shona says, flapping her hands at them. 'I'll wait here for you.'

He and Chrissie follow Sean into the pub and to the end of the bar, where two men are perched on stools, half-drunk pints in front of them.

'Walter, Pat… these are the folk doing the podcast. They want to ask you about the woman. About Jane. Behave.' Winking at Chrissie, he dumps the tray of glasses onto the bar and heads back outside.

One of the men – Walter, Cal thinks – leans over to them and offers a meaty paw to shake. The other just waves from his propped position, red cheeks suggesting that moving might be too difficult for him.

'She came in the bar at the hotel,' Walter slurs. 'When we used to drink in there. I was waiting for you to show up.' He looks at Pat. 'Always late.'

The other man takes another slug of his pint and shrugs.

'Are you sure you werenae pished? You'll be telling me you've seen Nessie in the loch next.'

Walter splutters on his beer. Cal worries he's going to choke, but he regains control. He can't decide if they're toying with them or imparting useful information.

'What did she look like?'

'Grey hair, walking jacket. Cannae really mind. Typical tourist.'

'She wasn't from round here?'

Walter shakes his head emphatically. 'Nah. Her accent was funny, like. No American but… something like that. She was a rare sniffy craiter.'

'So many of them with new kit and no commonsense,' Pat puts in. 'And look what happens to them – like that lassie this week.'

Both men shake their heads and Cal feels himself bristling on Lucie's behalf. They're not wrong exactly, but they didn't see her like he did.

'What did she go into the hotel for? Was she staying there?'

He holds his breath in hope, but Walter shakes his head.

'The shop was shut for a minute and she wanted a bottle of water. Didn't want to wait for it to open. Bought some crisps and all. Put them in her rucksack.'

'Her bag?'

'Aye.'

Walter signals the bar staff for another pint.

'I'll get this one,' Cal offers, digging his bank card out of his pocket and tapping it on the reader.

'Did she seem upset to you? Ill or depressed, maybe?'

Walter shakes his head slowly, side to side, like he's testing his neck still works.

'Maybe it was just that the shop was shut. But she seemed angry to me. Woman on a mission.'

'Any idea why?'

Walter shakes his head.

Cal senses that's all they're going to get from the men. As they say their goodbyes, Pat claps him on the back.

'That lochan's a dark place. My da used to say it was cursed. You be careful poking around.'

'Cursed?' The word seems cold in the hot bar. Cal thinks of the dark, deep waters of the lochan, of Lucie's strange mantra, of the hidden platform where Jane's remains were found.

'Aye. Cursed. Mark my words. Don't say we didnae warn you.'

—

They walk back in the semi-darkness, Cal and Chrissie sobered by their encounter with the men in the bar. The hills tower over Loch Tay, hulking and inky – the little lochan seems another world away.

'Cursed?' Shona laughs when they fill her in on the conversation. 'They don't really think that?'

'It is atmospheric up there.'

'You don't *believe* them?' She gives Cal a playful shove and he wobbles a bit, addled by tiredness and the pints he's drunk, though they were small fry compared to what Pat and Walter were putting away.

'No, of course not. Whatever happened to Jane happened at the hands of humans, but until we work out who she is, we've got no chance of finding out who wanted her dead. They did say something interesting, though.'

'What's that?'

'The woman had a bag she put her crisps into.'

'I don't understand.' Chrissie falls into step beside them.

'Jane wasn't found with a bag,' Cal tells her. 'So either Walter didn't see her at all…'

'…or someone took it,' Shona says.

Cal's mind spins up to that isolated place, where lichen clings to rocks in firework displays of blue and green, where the water is so deep and expressionless, where you feel that the landscape is concealing something, that people are watching you.

'I think we should look in the water,' Shona says, suddenly.

'You do?'

She shrugs. 'Let's be honest. There doesn't seem to be much to go on for Jane's case, with no samples to test. If you're going to have to tell Sarah it's a no go, then we should at least have tried everything we can, no matter how random. I think it might be good for you to go back there, too.'

Cal grimaces, relieved that Shona is game for another trip to the lochan, but dreading going back there. Now seems as good a time as any to mention his other idea.

'That's not the only thing I was thinking.'

His tone makes the others stop.

'I think we should apply to exhume Jane's body.'

CHAPTER EIGHTEEN

MORNA, 1952

For months their meetings both sustain and revolt her. She is fascinated and horrified at the way her body bends to his, as if she has no will of her own. But she can bear the self-hatred and the shame as long as he still needs her – and for a long time, he does. Slowly, though, she feels his attention slipping. Now, if she looks up from her seat at church on Sunday, his eyes will just as likely be on some other girl as boring into her, all-seeing, all-knowing. Even when she shifts position, fidgeting and inviting him with her restlessness, he keeps his gaze elsewhere.

Then there are rumours about him in the village. She hears them first in the shop and she almost drops the eggs she is holding.

'He'll soon be down the aisle himself, by all accounts.'

'Aye, he should settle down, right enough.' The woman who runs the store leans across to her friend, mischief in her eyes. 'A fine looker like that... He'll make some woman a good husband. I'd be in the queue if I were younger.'

'Well, I'd ay take him off your hands if you couldn't manage,' her friend retorts. The women's laughs echo to where she is standing, stock-still and hidden by the end of the shelf. Her body doused in ice.

'If gossip's to be believed, the young lady up at the castle is the one that's captured his attention.'

'And since when would you listen to gossip, Bridie?'

More laughter.

Mind flicking to the young woman she sees in the front pew at church on a Sunday. Golden curls and porcelain skin. She can't stop the gasp, though she presses her hand to her mouth to hold it back, as the women turn and see her standing there.

'Not a conversation for little ears,' the shopkeeper says tartly. 'And you can put those eggs back. Your last bill is outstanding. You'll need to tell your da to come and settle up before you take any more.'

'If he hasn't drunk it all,' the friend mutters, loud enough for Morna to hear.

The women watch as, cheeks burning, she returns the few groceries to the shelves and puts the basket back by the door. She does it slowly, numbed by the news and the shame. Her stomach rumbles as she leaves the shop and their laughter follows her down the street.

—

When her monthly doesn't come, a hand tightens around her heart. She waits, hoping it will simply be late. She's had less to eat this month; her father has been going to the pub every day and he has stubbornly refused to settle their tab at the shop, so maybe it is simply hunger. But, deep inside, she knows this is not the case. Sleep deserts her, the desire to eat vanishes and she picks at the meagre offerings, her father taking what she leaves without question.

What will happen to her? She's heard stories of disgrace; girls have vanished before and returned to the village later, wan-looking and dried out like husks. She can't even write to Betty to tell her. No one must know about them, she's promised. She needs to see *him*. He will know what to do. He will help her. He has to.

On Saturday, she goes to their usual meeting point at the ruin. She waits two hours in the drizzle, biting her nails and shivering at the feeling of watchfulness she always has there, trying not to think of the ghosts of the past clustering unhappily around her. By the time she leaves, she is wet through. As she crosses the grassy lawn, a stone dislodges inside the ruin and falls to the floor, shattering and sending an echoing boom into the air, scattering the crows nesting in the tower.

The next day is Sunday and his wedding is announced. She sits in church, lacklustre and desperate, and watches the smiling girl from the castle in the front pew, hatred and confusion pouring from her as the girl simpers at the congratulations tossed her way. There has to be some mistake, surely?

She watches his face, the side she can see of it from her vantage point, searching for some sign of coercion or regret. There is nothing. The hole inside from her lack of breakfast gapes wider.

The only way to catch him is to wait until after the service, to find him alone for a moment and pounce. She hovers in the graveyard, huddled by the wall under the trees, next to the leaning, moss-covered stones of the forgotten dead. She knows he walks this way, seeking solitude by taking the back exit from the churchyard, unlike most of the churchgoers.

When he sees her, his face hardens and his stride picks up, as if he will pass her.

'Wait! I need to talk to you, please.'

'What are you doing here?'

She quails at the rigid form of his face, the hardness she has always seen as strength until it is turned against her.

'I just need to speak to you.'

But the words are small and insignificant.

'We can't talk here,' he hisses, anger deepening the crags on his face, those long lines from his mouth to his jaw.

'But I waited for you and you weren't there.'

'Look.' He draws her to one side of the path, holding her arm away from him as if it were something soiled, pushing her back to the seclusion of the wall. 'You need to leave me alone now. That's enough.'

Her temples pulse. This can't be happening. 'But I need to see you. I'm...' Her words dry up and her hands fly to her belly. His eyes widen in disgust as he takes in the meaning.

'Were you not taking care of that?'

She takes a step back, physically staggered at the cold slap of his words. *How?* she wants to ask. *How would I take care of this? I don't understand.*

'My da will throw me out. Please. I don't know what to do. Who should I tell?'

'No one.' His eyes glitter like ice, reminding her of the lumps that formed on the loch one bitter winter, hard and unforgiving. 'You tell no one.'

At that moment a couple round the corner by the church and he startles backwards, his body language changing immediately, back straighter, more relaxed. He nods to her to fall in beside him and walks towards the gate. She presses one hand to the metal to steady herself, feeling faint and hot.

The couple are here, ready to pass.

'Wonderful service, minister,' the man says.

'Yes, quite beautiful,' his wife adds.

Unsteady on her feet, she clings to the gate until they have gone, and he sweeps past her. She barely hears the words he hisses.

'Saturday. Usual place.'

CHAPTER NINETEEN

Cal lies on the sofa in the cabin with thoughts of the lochan and the mystery bones circling inside him. Shona is exhausted and goes to bed, but he stays up to catch the news and falls asleep where he sits, addled by emotion as well as alcohol. In a dream, he travels from the hill to the graveyard, walking through the moss-covered stones to the quiet corner where Jane is waiting, ready to tell him her secrets. When he gets to her, the grave lies open, the earth yawning. She is gone.

He startles awake, a sheen of sweat on his face. His phone is vibrating beside him and he snatches it up to see the withheld number again. His body moves from sleep in an instant, adrenaline firing. Rocket lumbers from the sofa to the floor, flumping onto the carpet with a huff.

Rubbing his face to dispel the dream, he presses the answer button, heaviness settling into him as the situation with Jason Barr, with his damaged wife, comes rushing back.

'Naomi,' he whispers.

All he can hear is crying. She doesn't speak for long moments, during which Cal is filled with a mixture of sympathy and revulsion. This is a woman who wrote to convicted murderers in prison for kicks, who fell for one and married him. He just cannot understand what makes her tick. At the same time, he remembers Lucie, the relationship she had with Tyson, the madness it drove her to, and he cannot hang up on her.

So he waits.

'I don't know what to do,' she says. 'How do I escape from him?'

'You can leave him any time, Naomi. There doesn't have to be a reason. You're allowed to change your mind.'

'But he'll take half of everything. That's what he said. This house is my home. I'd have to move. I wouldn't have enough to live on.'

'I hadn't realised things were that tight,' he says.

'His defence... took almost everything.'

Cal wants to cry. There it is. The price of injustice. Barr's freedom bought for him by a woman deluded.

He sighs. 'It might be that the court would award you more assets, if—'

'If he committed a crime,' she says.

'What are you talking about?'

Her voice changes, shrewd and terrible. 'If he hit me.'

'Jesus. Does he hit you?'

'No,' she whispers. 'Not yet. He's smarter than that, but if I could make him... If I could prove it...'

Cal feels the swooping panic of a dangerous conspiracy. He cannot be sucked into this.

'Naomi, what are you talking about? This is madness. Just leave.'

His voice rises, loud in the quiet night. A moth batters itself against the light fitting, drawn in through the open door.

'He's coming,' she says. 'I have to go.'

CHAPTER TWENTY

He means to tell Shona about the call from Naomi, but they wake late and she has to rush to get ready for an online forensic strategy meeting. Instead, he takes Rocket for an amble in the woods behind the cabins and mulls the late-night conversation. Shona would tell him to talk to the police, to call Detective Foulds, who investigated and charged Barr with his sister's murder. But it's only one or two calls and if he does that, it will stir everything up again. He's not proud of the obsession he developed with Barr after the trial. He needs to put a stop to it, that's all. Move on and no one needs to know.

When he gets back, Shona is making iced coffees in her vest top and shorts, the smart top she donned for the call discarded. They find the only patch of shade on the deck to sit.

'I made the call,' she says. 'About Jane.'

Cal feels the thrill of a decision taken from his hands.

'What do we need to do?'

'Police Scotland won't block it. George Hunt left a trail of disasters behind him and so there's an unspoken agreement that redoing his open cases is not the worst idea. Any costs would have to be met by the podcast, though.'

'I'll talk to Sarah.'

Cal swallows, suddenly aware how seismic this could be.

'It will have to go to the Sheriff Court for approval. There's only one potential sticking point.'

Shona redirects her gaze from the sun-soaked view to Cal. Her hair is clipped off her shoulders and the days on the hills have turned her skin a light brown, with a smattering of freckles across her nose and cheeks. She looks beautiful.

'What's that?'

'The church. In the absence of family, it's their plot and their decision. If they're against it, then there's no point in pursuing.'

He pictures the minister in the quiet graveyard, lovingly tending the plot.

'What do you think he'll say? Tavish Dewar?'

'I don't know. People don't like exhumations. The idea of disturbing the dead. The community may not support it, and hostile locals are the last thing you need.'

She is distracted by the dog nudging her with his nose, seeking treats or back scratches from the softest touch, preferably both.

'It's not going to be easy, is it?'

'Even if you do get samples, the tests might not yield useful results.'

Cal stares at the expanse of the loch below them. What if this opens up a hornets' nest of pain for Jane's family, wherever they are? Are they robust enough to deal with it? There's no way to know.

'It's the perfect excuse, really,' he says. 'I can tell Sarah we've hit a dead end and I'm done.'

'You're not going to, though, are you?'

She knows him and his struggle between truth and comfort so well – is it better to know what happened to your loved one or live in ignorance? He used to be certain that it was better to know, but since he found out that his sister met Jason Barr on a dark country road and her body wound up buried in a scrapyard, he has tortured himself with the details of what she might have been through in the hours she was alone with him. Answers only bring more questions.

'I have to believe that the truth is better,' he says, finally. 'And Jane has no one else to push for her.'

Shona stands and paces the bleached boards of the decking. Cal watches her feet, the shiny pink polish on her toes gleaming in the light.

'Then talk to the minister,' she says. 'Unless you ask, you can't know.'

CHAPTER TWENTY-ONE

EPISODE TWO: WHAT LUCIE SAW

Today, there seems to be little reflection in the water of Lochan Nan Cat, despite the clear skies and baking heat. It's like it's sucking all light into its depths. As we reach the shore, conversation drops away. No creatures move, no birds fly. There is no one else in sight, just the occasional flash of people on the high peaks above.

This is the place where Lucie Barnes fell into the water, injured and delirious. What she says she saw could change everything. Forensic anthropologist Shona Williams has experience of recovering remains from all kinds of environments. She's agreed to take a look on behalf of Finding Justice. *Barefoot, she wades slowly into the water where Lucie's mobile phone and water bottle were recovered.*

'Talk us through what you're doing.'

'I've divided the bottom of the lochan into a grid and I'm going to walk along it, trying not to disturb the silt. There's a steep drop away when you get this far out. If you imagine a bowl with a wide rim – then Lucie's items were found quite near the lip where the lochan drops a long way. My colleague Cliff is over there, spreading out a tarpaulin where we can put anything interesting we find.'

After twenty minutes, Shona stops for a long time, staring at a particular point.

'What have you seen?'

Without answering, she plunges her arm into the water to the shoulder. When she's pulled it free, there is a long bleached bone in her hand.

'Is that what it looks like?'

'If you think it looks like a human femur, then yes, it is.'

For the next couple of hours, the team extract more bones, ferrying them to the tarpaulin and arranging the fragments. When they're finished, Shona's feet are bright pink with cold.

'Are the bones recent?'

'We'd need to carbon date them to be sure. They are certainly more than a decade old. Here we have part of a leg and foot. We're missing some bits of the foot – there are supposed to be twenty-six bones and we've got twenty, but you can see the shape. We also have a few bones from the other foot.'

'Where do you think the rest of them are?'

'My guess is that the body was resting on the edge of the drop. When it was disturbed, most of the skeleton must have gone over the edge. The only way to recover them will be divers.'

CHAPTER TWENTY-TWO

MORNA, 1952

It's late on Saturday when she gets home, dripping lochan water across the floor, her limbs shaking and her breath a frozen fog. She slips in by the kitchen door and finds the house cold, the stony damp seeping into everything. He's spilled whisky on the floor again and it sticks to her socks as she tiptoes across it, shivering. Bone cold and wraith-like. The fire is unlit, even though she cleared and set it this morning, so all he needed to do was light a match. There are dishes everywhere: it is as if he sets out to make as much mess as he can, just to spite her.

She stops by the table, scanning to see if there is anything left for her to eat, but there is nothing. It is then that she sees her mother's blue-and-white butter dish lying tipped over, cracked. Tears come to her eyes at the sight of it. The first she's properly cried today and they're over a butter dish. There is so much more to cry about than that. She can't stop shaking, her whole body jolting and cold. Her mind keeps looping over the things she saw, the things she did, the ways she has changed and can never go back.

Listening, she tiptoes to the doorway, peering into the small living room where two chairs sit before the cold hearth, expecting to see the bulk of him slumped and nasty. There's no one there, not even a pair of muddy boots with their dubs across the tiles. Heart pounding, teeth chattering, she crosses to the small staircase and ventures up into the darkness, step by step, ready to run if he's in one of those humours where he won't see reason and all she'll get is the thick end of his fist. Once, he hit her at the top and she tumbled to the foot. She was black and blue for a week.

At the top of the stairs, she exhales. From here, you can see into both the tiny bedrooms, and the filthy nest he sleeps in is empty. He must be at the pub. She lets out a long breath that turns into a moan. There is no way she can stay. He'll stagger in late if he's gone to the pub, too drunk to come and find her. If she leaves tonight, he won't know until the morning, maybe longer. Her fingers close tight around the solid item in her pocket. It feels warmer than flesh, and its value is as much as life itself.

In the bathroom, she strips and washes at the sink; the water must be cold but she can't feel it, can barely hold the flannel for shaking. Bundling her wet clothes into the corner, she dresses in the warmest things she has, but nothing stops the shivering. She doesn't have time for much if she's to avoid her da, so she takes only what will fit in a small hessian sack, tucking in the few clothes she has, secreting her stolen treasure at the bottom.

She's hungry but there is nothing to take from here. At the door she pauses, turning to look one last time. Already, her home looks smaller and even more filthy than usual. Locking the door behind her, she slides the key beneath it, thankful for once for the gap that lets the cold in. A sense of dread fills her as she creeps through the dark to the edge of the village. If Mr Bainzie will not help her she is lost. *No*, she forces herself strong. She will walk to Glasgow if she has to.

—

She sneaks along the side of the cottage to the back door and knocks in the darkness, softly — too soft perhaps, for no one comes. Losing her nerve, she takes a breath and studies the line of light at the window to the side of her. He's home. He has to be. Summoning her courage, she hammers hard with her fist. A second later and the door is thrown open.

'Who is it? Morna?'

'Mr Bainzie.' She sobs. 'I need your help.'

He lets her into the kitchen warmth, clutching her bag, her eyes startled and blinking at the glow, her flesh remembering warmth and bending towards the flame.

'Alastair?'

A sharp voice from the doorway. A woman stands in her apron, hands on her hips and suspicion in her eyes.

'It's okay, Beth,' he says. 'See to the bairn for a minute, would you?'

He crosses to the woman and kisses her on the cheek. Whatever passes between them must be trust, for his wife frowns at Morna but leaves the room, drawing the door shut behind her.

'Sit.' Mr Bainzie directs her to a chair.

'I'm sorry,' she says, her teeth chattering. 'I didn't know where to go.'

'You're frozen,' he says. 'Here.' He pours a cup of tea from the pot on the table and passes her a slice of buttered bread from a plate. 'What's happened? Was it your father?'

Morna shakes her head, realising from the sourness on his kind face how much he has guessed.

'I need to get to Glasgow,' she says. 'Can you help me?'

Mr Bainzie perches on the chair opposite her, leans close but does not touch her.

'Morna, are you in trouble?'

'Yes,' she says. 'I am.'

—

At the bend in the road, she wraps her arms around herself and looks anxiously for headlights, while pacing the verge. Maybe he's changed his mind. She thinks of her surrendered key and wonders if she can retrieve it. But she can't stay here after what she has done, so if he isn't coming, she'll have to hitch and make the best of it.

It's a good while after the time he told her to be there, when a car pulls up by the verge. She is sitting on a stump just into the tree line, so cold and tired she has drifted off and can barely move. She grabs her bag and stumbles towards him, tripping on the uneven ground. Hurrying around the car to the passenger side, she fumbles for the handle, hauling herself in.

'I'm sorry,' he says. 'I had to speak to Beth and then borrow the car from my pal Craigie.'

The heat and his presence are such a relief, she almost sobs. Mr Bainzie pulls the car out onto the road and the headlights illuminate the bends as they pick up speed. Terror creeps over her. She won't ever see Fearghas again. Just as she won't see the village that has disappeared behind her, the long stretch of the loch and the dramatic hills above. She clutches the bag to her chest. This is her only chance.

Numb, she tilts her head against the jolting door and tucks her icy fingers under her armpits. It's not so much sleep as delirium that she sinks into: churning waters and yelling, cold words and even colder realisations.

CHAPTER TWENTY-THREE

GLASGOW

MORNA, 1952

She jerks awake on the outskirts of the city, afraid and wishing for some intangible comfort. They arrive on a street of thin houses and discarded rubbish. The property they stop in front of looks the worst of a bad lot. This is nothing like the picture Betty painted in her letters. It has newspaper on the windows, some of which are cracked and all of which are blackened. Paint peels from a rotting door.

'This doesn't look right,' Mr Bainzie says, doubtful. 'Are you sure, Morna?'

She unfolds Betty's latest letter and they check it against the name of the street on the corner.

'This is it,' she says. 'Number fifty.'

'And she's definitely expecting you?'

'Oh yes,' Morna lies. 'She said just to knock quietly, as it's so late.' Forcing a smile onto her face, she turns to him. 'Thank you. Please, would you mind not telling anyone where I am. I'll be in touch with my da just as soon as I get sorted.'

Mr Bainzie sighs. After a moment, he nods. 'I'll keep the secret,' he says. 'I don't like this, Morna, but I know your father is not a… patient man.'

She wishes she could banish the anguish from his face. Only a few years older than her. The same sort of age as Fearghas. But he is a good man, and she can now tell the difference.

When she closes the car door and moves to the pavement, she waves him away and waits until she is alone in the deserted street. The sound of drunken singing comes from a lit property on the other side. Something scuttles in the corner of the front garden as she approaches, making her recoil and sending needles into her.

It is only a few hours until dawn. This is not so bad. Clutching her meagre bag, her stomach empty and growling, she settles down on the front step to wait for morning.

—

She holds herself together through the long night, through the shriek of Betty's landlady when she finds Morna cold and curled on the step in the grey dawn, through the look of shock and dismay on Betty's face when she sees her friend.

Morna stays calm when her friend bustles her down the street. Betty is dressed for work, her lips red and perfect as cherries, her hair curled and her skin clean. She keeps back the tears when Betty takes her by the arm into a small shop and buys her a cup of tea and a piece of toast.

'I've to get to work,' she says. 'I canny be late. The foreman's a devil. You canny stay with me, Morna, it's not allowed.' Betty's cheeks flush. 'I know I said it was my place, but…'

Sitting in her misery, unkempt and dirty from a night on the pavement, Morna feels the gulf between them splitting into a chasm. She needs to pull things back quickly or she's lost.

'I can get some money,' she says. 'I've something I can pawn. It's valuable.'

Betty's face clears. 'Well, if that's the case then maybe you could rent a room in the house – the attic isn't great but it's better than nothing. I could ask if there's a job going and all?'

Morna forces another fake smile onto her face but it wobbles.

'What's wrong?' Betty clutches her arm. 'Is it your da?'

She shakes her head, determined to keep her secrets in but, confronted with the kindness and familiarity of her old friend, she can't help it – the words jump from her lips, the whole sorry tale.

She knows from Betty's shocked expression that things are as bad as they can be.

'I need to be someone else,' she says. 'No one can know I'm here. If he finds me, he'll skin me alive.'

Betty nods. 'I won't breathe a word. We'll ask my boss for a job but give a different name, pretend you're my cousin, or something.'

Morna can't imagine ever laughing again – it feels as if happiness lies at the bottom of the lochan in the hills and she's never getting it back. This arrangement will buy her time, but it isn't enough of a plan to solve her problems forever.

'I can stay for a wee while, but I need to get far away. Further than Glasgow. If my da finds me, he'll kill me, Betty. What am I going to do?'

She doesn't tell her friend that's not the only thing she's running from.

Betty swirls her tea, staring into the bottom of the cup. After a long moment, she looks up and there are tears in her eyes.

'I don't know, Morna. But we'll think of something.'

CHAPTER TWENTY-FOUR

The bones are recorded, documented and transported back to Aberdeen with Cliff for analysis. It takes most of the day and Cal is thoroughly sick of the lochan by the time they leave it to trek home. His body screams at the exertion. When they reach the lodge, Shona goes straight into a lengthy strategy call with the police and other agencies needed for further recovery, while he calls Lucie to tell her the news.

She sounds groggy from painkillers, recovering from more surgery on her ankle.

'I didn't think you believed me. I didn't think anyone believed me,' she says.

'You were so sure. I thought it was worth checking.'

Lucie is silent for a moment and he realises she's crying. 'It's going to take me a while to feel normal after Tyson,' she says. 'It messes with your mind, being told you'll never be believed. I don't think I even believe myself.'

He thinks of Naomi. Of the weird, twisted way her mind works. Maybe it's not all her fault.

'It's because of you that we found the bones,' he tells Lucie. 'The police are talking about sending divers to the bottom of the lochan for the rest of them and that never would have happened without you. Maybe when you're better, I could interview you for the podcast?'

'Really?' She sounds excited by the suggestion. 'You're serious?'

'Of course I am. You could do a Reel for your account as well, if you like.'

Lucie squeaks at the thought. When she hangs up, he's still smiling.

Shona emerges from their room and Cal makes her a cold gin and tonic.

'Where's Chrissie?' she asks.

'She's gone to meet Sean and bring us back a takeaway. No one needs to cook tonight. How did it go?'

Shona squeezes onto the bench next to him and rests her head on his shoulder while he tops up their drinks.

'They're going to send divers down in the next couple of days and see if the rest of the skeleton can be located.'

'That's brilliant.'

'Whether any of this is related to Jane, I just don't know.'

The cold waters and the sheer drop lurk like nausea. Cal stares out into the middle distance then kisses the top of Shona's head.

'Maybe we'll never know.'

—

The next day is blistering again, little relief as he drives to the head of the loch with Rocket for company. Cal's stomach is a tangle of knots at the thought of the conversation that lies ahead. But Sarah is waiting for an answer.

Looking back down the long stretch of water, Ben Lawers is prominent on the skyline, hulking and watchful. In front of him is the church, surrounded by its cool, green graveyard. He clips on the dog's lead while he subtly assesses the site and how easy or difficult it would be to undertake an exhumation. Because of the walls, it's actually not that exposed and there's a gate at the back that would allow it to be done quietly, but the idea still makes him queasy.

As he stands by the grave, he becomes aware of an older woman watching from a bench further along. Despite the scorching weather, she is wearing a light padded jacket, a knee-length tweed skirt and thick tights. A William Morris-patterned tote bag rests on a walking frame beside her. When she glances over again, he raises a hand in greeting.

The dog pulls towards her, sensing the opportunity for attention. Cal yanks him back but the woman stretches out a hand and calls to him, so he lets Rocket lead the way. The Lab accepts the fuss with wild enthusiasm and then flops on the ground in the shade cast by the bench.

'He's lovely.'

'You've got a friend for life.'

'You were looking at Jane.'

She peers at Cal and he feels her assessing him, bright eyes beneath wisps of grey hair.

'Yes, I'm Cal Lovett. I'm making a podcast about the case, in the hope we can find out who she was.'

'I'd heard about that. I'm Rose.'

Rose looks out to the loch, her eyes watering. Her hand shakes as she reaches for a bottle of water in the bag attached to the walker.

'Here,' Cal says. 'Let me.' He pulls up the inbuilt straw and hands her the bottle. She drinks clumsily and he perches next to her. He's reminded of his own mother and her current state of frailty.

'Have you always lived here?'

Relinquishing the bottle, she nods. 'Since I was sixteen. I used to teach in the primary school for a time, but I gave it up when I had my son.'

'Do you remember when Jane was found, then?'

'Must be twenty years now,' she says, her face clouding over with the memory. She frowns. 'All on her own up there. It makes no sense.'

'Mother?'

Rocket scrambles to his feet and lets out a single bark. Tavish is striding along the path, sweating and uncomfortable-looking in his full ministerial garb.

'Oh, the minister is your son?'

Tavish's face creases in a smile at the sight of Rose petting the dog. Cal can see the affection between them immediately – so different to the relationship he has with his own mother. The man turns to him.

'Are you visiting Jane?'

'Actually, it was you I was hoping to speak to, but now is probably not the right time,' Cal says, half-relieved and half-disappointed that he will have to come back another day.

'I don't mind.' Rose flaps her hand in front of her face. 'I'd like to sit out here a bit longer. You could leave the dog with me.'

'If you're sure you're happy.' Tavish bends over and unfolds his mother's sleeve where it has risen and creased. She bats him away.

'Don't fuss.'

He gives Cal a look of patient amusement.

'Shall we walk and talk?'

Cal fixes Rocket's lead to the bench and watches as the dog rests his head in Rose's lap, then he follows Tavish round the side of the church.

'She's happiest out there at the moment,' he says. 'It's so hot indoors.'

'This heat is impossible.'

'What did you want to talk to me about?'

'It's a little delicate.' Cal takes a moment to frame his request. Tavish doesn't push him, just walks silently beside. 'To identify Jane, we had hoped to use a range of scientific techniques to see if we could work out where she grew up, maybe find some relatives.'

'What sort of techniques?'

'Tests on bone and hair samples.'

Tavish swallows. 'I see.' He looks out over the loch. 'She's lain here so long, that poor woman. She should have her name returned to her if possible.'

'Unfortunately, the samples that were taken at the time of Jane's recovery have been lost. We suspect they were accidentally destroyed after a particular lab closed. Without them we only have a basic DNA profile that is stored on the police system and there isn't a match on there.'

Cal takes a breath and turns to Tavish. 'There's no easy way to ask this, but we wondered if you might support the exhumation of Jane's remains?'

The man's mouth falls open, his smile dropping away. 'Oh. I see.'

From where they are standing, Cal can see the perfectly groomed grave plot, the care with which it is maintained.

'It's an upsetting idea, I know. But she may have a family somewhere, waiting for answers. There's a chance these tests can help us find them. That's the only reason I'm asking.'

Tavish puts a hand to his head.

'You're right. It's just... not something I'd considered.' He stares at the grave. 'We've never done that before. I don't know what people would think, in the congregation, that is.' He falters. 'I'm sorry,' he says, wiping his forehead with his arm. 'It's this heat. It's making me fuzzy.'

'Please don't feel you have to rush to a decision,' Cal says. 'Maybe we can send you some information about what would happen, and you can take some time to think about it and talk to the people higher up in the church that you'd need to seek permission from. The last thing we want to do is pressure you.'

Tavish's smile is sad. 'There's really only one higher-up opinion that matters,' he says. 'I will pray on it and maybe we can talk again in a day or two?'

'I'd appreciate that,' Cal says.

They walk in silence around the perimeter of the churchyard until they reach Rose and the dog in her shady spot.

'I'm afraid we need to go,' Tavish says.

Rose peers at him, frowning.

'We're going to visit my husband now, in the nursing home,' she says. 'He's not doing so well these days.'

'I'm sorry to hear that.'

The minister lifts the walker closer and holds a hand out to his mother.

'I can manage,' she says, giving Rocket another pat on the head. 'Don't fuss, Tavish.'

He watches the two of them make their way up the path to the church and disappear round the corner.

Before he follows, Cal crosses the dried-out grass and crouches by Jane's grave. Is this the right thing? He touches the lettering on the stone, acutely aware of how close to her he is. Only a few feet below him are her bones and the answers he needs. He just can't get to them.

CHAPTER TWENTY-FIVE

She calls again and it feels like his brain is swelling, ready to explode. He ignores her, but she tries over and over, the light flashing on his phone, illuminating the tiny bedroom. Cal tiptoes out to the deck, staring at the handset, trying to decide whether to answer or to turn it off. Rocket lumbers from his bed and follows, nudging Cal's leg with a wet nose.

'It's okay, boy,' he whispers.

The truth is, he's kept the line of communication open in case he learns something that could put Jason Barr in prison, where he deserves to be. The chance to seek justice for Margot has passed, but what if Naomi could tell him something else, something new? He thought for a while that Allegra Carlo might be the key, but there's no way in, it's a dead end. Now this diabolical idea of Naomi's – to lure Barr into making a fatal mistake – is something else entirely. He can't be a part of that. Can he?

He hates that this desire for revenge runs through him, corrupting him. Why won't she just leave him in peace? Feeling a flare of red heat, he drags the answer bar across the screen.

'It's late, Naomi. Please stop calling me.'
'We can help each other, Cal. We want the same thing.'
'I'm not the right person.'
'You're the only person.'

'Leave it. You need to leave it.'
'You don't know what it's like for me.'

Cal wants to scream.

'What do you want from me?'

'I want to be free. You can help me be free.'

He can't help it – fireworks of unfairness ricochet inside his skull, his feelings igniting.

'Naomi, why would I help you? You've propped him up all along. You are the reason he won that court case. You stood next to him and said he was good. You lied for him. You are the reason my sister has no justice, the reason I can't sleep at night.'

Silence. That just inflames him even more.

'You need to take responsibility for your actions. You need to stop calling me. I am not the answer.'

'But you could be...'

'LEAVE ME ALONE.'

And the line cuts, leaving him lost in the darkness.

Cal presses his hands to his face and screams into them. Every little bit of frustration and grief that has built up inside him has boiled over. Hot tears seep through his fingers, which are shaking as they still clutch his phone. He takes long shuddering breaths, trying to calm himself. Finally, his chest stops heaving and he turns, dropping his hands from his wet face.

Shona is standing in the doorway, watching him in horror.

'Cal?'

Her voice is heavy, laden with a thousand questions.

'Tell me that's not who I think it is.'

But he doesn't need to answer. She knows him too well. She spins away.

'Please,' he says, 'wait.'

When she turns back, there are tears in her eyes.

'How long has it been going on?'

He shakes his head, unable to remember when this started, unable to say it was months ago and that he's kept this secret for so long.

'All those times I've woken up and you weren't there, and I trusted that you were working or couldn't sleep... and you've been talking to her?'

Shona presses her hand to her mouth.

'I thought... I thought she could tell me something.'

'Look at yourself,' she hisses. 'What are you doing?'

He doesn't know what to say, fixed to the floor in shame.

There is a look of disgust on her face that he has never seen before.

'I'm sorry. I should have told you. Can we talk about this, please?'

'No.' She shakes her head. 'I'm tired, Cal. Right now, you're the last person I want to talk to. I need space.'

He deflates as she spins away from him. Shona doesn't bluff or attention-seek. If she says to stay away, she means it. Cal slumps onto one of the chairs on the decking, wondering if the whole holiday park heard their row. Rocket makes a noise somewhere between a grumble and a yowl. Instead of taking his usual place at Cal's feet, he slumps in the doorway, as if he is barring the way.

For hours Cal sits there, staring into nothing, hating Naomi, hating Jason Barr, hating himself most of all.

CHAPTER TWENTY-SIX

Cal is roused from the sludge of sleep by Shona shaking him awake. His limbs are tangled in the blanket, his mouth is dry and his head is banging.

'Is it late?' he mumbles, aware of the staleness on his skin, the traces of sweat and fear from last night, while she smells fresh, of daytime.

'We need to talk.'

She opens the door and sets off towards the forest. It's early, the dew still fresh on the ground, the air cool. Rocket bounds ahead of them, delighted at the early-morning adventure. Cal slips his feet into sandals. He feels the ground lurching beneath him; every step he takes is one into the unknown right now. He's betrayed Shona. They agreed to tell each other everything, to choose each other and not to feel trapped and obliged. If it was the other way around, he'd be devastated.

'I should have told you,' he says when he catches up with her.

'Yes, you should.'

She keeps striding and he scuttles to keep pace. He knows she's angry and she needs to walk and shout, and all he can do is be there and take what he deserves. The ground crackles under his feet, the usual bogs and mossy stretches desiccated and weary. Shona walks and walks and when they've been going for ten minutes, her tears start and he honestly thinks he has never felt more guilty than he feels right now.

'Stop, stop, please. Just stop.'

He catches up to her and takes her arms, pulling her gently into a hug. She beats her hands on his chest.

'You are so fucking stupid.'

'Agreed.'

'Foulds warned you. Wait. Does *she* know you're calling Naomi Barr?'

'I am not calling Naomi. I've never called her. But I do answer when Naomi calls me. I've tried to stop but I can't help it.'

'Why, Cal? You said you were drawing a line, moving on.'

'I know. I know I said that, and I meant it, I just… can't.'

Shona draws back, her eyes filled with a sadness that is far worse than anger.

'What were you thinking this would achieve?'

It's time for deep breaths and honesty.

'I was thinking she might tell me something and I could nail the bastard.'

Shona stares at him.

'She is never coming back. Margot is gone.'

'I know that. I do.'

'Foulds warned you to stay away. To stop obsessing. She said they'd have to charge you if you didn't leave them alone.'

Cal and Detective Foulds haven't spoken for months. Their bond is deeper than friendship but there's something fractured between them. The failure to achieve justice for his sister came at personal and professional cost to them both.

'I know it needs to stop, but this isn't just my obsession. It's hers. Naomi's. She won't leave me alone.'

'Then you need to report her.'

'You're right. The next time she calls, I will. You have my word.'

'I'm so angry with you.'

'I deserve that. I'm sorry.'

—

They walk back to the cabin in silence. Their hands don't touch and he feels how separate they are, how the trust between them has been wounded. It's all his fault.

Today he has a call scheduled with Sarah to discuss his future. He's dreading it, feeling stuck between wanting to carry on as he always has, and call a halt and upend his life. Maybe he needs to make some really big changes.

While Shona speaks to Cliff about trying to date the lochan bones, which have been confirmed as belonging to an adult male, he makes iced coffee, wistful for the old hot cup of coffee on a cold morning, steam rising into his face. The ice cubes clink as he crosses to the table and opens up his laptop.

He scans the emails, deleting automatically. Until something catches his eye. He undoes the action – it's an email address he doesn't recognise and it takes a moment for him to register who it is and what they're saying. When he does, he lets out a gasp, and the dog jumps to his feet and barks in surprise.

'What's happening?' Chrissie's head appears at the doorway.

'I've just had an email from Tavish, the minister at the church.'

At last some good news: a chink of hope.

'He's agreed to the exhumation. We can go to the sheriff and he'll support it.'

'That's incredible.'

'I know. Reading between the lines, it sounds as if his mother pushed him into it.'

'His mother?'

'Yes, I met her in the graveyard. She liked the dog.'

'Well, thank God for that,' Chrissie says, picking up the jug of iced coffee and pouring a glass. 'Literally.'

CHAPTER TWENTY-SEVEN

EPISODE THREE: EXHUMATION

In the darkness before dawn, minister Tavish Dewar says a prayer over the grave of Hillside Jane. Those assembled bow their heads, and even the loch lies perfectly still while the prayer is spoken and the gravediggers' spades strike the turf.

The moment is both solemn and hopeful. It's taken some time for the agreement to be reached and the proper processes to take their course, but last night a sheriff granted a warrant for Jane's body to be exhumed. This will allow examination of the bones and further tests to be done in a bid to discover the identity of the woman who died in the hills above the lochan more than twenty years ago.

A white tent has been temporarily erected to protect the site, and pathologist Samir Cole supervises as the men carefully peel back the turf with their spades and dig the hard ground. Heatwave conditions have made the earth rock-hard and it's slow-going. Even in the cool of night, sweat pours down their faces and they are forced to take regular breaks.

'You must see these kinds of scenes a lot in your role?'

'Actually, exhumations are less common than you'd think, and this is a more orderly recovery of remains than is often the case. Jane was buried in a hardwood casket donated by the community here and so we're hoping it won't be degraded and may be able

to be lifted out relatively intact. As long as that's the case, we'll transport it to our facility directly.'

It takes several hours until the coffin is recovered. Photographs and measurements are taken, and the box is then carefully lifted from the open grave. We wait for the environmental health officers and pathologist to confirm the casket is intact before the coffin is transferred to a waiting vehicle to be taken to the lab. As soon as the examination has been done and samples taken, Jane will be returned to her resting place, raised only for a couple of days.

Samir will be looking carefully at Jane's skull, hoping to shed more light on her death.

'We'll know more when we are in the lab, but on the post-mortem photographs from 2004, the woman's skull is clearly fractured and damaged and we believe that has occurred pre-mortem, rather than as a result of later animal interference. That's really all I can say at this point. Once we've taken some measurements and a closer look, we will try and map those injuries to the place Jane's body was found.'

By the time the coffin is secured, the sun is up and, even in the shaded graveyard, the atmosphere is sticky and close. The date of the exhumation was kept secret to discourage onlookers, but as Jane's remains are driven slowly out of the village, a group of local people emerge from their houses and line the narrow road to watch. Several of them bow their heads. One makes the sign of the cross.

We don't know who Jane was yet or where she came from, but she has found a home here and it's waiting for her to return.

CHAPTER TWENTY-EIGHT

MORNA, 1952

The boat takes four weeks but it feels like forever. Morna is sick every day, unable to adapt to the lurching movement of the vessel, or that's what she tells herself. The constant queasiness means she spends as much time as possible in her cabin, curled on the bunk, praying the nausea will vanish if she stays still. The sickness isn't caused only by the boat, she knows that, but she presses down the knowledge and grips her hands in tight fists – for the first time in her life, she is utterly alone.

'You all right, doll?' The woman in the lower bunk asks her the same question every day, frowning when she sees Morna still curled in a ball. 'Come on, now.' The woman's concern forces her back into reality and stops the descent into grief and regret that would be so easy. 'What's wrong?'

'Seasick,' she lies. The word's a whisper that tastes curdled on her tongue.

The woman – a Mrs Lydia Dawson – brings Morna bread and water when she refuses to leave the bunk, barely caring what happens to her now, cursing the decision to leave dry land and surrender to this hellish existence of always-motion.

The woman wipes her brow with a cool cloth like she's fevered, and maybe she is. Sometimes it seems that Mrs Dawson is on the verge of saying something – her eyes rake Morna's small frame with sadness, but each time she bites her tongue.

'Eat,' she says instead. 'You can always go back,' she adds when Morna stares up with glazed eyes. 'It doesn't have to be forever, lass.'

She closes her eyes tight as hunger growls inside her. She can never go back, never. No one can reach her here. Except the devil. She watched the shore as the ship drew away, waving at Betty on the dockside and taking a last look at her home, trying to impress Scotland on her memory forever. Relinquishing who she was. It took weeks to send away to Edinburgh for her passport, even after they'd persuaded Betty's gaffer to write a letter confirming her identity. Now she will have to abandon her name, too. No one can find her.

She will become a new person. Two new people, before long. The sickness slops inside her at that thought. Of what it means and how the baby will have to come into the world. She doesn't want to think of it, can't bear the idea that what had happened to Ma will happen to her. Her younger brother was born quickly: slick and silent. His death 'a punishment from God'. Her mother never really recovered and followed a few years later.

And she deserves to be punished, much more than Ma, doesn't she? After what she's done. She rubs her arms to feel some warmth, chilled to the bone even in this stifling cabin, and she hates that she still craves his touch. There's something wrong with her.

'You should come up into the sun,' Mrs Dawson tells her every day as she herds out her quiet children with their watchful eyes. 'Come for some fresh air.' But Morna can't. She will have to look at the water then, remember what happened at the lochan. Saliva pools in her mouth.

How did it come to this? As the ship pitches in the night and sleep evades her, strange images flood her mind, memories taking on a hallucinatory quality, colours firing behind her eyes. Things used to be all right, but when wee Owen died, Morna started to anger Da just by being around, as if her presence was a reminder that the longed-for boy had not lived. Before Owen, there were few kind words; after, there were none.

At least here, on board the ship, she is free from her father's fists. She has never lain this still, this sick, this long. She can still hear their voices in her head. If anything, they're getting louder the further from them she travels. A reminder that you cannot escape, no matter what.

But as the ship sails into a new hemisphere, the voices become fainter. Her father can't find her. She could write to him later, when she's out of reach. But she won't.

The cabin is quiet, all the other bodies up on deck. Morna sits up, pressing her hands to her belly. For the first time, she feels better.

Out on deck, her eyes are blinded by the brightness. Shading them, she keeps her gaze firmly averted from the water and staggers weakly along the ship.

'Lord! She's alive!' Mrs Dawson shrieks, beckoning her to sit beside her. 'Feeling better, doll?'

Morna nods, too overwhelmed by the light, the noise and the life around them to speak.

'You haven't even told me your name.'

She looks around, taking in the ship powering them towards a new life. She makes her cracked lips part, pulls them into a smile. 'It's Violet.'

CHAPTER TWENTY-NINE

They're back in Aberdeen while Shona helps with the examination of Jane's remains. A ferry accident off Orkney has delayed the dive plans for the lochan so they decided to come home until they can take the next steps.

Shona calls from the lab as soon as she's finished her analysis of the bones.

'We've taken the samples we need and Cole is sending them off to the labs we have lined up. Now we just have to wait and see.'

Cal feels a swelling of hope at the progress. Maybe they can inch their way towards an identity for the woman.

'Did you have the chance to examine her injuries?'

'Yes, and her skull was a mess. Multiple fractures consistent with being hit with a large object. There's a strong likelihood she was murdered, Cal. They just aren't consistent with a single fall.'

His mind jumps to Lucie, now recuperating at her parents' house in the Cotswolds, posting cheerful pictures of her foot in a protective boot. Her injuries from her fall weren't fatal but were more extensive – ribs, ankle, concussion. They make Jane's seem strange by comparison.

When Shona rings off, he sits and stares out of the window, taking in the implications. Was someone on the hill with Jane that day? Did they strike her on the head, take her bag and leave her for dead? Why?

—

In the evening, Cal is outside, chopping logs, his T-shirt drenched by physical exertion as well as the ongoing heatwave. Fires are the last thing on their minds, but the wood is bone dry and they're taking the opportunity to stockpile as much as they can before winter. The ground is strewn with raw splinters, the scent of which always relaxes him, their richness mingling with the clean air and the farm smells from the fields that border their property.

He hefts the axe above his shoulder, appreciating the hardening in his muscles, the strength building after so much practice. His haphazard initial attempts had Shona bent double with laughter when he carried them in and presented them, but now his kindling is even and his stroke swift.

He's lobbing the split pieces into a basket when Shona appears at the door, her hair wet from the shower. He's definitely not forgiven yet, but he's working on rebuilding the trust between them. His phone stays in the other room at night and Naomi hasn't called since he lost his temper with her.

Shona says his name twice before he registers she's there, so lost in his thoughts of Jane and lulled by the hypnotic swing of the axe. She holds out his phone.

'It keeps ringing. I think it's Detective Foulds?' She frowns. 'Did you call her or something?'

'No.'

Cal brings the axe down in a clean sweep, embedding the blade in the stump. He wipes his hands on his jeans and reaches for the phone. Shona smiles as their fingers touch, though the movement fails to reach her eyes. He hates the caution he sees there.

'Cal.' The detective's voice is frosty, he thinks, unlike her usual tone.

'Sorry, I was just chopping wood so I missed your previous call. Calls. Shona brought me the—'

'Cal. Have you been speaking to Naomi Barr?'

So that explains the palpable chill.

'Er. No, well, yes. But I haven't been calling her... *She's been speaking to* me.'

'Oh my God. Cal! What the hell?'

'She started calling me and she won't let up.'

'And you didn't think to mention this?'

'I did, I just... I couldn't. You told me not to have anything to do with them.'

'Exactly. I'm looking at her call logs and there are fifty calls to you over the past months. This is insane. You should have called me as soon as she got in touch.'

Cal swallows. Foulds sounds truly angry. He's seen her mad before, but never at him. He remembers the dread he felt the first time Naomi Barr called.

'I'm sorry.' The words are inadequate and do nothing to quench her anger.

'What has she been calling you about?'

He can't tell her what Naomi said about provoking Barr.

Cal's pacing the stretch of dried out lawn, one hand pushing his hair off his sweating forehead, immune to the view before him, not seeing the distant trace of Bennachie, Aberdeenshire's most distinctive hill.

'I'm not sure. One minute she seemed to want my help, the next she was messing with me, like she wanted to get me into trouble...'

'That's why I would have expected you to tell me immediately. I thought you'd know better than this. You're supposed to be smart, Cal. What does she say to you?'

'Just a load of stuff about regretting marrying him but still being in love with him, that she's frightened of him but can't leave, that he's changed but hasn't.'

'And you didn't think she might need help?' Foulds sounds shocked, despairing. Cal is barely aware of Shona poised on the doorstep, watching and waiting. She was right. He's a disaster.

'She married a convicted criminal. Someone with a track record of violence against women. Who does that?'

'A vulnerable woman?' Foulds says, sarcastic and cold.

But Cal doesn't care. He is on a roll and can't stop the words pouring from him. 'She went in with her eyes open. Worse than that, she legitimised him. She funded his lawyers, his media campaign. He got off because of her. You know that! How can you feel sorry for her? She made her bed.'

Foulds sighs. 'I'm going to need to take a statement, Cal.'

Something thrums inside him, the unfairness bubbling like oil. A flash memory of his sister sitting on the closed lid of the toilet while he played in the bath, reaching her hand into the water and splashing him. This is a new memory – he didn't think there were any left to rise to the surface but it does, stunning him. He can smell the Matey bubble bath, hear her laughter. He can only have been four years old. Tears come to his eyes.

When he tunes back in, Foulds is saying his name. 'Are you still there?'

'Yes.' He clears his throat. 'Sorry. Still here.' The shock subsides and the chill seeps in, bringing back some of his senses, his thoughts. A shot of foreboding. The question he should have asked right away.

'Wait. Hold on. Why do you have Naomi Barr's call logs?'

He looks up and his gaze meets Shona's blue eyes, the only things that anchor him as he experiences a sudden sense of falling, of inevitability.

Foulds sighs. 'I don't know how to tell you this, Cal. Naomi Barr has been reported missing.'

CHAPTER THIRTY

There's a rushing in his ears, making it hard to hear her. He must have misheard.

'What?'

'She's not been seen for two days. You might be the last person to have spoken to her.'

Cal sinks down until he's perching on the log-cutting stump, nestled close to the axe, feeling the old tree's scars through the seat of his shorts.

'I don't understand.'

'Don't you?' Foulds is still sharp but softening slightly.

'Please. Tell me what's going on.'

'Naomi always went to visit her elderly mother in her care home. Every day.' Cal swallows guiltily. He does not do the same thing for his mother. It's just not possible when he's so far away. 'Yesterday, she didn't show. The home couldn't contact her. Her mother, it turns out, has a lot more sense when it comes to men than her daughter. She, apparently, has never liked Jason and reported the no-show to us. We did a welfare check and she isn't at her house.'

'What does he say has happened?'

'He says they haven't been getting on and she's gone away to cool off, without telling him where. Wouldn't let us in, though, said he didn't want us messing the place up.'

'Can you get a warrant, trace her phone?'

'Yes, thank you, Cal. I do know how to run an investigation.' He's relieved that there's a hint of her usual sarcasm in among the displeasure. 'We're on the case but her phone doesn't seem to have been turned on. However, I pull the records and, lo and behold, you show up.'

'Oh.'

'Oh, indeed. It's time to talk, Cal, I need to know what's going on.'

Cal takes the phone down the hall into the bedroom, barely registering Chrissie's wide-eyed concern on the way past. He sits on the bed. This is where he wakes when Naomi calls him in the night. There's a terrible hollow sickness in his gut. How could he have allowed himself to be blinded by his hatred of Barr? How could he have looked at her cries for help and only seen what was in it for him? Why didn't he see this coming?

He swallows and when he speaks, his voice sounds small. He lays it all out for Foulds. From that first call to the regular night-time wakings, the way Naomi's words would lurch from self-righteousness and goading to fear and demands.

'Why did you keep answering?'

'I don't know. I don't know,' he moans. He can almost feel the ghost of his sister in the air around him – what would she think of him? Shame creeps up his throat and he coughs to dislodge the lump but it won't go. 'It just felt so final. Like that would be saying Margot was gone. I know that's stupid,' he adds before Foulds can tell him.

She exhales. 'I don't suppose you recorded any of these calls, did you?'

'No, I'm sorry. They were always in the middle of the night.'

'And, I have to ask. Where have you been for the last couple of days?'

Cal's hand feels unsteady. He's in a nightmare. 'I'm in Aberdeenshire.'

'And that can be verified?'

'Yes. Chrissie's here with me – and so is Shona, before work and in the evenings.'

'Good.'

'You don't think I would...'

'No. I don't.' She sounds exasperated, as if this should be obvious. Nothing is obvious to him right now, though. 'But I can imagine if the press got hold of this, someone might ask the question. You know... an eye for an eye.'

Cal's laugh is hollow. 'But he's innocent, remember? In the eyes of the court.'

'In the eyes of the court,' Foulds repeats.

'He wouldn't be so stupid, would he? After getting away with everything?'

'I hope not.' Foulds sounds hollow too. 'This is not how I want to finally get him.'

'I'm sorry. I told her to leave him, to get help. But I didn't believe her. I should have done more.'

Foulds pauses. 'She wasn't... isn't an easy person to help.'

When they say goodbye, Cal sits on the edge of the bed, not moving, the phone still in his palm.

There are stories you tell yourself about the kind of person you are, your values, your principles. His whole life, he's been driven by what happened to his sister. He's dedicated his career to finding justice for people, women most of all. He's believed their stories, fought for the truth.

Except this time. If Naomi Barr has died because he failed to act, then he has blood on his hands. He's betrayed everything he believes in. Margot most of all.

CHAPTER THIRTY-ONE

Dinner is almost silent. Cal stirs the pasta on his plate with his fork, thick strands of tagliatelle coated in carbonara sauce. He tries a mouthful but the food seems to expand until he feels like he's going to choke on it.

He looks up to find both Shona and Chrissie watching him. They immediately drop their gazes and focus on their own plates. From the rug by the fireplace, the dog huffs a sigh into the quiet.

'Sorry. I just can't believe it. I don't know what to do.'

Chrissie looks at Shona, as if hoping she'll speak first. Cal can feel how much they're both floundering to help him: no one anticipated this.

'You can't *do* anything, Cal.' Her voice is soft and sympathetic but he can't feel the warmth he should feel from her reassurance. Nothing is penetrating the smothering darkness around him. 'You told her to get help and she wouldn't. I don't know whether Barr was in on these calls or not, but it sounds like she got some enjoyment from tormenting you.'

'But what if he's done something to her?'

'Then it still won't be your fault. She chose him, married him and refused to get help. Other people should have stepped in, but not you. Of all people, not you.'

He sets his fork on the plate and reaches for his glass of wine. 'I should have spoken to Foulds, told her Naomi was ringing.'

'Yes,' Shona agrees, 'but we don't know if they'd have taken you that seriously, even if you had. It still doesn't make this your responsibility.'

'And anyway. I just can't believe he'd be that stupid,' Chrissie says. 'He must know he'd never get away with it.'

'Why not?' Cal's voice croaks as he speaks. 'He's got away with all sorts of things you'd never think possible. Why not one more?'

'Maybe he's telling the truth for once,' Shona says, standing and gathering their plates together. 'Even a stopped clock is right sometimes. She might have walked back in by now for all we know.'

'I guess so.' Though in his gut Cal feels a deep and horrible certainty. If he closes his eyes, it's the ex-bouncer's strong arms he sees, the shark-like deadness in his gaze. When it comes to Barr, there are no rules of decency.

He can hear whispers in the kitchen and he turns.

'What's going on?'

'Look what Chrissie made.' Shona uncovers a beautiful chocolate dessert while his daughter gets out bowls and spoons, a look of pride on her face.

'I did it before we knew...'

He doesn't want her to apologise. 'That looks incredible. What is it?'

'Chocolate mousse cake. Can you eat some?'

He looks into Chrissie's worried eyes and resolves not to do this. Naomi Barr should be a private pain, not something that damages his family. 'Just try and stop me.'

'You can't let this derail you, Cal,' Shona says, almost like she can hear his thoughts, as they cut fat slabs of cake and douse them in cream. 'It looks like the dive is going ahead next week at the lochan. Come and observe. Don't let Barr mess with your life anymore.'

Shona looks at Chrissie expectantly, as if urging her to speak.

'I'm not sure today is a good—'

'What is it?' He spoons a mouthful of cake into his mouth. It melts on his tongue, rich and soothing, like a hug. 'Oh my God, this is amazing.'

'It's sort of bribery cake, Dad...'

He pauses, spoon dug into soft chocolate.

'I'm kind of hoping I can come with you again and help on the podcast. Officially, this time.'

He's taken another delicious mouthful, so he can't immediately respond.

'I talked to Mum,' Chrissie says before he can speak. 'I have her blessing. Not,' she adds, 'that I should need it.' Cal is glad to see the stubbornness and heat mixed with the persuasion – more like the daughter he knows.

'It would be good for you to have an extra pair of hands,' Shona puts in.

'Why do I feel like you two have been talking about this without me?'

'Because we have...' Chrissie says.

Cal smiles at them both. They're right. He can't look back. He has to press forward or he's going to be dragged back under again. Going back to Loch Tay, seeking answers for Jane, will give him the purpose he needs. He is not going to sink into the Barr quagmire, not this time. There, he can escape it.

'Fine,' he says. 'Let's do it.'

CHAPTER THIRTY-TWO

With local interest in the lochan bones high, the day chosen for the dive is kept quiet. Shona has secured permission for Cal to attend and document the search so they meet the small team in the car park early in the morning. He scrolls the news as they wait for the dive team to double check the equipment in their specialist vehicle and to receive a briefing from the police search adviser.

Naomi's disappearance has hit the news and he feels sick every time he thinks about her. Shona puts her hand on his arm.

'Foulds will let you know if there's anything significant.'

Cal nods. She's right – he needs to stay calm.

Things are still complex between them. Naomi's disappearance broke into the stalemate, but his secrecy over his calls with her has rocked Shona's trust and he hates that.

He pockets the phone and resolves to focus on Jane and the podcast.

'Will there be enough air cannisters to do a complete search?' Cal asks Amir, the head diver, when the briefing is finished.

'That's the question,' he says. 'Ideally for a big search we'd try and set up an air supply station but this location is too remote and hard to access. We've assessed the water depth as just over thirty metres so it's on the border of what we'd use normal SCUBA for without decompression planning.'

'It sounds complicated.'

Amir smiles.

'It helps that we have a very defined place to focus. Maybe we'll get lucky and find the rest of the skeleton intact on a ledge just below the place where you found the leg bones... be home for lunch.'

A stocky man who looks like he's ex-army snorts. 'Dream on, pal, dream on.'

The man hasn't introduced himself or made eye contact with Cal, so he tries to engage him now.

'I'm Cal,' he says, holding out a hand to shake.

'I know.' The man ignores his outstretched hand, turning away and busying himself with sorting equipment. Cal looks at Amir, who shakes his head and rolls his eyes.

'Cal, meet Greg.'

Cal shrugs. Journalists are used to being the unwanted presence.

Another diver, Hannah, has been listening in. She must be in her twenties, strong and muscled. Tying her long brown hair up in a messy topknot, she swings her pack into the back of the Land Rover they'll be travelling in, then continues the conversation as if the snub didn't happen. 'Would be nice if it were that easy.'

As well as Cal, Shona and the five-strong diving team, the crime scene manager Ruaridh, police search adviser Alison and two officers from the mountain rescue team are accompanying them to the lochan. Anything found will need to be documented and photographed carefully.

The group sets off from the car park at six, after waiting for a farmer to unlock a gate that allows the vehicles to bump up a winding track along the side of the hill towards the small dam. Sheep scatter before them.

After forty minutes they reach the dam and there is a buzz of activity as the divers and officers debate the route ahead of them, confirming the plan to walk the final stretch, while they unload the kit. Cal helps Shona to check and recheck her pack, and then swings his own heavy rucksack onto his back, loaded up with food, water and the other equipment he needs. He's promised Lucie he'll take some video footage, as well as his audio recordings.

The divers and officers are fitter than he is, but weighed down by a lot more equipment, so he is able to keep pace and listen to the team's stories about dredging canals and finding bloated bodies in rivers. With the exception of Greg, they have an easy way about them, perhaps used to maintaining their equanimity amid tragic searches, and Cal slots in next to Hannah, who seems happy fielding his questions.

'Finding bones feels a bit easier than looking for recently missing people,' Amir tells him, overhearing their conversation. 'It can be soul-destroying sometimes.'

'I'll bet.'

'That ferry was the worst,' Hannah says quietly. 'I knew we were unlikely to find anyone alive, but still, I'd hoped...'

They lapse into silence at the thought. As they climb further, the conversation and banter stop: everyone is breathing heavily and putting their energy into getting to the lochan. Cal's relieved to find that the other trips have strengthened his muscles and the ascent isn't as excruciating as the first time he did it.

They arrive mid-morning and trek along the shore to the place Shona marked the last time they were there. Cal sees the atmosphere has the same unsettling effect on the diving team and officers. He averts his eyes from the peaty mound that marks the place where he found Lucie. He doesn't want to see that hollow and remember how close to death she came.

After a drink and a brief rest, the team start kitting out to go into the water. They conduct pre-dive safety checks and set up a shot line, which Amir tells Cal would usually be taken out by boat to the centre of the search area, but here the rope and weight are attached to a large rock on the shore so the divers can descend in a controlled manner.

Hannah and grumpy Greg are going in first, with Alison and Amir masterminding the operation from the shore. Shona and the other officers unzip a rucksack with the bags and labelling equipment they hope they will need. Alison stands ankle-deep in the cool water, snapping pictures of the divers as they wade out to where the rope goes over the drop.

Before long, the diving duo are floating, masks on. They nod to each other, tuck their respirators in their mouths and start to follow the line down, making surprisingly few ripples as they submerge.

The sky shimmers in the water's glassy reflection and those left on shore cluster around the small screen Amir is monitoring – Greg is wearing an underwater camera and it gives a hazy view of the steeply dropping shelf as the divers sink slowly, scanning for anything resembling a skeleton. Cal feels a twist of envy for the pair in the cool sanctuary of the lochan. The heat is unforgiving, his clothes sticking to him.

'It's surprisingly deep for a relatively small body of water,' Amir muses as he watches. 'And steep. I suspect anything that fell off that lip has gone a long way down, unfortunately.'

'Does that make things harder to find?'

'It depends how much silt there is on the bottom. It could be metres of murk or pretty clean. Our tests suggest there is some silt on the floor but that it's not too bad. They'll check that with weights and then lay some guide lines along the search paths we've planned.'

It's peaceful on the shore, though the anticipation is making the atmosphere tense.

The divers must almost be at the bottom when the camera suddenly swivels away from the side to show the middle of the lochan.

'Hang on,' Amir says, pushing his sunglasses onto his head.

The water is relatively clear but it's still not possible to make out what the divers have seen as they move away from the side. A shape looms, dark and unusual.

Amir shades the screen with his hand and Alison bends in closer to see.

'What is it?' Shona asks, as everyone clusters around the screen in the beating heat, alerted by Amir's tone that something interesting is happening.

'Is that…?' Cal asks, unwilling to say the word, feeling foolish for even thinking it.

'It can't be.' Amir rubs his eyes. Shona slides in front of Cal to see better.

At that moment, the camera angle changes and it's clear from the screen that Hannah and Greg are coming back to the shot line and ascending to the surface. This was not the plan. The shore group turn as one to the lochan and

Amir wades out into the water, seeming alarmed, slipping a little on the submerged rocks as he hurries to meet them.

The divers break the surface, hands on the line, and Hannah is first to pull her respirator from her face.

'Did you see that?' Her voice is loaded with disbelief.

'We couldn't quite make it out,' Amir tells her, reaching an arm to help Greg up onto the lip. 'I might be going mad, but it looked like—'

'A plane,' Greg finishes, a trace of glee in his voice. 'There's a fucking aeroplane down there.'

CHAPTER THIRTY-THREE

Everyone starts talking at once, until Alison calls for quiet so she can radio the SIO. Cal scans the valley around them, chilled at the secrets that lie in these baking hills. A hundred questions leap into his head.

He and Shona listen as Amir and his diving team confer with Alison and Ruaridh.

'We've planned for the bones, not anything else,' Alison says, sighing. 'The SIO is getting onto the AAIB now. They'll need to be involved in the next steps.'

Greg strides forward. 'Do we have any record of there being a plane wreck in this lochan? Maybe it's a known wreckage? Recovering it from here would be damn near impossible so perhaps they decided to leave it down there.'

'I've been researching this lochan and these hills, looking for anything unusual,' Cal says. 'There's been no mention of a plane crash. Definitely not.'

They all turn back to Alison to wait for a decision from the SIO. It's going to be his call. The radio crackles and she walks away from them as they strain to catch a sense of what's happening. If this was a disparate collection of people before, it's now one coherent team.

'Right,' she says, eventually striding back. 'It's been bloody difficult to get everyone up here so we have to make the most of it while we wait for more information. We're splitting into two mission objectives. Plan one is the original objective of trying to locate the rest of the remains and transporting them out of here. Mission two is to use any remaining oxygen to photograph the aircraft and gather information.

'However. We do not yet know if this is a military or civilian aircraft so do not disturb the wreckage. Is that clear?'

She looks at Greg and Hannah. Hannah nods her understanding, but Greg is already pulling on his mask and heading for the water.

As the divers sink out of sight along the shot line, Cal searches the hill above for the place where Jane was found. He locates it after a few moments, recognising the flat grassy platform sheltered by rocks. He remembers standing up there, knows it offers the perfect view of the lochan. Impossible to know that this deep water was concealing something so significant. Silent and secretive. No wonder Lucie was afraid, alone in the dark with the ghosts of the past.

Could Jane be linked to the lost aircraft? That seems far-fetched, and yet so does the likelihood of two mysteries surrounding this one small body of water. Did she know it was here?

Watching the screen intently, they can tell when Greg and Hannah reach the bottom. A few times, the camera turns to show the bulk of the aircraft, resting tail up against the steep wall to the lochan floor in the fuzzy image. There is another world beneath, further drama in an already dramatic landscape. It shows the way the land has moved and broken over time, creating these incredible folds and crevices. The surface group watch as the two divers lay weighted lines and search along the bottom, though they rapidly stir up silt that makes it hard to see.

After a while, Amir checks his watch.

'They'll be coming up any moment,' he says.

When Greg and Hannah surface, it's with good news.

'We think we've found something,' Hannah tells them. 'The silt isn't that deep. There's rock beneath. I think there are pieces of bone but we were running out of air so we've marked the spot.'

'Let's go back,' Greg says as Amir helps him to shore.

'Break first,' Alison says.

Greg looks like he wants to argue, but the PolSA's words brook no opposition so they stow the kit on the rocks and everyone sits on the tussocky grass to eat sandwiches and rehydrate. Cal passes around a pack of biscuits and even Greg deigns to take a couple. His face is softer, less hostile than when they began. He's invested now, like they all are.

Cal takes the opportunity to record some observations and to interview Amir about the finds so far, while the second diving pair get ready to descend. He wipes sweat from his forehead and pulls his hat down more securely, trying to create shade. The heat is a constant assault. What have they started with this investigation? What will the local community think?

This time, the divers work without further incident, collecting the fragments of bone in special pouches that will protect the remains when they're brought back to the surface. The silty landscape on the screen is hard to interpret but occasionally they see the defined shape of a hand in the gloom as the pair work methodically.

When the divers resurface, Amir and Hannah help them to shore, while Shona and the officers take charge of the pouches of bones. Everyone is hot and tired. They move impatiently, conversation limited and clipped.

'Right, last dive,' Alison tells the team, looking at her watch.

Once more, they watch from the surface as Greg and Hannah drop to the prone corpse of the small aircraft, propped in its undignified position on a rocky outcrop that is stopping it falling to the bottom of an underwater chasm.

Cal studies the screen closely as they swim to the plane. The image is fuzzy, but it seems the craft is surprisingly intact, covered by a green slick of algae. He searches the screen for identifying numbers or details but he can see now that the tail has sheared off and must have sunk lower.

The divers glide along lines towards the fuselage, sliding deeper towards the cockpit. The cool, dark world they inhabit is so different to where they are standing, above the surface, that it feels like another planet. All the while, Amir's gaze is fixed on the shapes of them taking photographs, capturing the details before they return to the surface and burst back into the light.

It's hard to see on the small screen, but Cal thinks he can see part of the cockpit collapsed in on itself, or maybe the canopy is missing. Everything seems different down there beneath the weight of water – almost impossible to tell what's going on. But then Greg shines a light to illuminate the inside of the plane.

Cal vaguely makes out the shape within but at first cannot fully tell what he is looking at. Beside him, Shona and Alison fall silent. The water laps at their feet. A collective gasp as they all realise together. Scraps of cloth, bone, skull and flight suit, before the camera pulls away. The image sears into Cal's vision, his mind filling in the gaps.

The two divers seem to be signalling to each other, before Greg turns back and delves into the cockpit, Hannah tugging on his arm, trying to pull him away.

'What are they doing?' Cal asks Amir.

He frowns. 'I've no idea.'

They wait, silently, for the pair to return along the lines and reach the surface. When they do, their heads pop up fast, like bobbing corks. Immediately she has her respirator out, the previously relaxed Hannah is shouting at her colleague.

'I was telling you not to disturb it.' The words reverberate across the lochan, bouncing off the protective walls of the mountains around them.

'I didn't know what you meant,' Greg shouts back.

'Bullshit.'

Greg's face purples and he gulps furious gasps of air. 'It's done now. Just help me with this, would you?'

Alison wades out to meet them. Her voice is loud, her previously even temper fraying at the edges. 'What the hell is going on? Did you not hear me, Greg? I was very clear that the aircraft was not to be touched or tampered with.'

Greg scowls. As they come closer to shore, the divers lift a small metal box from the water, drips streaming from its dull surface.

'Fuck's sake,' Alison exclaims.

She hauls Greg to one side, berating him for ignoring orders.

Cal and Amir help Hannah from the water.

'Did you see?' Her face is grave.

Amir nods. 'Looks like the pilot was still in there?'

'There was no sign he'd tried to escape. Still belted in.' Hannah frowns. 'But the cockpit had already been breached. Greg didn't touch that.'

'Maybe that explains the second set of bones,' Cal suggests. 'Maybe someone made it out and tried to swim for it.'

He looks across the water, imagining the lochan at its full height, shrouded in darkness or foul weather. It could be a dangerous and forbidding place, not this sun-soaked version.

'I think we should be recovering the body,' Greg says when Alison's finished her dressing down. 'We can't just leave it there.'

Shona steps forward. 'We don't have instructions to do that, or the proper equipment to transport the remains. That would need to be agreed with the AAIB or the DAIB if the plane is military. It's illegal to tamper with it.'

'We have a body bag,' Greg counters, his face transformed by a deep scowl. 'We could do it while we're here. The pilot deserves a burial.'

'No,' Alison says, holding up her radio. 'Boss says we do what we came to do and that's it. There's procedure to follow.'

Greg makes a sound of frustration, his whole body telegraphing his disagreement.

Hannah glances from one to the other of her colleagues. The atmosphere of success has frosted over and the energy is low.

'Are we going to see what's in the box?' Cal asks, tentatively.

Everyone turns to look at the object, forgotten amid the tensions.

Alison makes a noise of frustration and glares at Greg.

'Now that it's up here, I guess so.'

They carry it to a tussock of dry grass. The box is small but weighty. Alison directs another officer to photograph the box while Shona records its measurements.

Impatient, Greg leans in and urges them to hurry.

Eventually, gloved, Shona opens the catches and works them back and forth to free the seal.

'Careful,' Alison winces.

They jerk open. Slowly, Shona lifts the lid.

Cal gasps. The metal before them gleams in the light, like a dream, or something from the pages of a child's adventure story. Whatever he was expecting, this wasn't it.

In the box lie three bars of gold.

CHAPTER THIRTY-FOUR

By the time the vehicles have bumped down the long track off the hill and clattered over bone-shaking cattle grids, Cal is dusty, stinking and exhausted. Shona will be accompanying the bones to Aberdeen, while the gold is securely stowed and transported by the police. Under orders from the distant SIO that Alison has been radioing, the gold bars are to be kept a secret for now. Cal is not permitted to report on them.

It feels lonely back at the lodge with Shona gone, but it doesn't take long for the calm to be pierced. Chrissie bursts through the door with Rocket, bearing ice-cold cans of lemonade from the shop.

'I heard,' she says breathlessly, 'that there's a plane with another dead body in it at the bottom of the loch? God, it's hot in here.'

This is not a property built to cater to extreme heat. He has all the windows open but there is no breeze. The fan is circulating hot, soupy air in the dim and stifling structure.

'That was fast. Where did you hear?'

'The divers went to the pub. Sean called me.'

Cal studies her. 'What else did they say?'

'What do you mean?' Chrissie frowns. 'Nothing…'

At least Greg hasn't spilled the beans about the gold.

'And what's the general take on it?'

'Some people are interested, others think you're—'

'Stirring up trouble?'

'You *are* a troublemaker, Dad.' Chrissie hands him a drink and flops down on the sofa, cracking open the other can. 'I'm meeting him for a drink this evening, so I'll get the gossip, check out which stake they're planning to burn you at.'

'Very funny.'

When Chrissie leaves him to it, Cal pours a glass of wine and moves outside. Around the holiday park, the smell of charcoal and cooking meat spirals into the air, and children pelt around on their bikes or crawl into dens they've made in the bushes. All of these holidaymakers seem oblivious to the drama playing out in the hills above.

Cal's phone buzzes with a voice message from Lucie, asking how the day went. Before he can answer, she video-calls him, her perfectly made-up face and plaited pigtails filling the screen. She bats away his questions about her recovery, and her effervescence immediately buoys him.

'Did you find the rest of the bones?'

'We did.'

She cheers. 'That's such a relief.'

'We found a bit more than that.'

Lucie screeches with disbelief when he tells her about the plane and the second set of remains. He decides against revealing the presence of the gold bars, thinking sunken treasure might just tip her over the edge and he'd be in a lot of trouble if that ended up on social media.

'I don't understand,' she says when she calms down. 'Is any of this related to Jane?'

He ignores the gut feeling he has that the plane is too much of a coincidence. He should be dealing in facts and certainties, not hunches.

'I don't see how that's possible,' he tells her. 'It must have been there a long time to have happened off the radar, and Jane only died twenty years ago. By the looks of things, it must be a post-war accident, when flights weren't so tightly regulated. We're hoping to establish where it came from soon.'

'I can't stop thinking about her out there in the hills, alone. It's really haunting me. It won't stop people focusing on her, will it?'

Cal is struck by how much Lucie has identified with Jane. How personal this is becoming for her.

'If anything, the plane's discovery works to our advantage. It brings more media attention, makes Jane even more of a story, as horrible as that sounds.'

Lucie visibly relaxes.

'I'm working on a Reel about her. I'll send it to you now.'

—

When Lucie rings off, Cal finds his mind automatically returning to Naomi. He's checked and rechecked the news, and there's no progress on her case so he makes himself a meal of leftovers and sits down to research plane crashes in Scotland to distract himself. He finds lists of hundreds of military crashes, but scrolling through them all isn't helpful. He has nothing to go on. No way to narrow it down. Could the plane be military? Surely, it would be known about if that were the case?

He makes notes of questions to ask the experts. Gradually, the air cools and the night becomes pleasant and relaxing. The park quietens; exhausted and heat-soaked children are given baths and put to bed. He wonders when

Chrissie will be back, if he should wait for her. It's hard to fight the instinct to protect.

After speaking to Shona, he sends a text telling Chrissie he's going to bed. He's just turned out the light when he hears the front door go, so he slips out of bed and sticks his head round the door. His daughter is sitting on the sofa, alone, her head in her hands. She hasn't seen him and he's about to move towards her when he realises she's crying, pressing the heels of her hands into her eyes to hold in the tears.

Cal swallows the lump in his own throat, hating the horrible sick feeling that grows inside him at the knowledge that he's spying on her private sadness. Frozen for a moment, he gradually comes back to himself. He steps carefully back into his room, closing the door silently, breath held, though he waits with his fingers on the handle for a moment, uncertain. Should he go out there and ask her what's wrong? He should, shouldn't he?

He decides one way and then the other, but something glutinous prevents him from showing himself. They have a good relationship these days, he and Chrissie. When she's ready to talk to him, she will. He has a horrible feeling that this quiet private sadness is linked to the other changes he's noticed, such as the strange turning away from her art. He resolves to speak to Allie, to ask his ex-wife's advice on what to do. He's lost on his own.

Sleep refuses to come. He hears Chrissie go to bed, turning out the bathroom light, closing her door. The lodge falls silent, and only the occasional creaking and snuffling from outside the open window filters in, a reminder of the world beyond.

Cal lies there, a million thoughts bombarding him, fears and worries, guilt and sadness. He thinks of Naomi, of Foulds searching for answers as he searches for Jane. There's a constant nagging feeling in the back of his skull, a sense that he's forgotten something important.

Perhaps he dozes, slipping in and out of thought and dream, strange shapes and movements in his mind. It feels like he doesn't sleep at all; he just opens his eyes when dawn comes, a relief to have made it through the night.

CHAPTER THIRTY-FIVE

EPISODE FOUR: THE SCIENCE BIT

We've always been convinced that science can help us unlock some of the doors to Jane's identity. Unfortunately, with bone and hair samples lost, it took exhumation of Jane's remains before we could use up-to-date tools and analysis. If she had been cremated, then the opportunity would have been lost.

Now, in partnership with Police Scotland and thanks to scientists at the University of Glasgow, we've been able to use isotope analysis on those samples and the insight they offer is transforming our approach to the case. This testing, conducted by geologists, can be done on hair, teeth and bones. It gives us information about the environment where a person was raised and lived.

Geologist Mira Sayed explains, 'The isotopes in our bodies are different atoms of elements that we absorb through our diet and environment. Luckily for us, these isotopes are specific to geographical areas.'

'What does this mean for our investigation into Jane's identity?'

'Using this technique, we can narrow down both where Jane was raised and also where she was living around the time of her death. For example, in analysing Jane's teeth, we can determine the general area where she lived as a child, as teeth form early and so contain isotopes from that time of your life.'

'And you have results for us?'

'Yes, we have. We found that Jane spent her early years in the Scottish Highlands, in an inland area, rather than near the coast. The oxygen isotope ratio shows the drinking water there was primarily rainfall-fed.'

'So, theoretically, it's quite possible that Jane was born and raised near where she died at Loch Tay?'

'That is possible, yes.'

Clearly, this throws out a lot of questions that we and the local community have already been asking, such as why no one has missed her or come forward to claim her. It seems impossible that someone could live so off-grid that no one would notice they'd gone.

However, the next bit of information that Mira's team discovered sheds light on why that might be the case. In fact, we may have been looking in entirely the wrong place.

'The fact that hair continues to grow makes it different when it comes to isotopes. Hair can tell us where a person has spent their last few months. In fact, it can be really quite specific, even showing if someone has been moving between different places during that time. We obviously can't give an address, but we can narrow the field to give more traditional detective work a chance.'

'That's incredible.'

'It is. And what we found in Jane's case is that she was almost certainly living in Australia in the months and years leading up to her death.'

'Australia?'

'Yes. Australia has distinct oxygen isotopes in its water. Along with the strontium, carbon and nitrogen isotopes, they tell us that's where she was. What's more, the high level of sulphur isotopes also suggests she was living by the coast there.'

This is hugely significant. Detectives investigating Jane's identity have long suspected she'd travelled to the area from abroad, *but hadn't been able to narrow down the search, partly because of the time that elapsed between her death and her body being found. Thanks to these isotopes, we have a good lead to follow.*

So now, we know we're looking for someone who was born in Scotland and likely spent their childhood in the country, before emigrating to Australia. The question is why Jane came back, and why her life ended on an isolated hillside in the land of her birth.

Finding Justice *consultant Dr Shona Williams says the significance of this is massive.*

'Someone out there must be missing this woman. We know that she'd given birth to at least one child. We can now take the next steps to finding out who she was and what she was doing here.'

'How do you feel, hearing this news?'

'I feel quite emotional, to be honest. We've always said looking for Jane is like looking for a needle in a field of haystacks. Now, we've got one haystack to focus on.'

CHAPTER THIRTY-SIX

MORNA, 1952

The last week of the voyage, encouraged by Mrs Dawson, Morna is able to stagger weakly to the deck and sit in the sunshine, sickened only by the sight of small children playing on the smooth boards around her.

She averts her eyes and looks instead at the rushing of the waves. The water is different to the stillness of the lochan. It's bigger and bluer and rolling like a beast at play instead of stealthily watching her. She's able to sit with her eyes shut, the orange light flooding her through closed lids. She's able to eat a little more, to take the brine of the air into her lungs.

None of this solves the problem of what she is going to do when they dock. The government has promised jobs and opportunities, but she is a single young woman, barely more than a child, with challenges ahead. What can she do? When these thoughts rise, she tamps down panic, making herself breathe deeply. One step at a time, that's all there can be. There are only so many options open to someone in her situation. She will have to do what it takes to survive.

The land appears and it seems the entire ship's population clusters at the railings, watching this strange country, its turquoise waters and foreign trees in new shades of green, advancing towards them. There is excitement, chatter, song. She feels only a blankness. Neither anticipation nor regret, just a clean white sheet of nothing.

As the ship glides into port and is made fast, Morna returns to her cabin and gathers her few possessions into the hessian sack. Mrs Dawson watches her. 'Some colour in those cheeks now, Violet, lass.' Kindness chafes like new shoes on raw skin but she would not have survived without the woman, so she smiles.

'Where are you going now? Do you have a place? Friends?'

Morna shakes her head. Watches Lydia Dawson hesitate.

'We're meeting my husband and his brother. The authorities will give you a hut to live in, but they'll be crammed. You could bunk with us for a short time?'

She doesn't deserve to be taken in by this kind family. But there is little alternative, so she grasps tight to the help that is offered. When they leave the cabin, she takes the hand of one of the smallest children, following in Lydia's wake into the bright new world.

—

Lydia's husband Danny doesn't want her there. Morna can tell this as soon as he looks at her, his brow furrowed over his brown skin.

'How long for?' he asks Lydia, under his breath but loud enough to hear. He stares at Morna, taking her in. Lydia kisses her husband. Morna looks at her shoes.

'Just a short time,' she says, 'until she's on her feet.'

Danny scowls, but he has not seen his wife for so long that her kisses quickly distract him. Morna averts her eyes from the sight of Danny's hands on Lydia, struck by the flashback of hands on her own body – insistent, grasping, finding the warm places on the bleak hillside.

She sits on the step outside their hut, faint with heat, and the weight of the brother, Lucas, watching her, sizing her up in a different way. Less a burden, more potential. She shudders at the thought. He spits on the ground but his eyes stay suckered to her body, barely straying to her face as he continues his assessment.

Morna stands, dusting off her hands, uncomfortable with both the scrutiny and the pungent eucalyptus, needing to get away.

'Where's the beach?'

Lucas points. 'Want me to show you around? Get to know you?' His voice suggests a different kind of acclimatisation.

She shakes her head, wary of the thoughts visible on his face. She's seen them before. 'Can I come?' Lydia's eldest daughter, Alice, a girl of twelve, looks up from where she and her three siblings are scratching marks in the dust. 'Please?'

As soon as she acquiesces, the others clamour to join them. She'd have liked to be alone, but at least this will protect her from Lucas's advances, while Danny and Lydia are busy inside. Morna and the children trail across the road and through scrubland towards a golden beach. The ground is still moving beneath her feet, rolling like the boat on the water. Shading her eyes, she feels a kick of awe inside her at the sight in front of her. It's postcard-beautiful, with families lolling on the sand and kids in bathing suits splashing in the shallows.

She and Alice help the younger ones off with their shoes, and Morna sinks onto the sand and watches them run towards the waves to wet their feet, kicking up puffs of yellow sand as they go. At least for a few moments she has time to breathe, to work out what to do. She needs to find a job soon; her carefully hidden notes won't last that long. Should she take a place in a hostel, or stay with Lydia's family? What is she qualified to do? She was good at school, could teach, maybe do secretarial duties or pick fruit. But only for so long. What then? Tears draw to her eyes at the hopelessness of it all, the heat and tiredness overwhelming her.

'Hey, don't blubber. You're not a whingeing pom, are you?' She looks up into the smiling face of a tall and slim young man, so brown he makes her feel like milk, though her skin is already smarting in the fierce Aussie sunshine.

'What's a pom?'

'You are.' The man grins. 'Although maybe not, with that accent. Where are you from?'

'Scotland.'

'When did you get here?'

'This morning.'

'You should sit in the shade, then.'

Everything he asks sounds like a question, but she immediately feels at ease with him. Safe. He helps her carry the shoes to the dappled shade of a tree further up the beach and she waves at Alice to indicate where she is sitting.

'Those your brothers and sisters?'

He nods in the direction of the younger ones, who are giggling, knee-deep in the surf.

'No. I'm just watching them for my friend. I'm on my own.'

He frowns and his voice is gentle when he asks: 'Mind if I sit?'

'Sure.'

The easy smile doesn't leave his face for long and his gaze rests on her like she's even more beautiful than this paradise she's landed in. Morna feels guilt echo inside her, tempering the enjoyment.

'What's your name?'

'Violet.' She lies, twisting a strand of her Scottish hair around her finger on this Australian beach.

'You in the Nissen huts back there?'

She nods, daring now to meet his gaze and see the brown of his eyes, flecked with honey. The tension of the voyage leaves her muscles; the sense of listing she's had since she set foot on this land, the ground swaying beneath her, dissipates.

They sit together, talking. She tells him about the death of her family, the fact that she's alone in the world, that she's staying with Lydia but isn't sure she's welcome. As she spins the lies, she steps fully into them, leaving the girl she was behind her like a mirage.

He listens. Properly listens. And she realises how tired she is.

'I could ask around for you? The government will give you a job but it might be harvesting sugar cane. There are some administrative openings here and there. Can you type?'

She lies again. 'Yes.' How hard can it be? Harder than this?

The children run up the beach, wet and sandy. They're hungry. It's time to take them back.

She looks regretfully at him, lets her eyes linger on his, drawing him in.

'There's dancing,' he says. 'In the hall on Saturdays. Will you come?'

She thinks of her faded 'good' dress, stuffed in the sack. Of the flickering inside her and the time running out.

'Yes,' she tells him. 'But... what day is it now?'

He laughs. A long, clear sound like a bell. 'It's Thursday.'

Morna blushes and nods. The young child tugs on her hand. 'Violet!'

'I'm coming.'

She realises, as they cross the road and attempt to locate their hut in a sea of similar buildings, that she didn't even ask his name.

'Violet's got a boyfriend!' The youngest boy spills the beans as soon as he sees his parents and Lucas, who is smoking a cigarette outside of their hut.

'Good,' Lydia says, scooping him up and planting a kiss on his cheek. 'You can stay for a bit,' she whispers to Morna. 'A few weeks at least. I'll work on him.'

Morna blushes, daring to glance at Lucas a moment. Enough to see his face of thunder.

CHAPTER THIRTY-SEVEN

MORNA, 1952

The Saturday dance is a square dance. Lydia is keen to go too, and works hard on Danny.

'Please?' Morna comes to her aid, sure she cannot just walk into a dance hall alone here, but knowing she must go, that she has to see him.

'Your young man's going to be there, is he?' Danny gives in eventually. Even in the space of a few days, Morna has seen that Lydia can twist him around her finger but it's a delicate balance and if she twists too far, he snaps. 'I suppose we could give it a try. What about you, Lucas?'

'No chance. You won't catch me at those things.' His black mood has lasted since they arrived. Maybe this is just the way he is.

'You can watch the little ones,' Lydia jokes, though they all know full well that Lucas will be at the pub spending his wages and staggering in late, peeing against the side of the hut so the air smells of hot piss. Morna has to keep the family sweet, but being nice to Danny's younger brother makes her skin crawl.

She and Lydia spend an hour pressing their dresses as best they can, fixing their hair. Lydia has a powder compact and a lipstick that they dab on their cheeks as well, peering into the small mirror propped up in the hut, while the children prance around them and Danny sits outside with a beer. Lucas is nowhere to be seen.

Morna's heart flutters in time with her belly as they walk along the beach to the community hall, where what seems like hundreds of people are packing into the building, and the twang of the music and the caller's cheerful voice drift out to them. She smooths her dress, sucking in the small bump that she hopes no one else can see. It won't be long now, and everything will change. Lydia, noticing, clasps her hand a moment.

It is packed inside and she cannot hope to find the man she can only vaguely picture: white teeth and brown skin, a kind smile and honey-flecked eyes. But then he's there in front of them, beaming like he's been watching for her.

'I didn't know if you were coming,' he says.

Ian. His name is Ian.

She introduces him to Lydia and Danny, and they buy drinks and stand and watch the dancers for a time, people moving in unfamiliar sequences.

Morna is nostalgic for the kilts and sporrans of home, the passionate music of the fiddles and the strong arms lifting you off your feet and whirling you. She feels sick with sadness.

But the longer she watches, the more she sees it's just like a ceilidh – the caller is telling the dancers what to do. When Ian asks if she wants to try it, she nods, giving him her hand and letting him take her into the dance, surrendering her fear and control.

The music swirls and the caller sings directions, and for a very short time, Morna is free. She has to concentrate so carefully on the steps and the strange-accented directions that she cannot think of her worries. Every time she looks up, Ian is fixed on her, the glow of adoration on his face.

CHAPTER THIRTY-EIGHT

Cal dresses and heads into the open-plan living area. Chrissie is still asleep and the cabin feels tranquil in the early morning, the day an open possibility.

Shona's already messaged to tell him Police Scotland have been in touch with police in Australia to run Jane's DNA sample against their system but it hasn't yielded a result. As a separate line of investigation, Cal and Sarah have been in touch with an Aussie ancestry site, appealing to them to enter Jane's full profile into their database and see if there are any hits.

The rules of the site are that you can only enter your own data. While the US is deploying genetic genealogy in high-profile cases, not all countries have resolved the ethics of using ancestry sites for police investigations. However, the fact that this is a missing person case seems to be working in their favour – the general consensus is that identifying a victim is a less controversial use than pinpointing a killer using their familial connections.

Co-ordinating all parties has been an exacting task and he's sure it wouldn't have been possible without Sarah's determination and ability to wear people down. It's been a relief to see her skills deployed against someone other than himself.

Of course, they could just break the rules and submit Jane's profile themselves, but he's conscious that Shona's participation in this podcast puts her at professional risk so he's not prepared to cut corners unless they have to. Getting the company on board might take longer, but it's a better bet. There must be an Australian family missing someone, waiting for answers.

His phone pings and he grabs for it, expecting Shona. Instead, it's a text from Detective Foulds. *Appeal for Naomi going live in ten.*

Cal stares at the words, nausea and guilt resuming their churning in his stomach. Thoughts of Jane retreating, he reaches for the remote control and sits down to wait. He's been praying it was all a mistake, that Naomi would have walked back through the door by now, seeking a reconciliation with Barr, but it's increasingly looking like that's not the case. The more time goes on, the more he worries she's done what she suggested and provoked him into violence.

The appeal is heart-wrenching. Naomi Barr's mother is silver-haired and frail, her features angular to the point of gaunt. She walks with two sticks to the row of seating, helped by Detective Foulds, light ricocheting off her hunched frame from the cameras clustered to hear what she has to say. Cal anxiously scans the lines of people. Jason Barr is not there.

Detective Foulds leans into the microphone.

'Good morning. Thank you for being here. Today we are making an appeal for Naomi Barr, or anyone who knows her current whereabouts, to come forward. We've circulated a picture of Naomi and her details, including what she was wearing when she disappeared. Naomi was last seen seven days ago when she visited her mother, but she did not return home after that visit.

'Naomi, if you're watching, you're not in any trouble. We understand you may wish to have some privacy and if that is the case, we respect your wishes, but please give us a call so we can establish that you're all right. To anyone else who may be holding Naomi against her will, we ask that you release her to her family.

'Naomi's mother, Susan, will now say a few words and then I'll take a couple of questions.'

She angles the microphone across and down so that the older woman can reach it. There's a pause as Susan looks out at the sea of jackals while they wait for her to speak.

'I'd like to ask anyone who has my daughter or knows where she is to please let her come home,' she says, her thin voice wobbling. 'She visits me every day. This isn't like her and I need to know that she's safe. Please.'

Cal watches, feeling like he's sliding on pebbles, unable to get a grip on his thoughts. With every new piece of information, Naomi becomes more human to him. He failed to help her.

Foulds opens up to questions, pointing to an unseen journalist at the back.

'Is Jason Barr a suspect in Naomi's disappearance?'

Cal holds his breath.

'We have no reason to suspect any harm has come to Naomi,' Foulds says. 'We expect to find her alive and well.'

'But you're searching her home,' another journalist butts in. 'You must think there's evidence there.'

'That's not a question,' Foulds says, calmly. Hundreds of miles north, Cal smiles.

'Do you think there is evidence against Jason Barr?'

'We will be conducting a thorough investigation and following all leads,' she says. 'Last question.'

'Has Jason Barr been arrested?'

Foulds' face is a mask. 'No. He's helping us with our inquiries, that's all.' She pushes her chair back as she says, 'That's all we have time for.'

The last shot shows her offering a hand to Naomi's mother, then the camera cuts back to the news crews outside the Barrs' home. There's a hive of industry visible – officers trudging in two by two, some dressed in protective overalls. Two more emerge from the house, plastic bags in hand and faces painted serious. Is that a laptop in one of them? A hard drive?

Rattled, Cal stares at the television and reality swims in and out. The blood speeds through his veins, making his head light. But gradually, it is starting to sink in: Naomi Barr really is missing, this isn't a hoax. He watches transfixed, as Jason Barr's carefully constructed life is taken apart in front of him, piece by piece.

CHAPTER THIRTY-NINE

While he waits for any news from Australia about Jane, and while he tries not to beat himself up for Naomi's disappearance, Cal turns his attention to the plane. Since the AAIB and DAIB have taken over the investigation, he's been shut out and all he knows is the little Shona has been able to tell him. Discussions are ongoing about Salvage and Marine Operations undertaking the recovery of the body from the aircraft, and whether or not it is feasible for them to raise the plane.

All day, he sits in a local cafe, ordering drink after cooling drink and using their fast Wi-Fi for research, but the maze of aviation websites and forums is impenetrable. He sends off various appeals for help, hoping someone comes through. Above him, the secretive hills are orange and brown instead of green and purple, parched and desperate for a drink of the water that sits at their feet.

Finally, just as he's giving up hope, he gets a reply from an aviation expert based in Lossiemouth, on the coast in Moray. The man retired after years as an RAF engineer and has a small museum in an old hangar. By all accounts, he's the font of aviation knowledge needed – he's a regular on one of the main forums and the rest of the members seem to defer to him. Cal gives Bobby the bones of the problem and they arrange for him to drive up to visit him in his hangar museum the next day.

By the time he makes his way back to the cabin, it's getting late and he's exhausted. Chrissie is outside the lodge, wearing a green sundress and with wet hair, curls drying around her face. A bowl of salad and a loaf of bread sit on the picnic table and she's just turning off the barbecue, removing fillets of grilled fish. When he approaches, she throws her arms around him.

'You cooked?' He sets down his laptop bag, still feeling stunned whenever she proves herself to be no longer a child.

'I did more than that. I caught the fish!'

'You're kidding.'

'Nope. Went out on the boat with Sean for a bit today.'

He smiles, burying the urge to ask what the deal is with her and the young barman. It's just a relief to see her relaxed and happy. They sit and eat the meal she's prepared. Cal drinks a long, cold beer and feels the frustrations of the day slip back into perspective. He fills Chrissie in on his contact with the aviation expert and together they listen to the recordings she's been taking with local people so they can start editing them into a script. He's always been a lone wolf, but he likes working with his daughter.

They settle into a comfortable silence, watching the long loch and the families around them. He can't let this opportunity pass, though. It may not be appropriate to ask her about her love life, but Cal's determined not to keep ignoring the elephant in the room.

'Have you been doing any drawing here?'

She shrugs. 'Not really, no.'

'You don't seem to be doing as much these days,' he says lightly.

Chrissie is still for a moment, her face turned to the loch view so he can only see how troubled she is in profile.

'I don't know, Dad,' she says quietly. 'I seem to have lost the love for it.'

She looks back at him and her unshed tears make her eyes bigger, tugging at his core. How to fight the urge to fix when you can't.

'Is this a new feeling? Did anything particular trigger it?'

She thinks for a moment then shakes her head. 'Honestly, no. It's been coming for a while now and I've been pushing it away.'

Cal pushes his plate aside. 'What do you want to do about it?'

She takes a breath. 'I'm thinking about changing course.'

He keeps his face deliberately neutral. 'What to?'

Chrissie looks down at her fingers, shredding the piece of kitchen roll she was using as a napkin. 'I'm not sure.'

The anxiety to make everything all right is intense and he fights the urge he feels to intervene. This is something she has to figure out for herself.

'Well, you've got time to think about it. Let it percolate.'

She looks up reluctantly, as if scared of what she might find on his face.

'You're not mad?'

He smiles. 'No, I'm not mad. Why would I be mad?'

'Do you think Mum will be?'

Art is Allie's vocation and something that has always bound her and Chrissie together. He can see why she's worried what her mother might say.

'No,' he says, definite. 'She just wants what's best for you, love. We both do.'

He gets up, moving to her side of the table to hug her.

'Thanks, Dad,' she says, her face buried in his chest, her voice muffled. He kisses the top of her head and releases her, overwhelmed by how much it's possible to love someone.

—

As they've been talking, the dark has fallen, so they clear up the dinner things under the light of the rising moon, which this evening is swollen and close.

Cal should just go to bed, but can't resist opening up his laptop to check his emails and the news. It's a terrible habit and one Shona is always trying to train him out of, but he's desperate to know what's going on with Naomi's investigation, terrified that news of a body being found will break. He opens his inbox, promising himself he won't get drawn into dealing with anything tonight.

But what he sees blasts him wide awake, sending adrenaline pelting through his limbs.

'Chrissie?!'

She sticks her head out of the bathroom, toothbrush held to one side. 'What?'

'The ancestry site in Australia… They've got a hit.'

'Oh my God. Hang on.' Chrissie darts back into the bathroom and he hears the sound of her toothbrush hitting the sink. She's by his side in seconds. 'Show me.'

Together, they scan the email, eyes skipping over details until they parse the information and land on the salient point.

'Is that…?' Chrissie points at the screen.

'Yep,' Cal says as he stares at the words in disbelief. 'They've got a grandchild on their system. It looks like we've found her.'

CHAPTER FORTY

Cal makes the journey to Lossiemouth, bleary-eyed after he and Chrissie called Sarah late last night and discussed the next steps into the early hours. They are impatient for details but under their agreement with the Australian genealogy company, the police will be making the first approach to the family and breaking the news.

Now that it's a reality rather than a hypothetical, Cal feels a burn of anguish for the family about to discover that their loved one met a violent end so far from home. He knows how it feels to have that news delivered. He knows you can never recover from it.

The hangar isn't far from the coast, on the edge of what looks like a manufactured forest – the trees all in perfect rows, like soldiers standing sentinel. A field and a small runway sit before it.

As Cal gets out of the car and breathes in sea air and hot pines – an intoxicating scent more reminiscent of the south of France than the north of Scotland – a man in a navy boiler suit emerges from the open doors of the hangar, wiping his hands on a dirty rag. He's grey-haired but tall and upright, a military bearing about him that gives away his RAF pedigree.

'Cal? I'm Bobby. I won't shake your hand.' He shows him the grease marks by way of explanation.

Behind Bobby, Cal catches a glimpse of several light aircraft, one of which has tools and a small ladder arranged near the tail. As he follows the man into the hangar, he closes his eyes and breathes in the new smell, immediately plunged back in time to his grandfather's garage – oil and sweat and machines combined in perfect nostalgia.

He is struck by the dedicated but homespun nature of the exhibits, the neatly stencilled signs and the simple money box on the chair.

'Great set-up you have here.'

'Keeps me out of trouble. I've been fascinated since I was a bairn. All I ever really wanted to do. I was an engineer at Lossie for thirty year but you have to make way for the new guard eventually.' Bobby shrugs and in the movement Cal reads the regret and loss.

He holds out the box containing the bottle of Ardbeg and sets it on the desk beside them.

'A little thank you for your time.'

'Much appreciated.' Bobby's eyes gleam when he sees the whisky. 'That's a good year.'

'I have to confess to having done some internet stalking to discover your poison.' He laughs.

'So, you found this wreckage, then? I saw a news story on it but there's not been much information released.'

'Sort of. We stumbled across it when working on a podcast about a woman who was murdered in the hills. She was never identified and we're trying to discover who she was, find her family and maybe work out who killed her. This was an unexpected development.'

'Any chance of retrieving the plane? Have the salvage guys said?'

'I'm not sure. The decision is with the authorities, so you never know. There's a body in there, I'm afraid. Bones of a second body were found in the lochan. Whether or not they're connected, I don't know.'

Bobby's expression sobers, his eyes go a little distant at the thought of the downed aircraft.

'What do you need from me?'

'Well. The details we were able to gather have gone to the authorities but of course they're being tight-lipped about the plane and where it might have come from for now.'

'And you're trying to see if it could be linked to your dead woman?'

'It's a long shot I know, but we're pretty stuck. Without knowing who Jane is, we have no idea who would have wanted her dead.'

'I'll help if I can.'

'I've got some printouts of the underwater pictures.' Cal gestures to his bag. 'I'm hoping to work out what sort of aircraft it is and how long it might have been down there. Maybe we can establish where it came from and who was on board.'

Bobby clears papers and rubbish from his desk, shoving things out of the way to make a clear space. Cal takes the folder of pictures from his bag. He's had them blown up and printed out and he lays them in front of Bobby now. Luckily, he took these before the authorities shut him down, and no one remembered to ask for them to be deleted.

'The water's clear.'

'Yes, fresh mountain water. It's very clean, as there are few pollutants up there. We think that's preserved the wreckage. The lochan is incredibly deep. If the heatwave hadn't dried it out a bit, the first set of bones probably wouldn't have been spotted. That find led us to the plane.'

Bobby peers closer, sucking in a breath as he scans the pictures and clearly experiences a flash of recognition.

'That looks like a Chipmunk.' He studies the images, then picks one up, holding it in front of him. 'Yes, look. See the low-mounted wing and the two-seat cockpit with a clear canopy. I'd swear it is. These started to replace the Tiger Moth after the war – came into service in the 1950s. They were used for training a lot – Canadian design. Could easily be flown solo.'

Cal wonders what this means for the other set of bones – are they connected?

'But how could it crash without anyone knowing? It must have come from an airfield and been missed by someone when it didn't come back?'

Bobby purses his lips. 'If it was flying in class G airspace, they wouldn't have had to register a flight plan, and if you were flying low then you'd be under the radar, so... it's possible it crashed and was missed but no one knew where to look.'

'It seems unbelievable no one would have seen it go down.'

'Aye. So many planes have gone down over Scotland, though – not just during the war. Mostly they've been found, as they're pretty obvious. It's wild out here but not exactly the Colombian jungle.'

Bobby carries on, waving his hands in the air as he warms to his theme. 'They used to be left where they lay and there are still places where planes remain intact as a memorial. Though these days there's always some idiot wanting to take bits away with them, or posing for social media.'

Cal leans in to refocus him. 'Would it be possible for a plane to go into water and there to be no trace, though?'

'It's possible that a plane could be going down or lose power and the pilot might try to land on water if there was no other option. Theoretically, you could hit the loch and sink. It can't have been going that fast, though, if you say the plane is almost in one piece.' He shakes his head. 'My money is on an emergency landing that went awry.'

'They couldn't eject?'

'The Chipmunk didn't have ejection seats. You could open the canopy and bail out, though. Military aircrew would generally fly wearing parachutes.'

Bobby has returned to the pictures.

'Hud on.' He ducks into an office that Cal hasn't really noticed before. It looks like a store cupboard, crammed with books and files. There's a lot of banging and swearing.

'Need a hand?'

'No, no. All fine.' Bobby emerges with a thick file covered with dust. 'How long have you got?'

Cal grins now. This is his sort of obsessive. 'All day.'

Apart from a break when Cal goes out to buy them sandwiches, he and Bobby study lists of planes and flight records for hours. It's sweltering inside the hangar, so they retreat to the shade of the movie-set pine trees and sit on a couple of camping chairs while they scan page after page. Cal largely acts as a scribe for Bobby, as the man flicks from one file to the next, clearly in his element. Occasionally, he hares off inside for another book or document, determined to work out where this plane might have originated.

It's mind-bending work, and with all the numbers and details, Cal would be lost at sea without Bobby.

'Hang on,' the older man says suddenly, his finger stopped at a footnote in a self-published book with a very small font. 'This refers to a missing Chipmunk from Dalcross airfield.' There's a note of excitement in his tone, the pair of them on the search for treasure.

'Could that be it?' Having seen the wealth of data and the sheer number of things to plough through, Cal is pessimistic about their chances of identifying it, but Bobby has scientific patience and a methodical approach.

By way of answer, Bobby pulls an ancient Nokia phone from his boiler suit and starts clicking through the contacts.

'Sandy? Is that you?' Cal glances at the book sitting upside down on Bobby's knee, the spine bent back. Then a series of 'Aye, aye, aye… aye,' that seem to go on forever before Bobby gets to the point. 'Well, I'm just thinking. That Chipmunk in your book that went missing in the 1950s. Was there ever any theory about where it ended up?'

A small pause.

'And who was flying it?'

Cal strains to hear but can't decipher the words.

'Aye. That would make sense.' There's a long pause and Cal leans in, feeling the tension stretching infuriatingly inside him. 'Well, now. Maybe. Maybe.' Another long series of protracted chat and Cal wants to scream. Finally, Bobby seems to be wrapping up. 'Aye, well I will now, Sandy. You'll be the first to know. Aye.'

Bobby clicks the button on the phone and looks at Cal.

He hangs there, on tenterhooks. 'Well?'

'We might just have it.'

CHAPTER FORTY-ONE

EPISODE FIVE: WHAT'S IN A NAME?

It's as warm as a Spanish beach in the heart of Perth. Local people have covered the once-green Inch, the park by the river, and two ice-cream vans are doing roaring trade. But there's no time to stop and take in the view. Finding Justice *is here to finally learn Jane's real identity. With me is Lucie Barnes. Lucie has been helping the podcast with publicity since she was rescued from the same hills where Jane died. She feels a strong affinity with Jane, as I know do many listeners.*

It's an emotional moment, knowing we will finally hear her real name.

DS Matthews, who we've been liaising with at Police Scotland, leads us through to an interview room. The fans aren't working, so we leave the door open and you may hear the sounds of the police station in the background. For those of us in the room, however, the noise fades into the background.

'Well. Here we go. Are you ready?'

'I think so.'

'Jane's real name is Violet Martin. Maiden name Reed. Take a look in the folder. It came across from the Melbourne police this morning.'

When we open the file, there's more than we expected to find. There's a picture.

It's hard to convey how moving it is to finally see Jane as she was and should have been. Violet is slim and straight-backed, with blue eyes the colour of Loch Tay in the sunshine. Her grey hair is twisted up in a French knot, a couple of strands hanging artfully, and she wears sensible trousers and a striped T-shirt. Her face is healthy, her forehead lined. She looks wiry and strong, like someone who could walk a long distance. She does look a little like the artist's impression that was created twenty years ago, but only in particulars. This woman is flesh breathed into a line drawing.

There's a man in the picture too. He has a kind smile, crinkles at the corners of his eyes and sunglasses perched on his head. He leans in close to Violet, his arm around her shoulders. In front of them, three adult children – one with a young child on her lap. They're all beaming at the photographer, except Violet, whose smile has a distance that isn't present in the rest of the faces.

'This is her family? Her husband?'

'Yes. She had been in Australia all her adult life apparently. She took a boat from Scotland in the 1950s and married an Aussie so never left. They had three children. He died before she went missing.'

'What did they think happened to her? The family.'

'They thought she'd wandered off into the bush. She made it seem that she'd gone on a local hiking trip. Now it looks like she laid a trail then vanished. They had no idea she'd left the country. She must have gone to great lengths to conceal it, as there is no record of anyone by the name of Violet Martin or Violet Reed entering the UK. We'll be looking into that further.'

'When did she go missing?'

'In 2003. The right timeline for us. We know she lay undiscovered for around a year, so it fits. Congratulations. You did it.'

'Can we talk to the family?'

'They're shocked, according to the New South Wales police. It's understandable. But I believe the son indicated he is going to give you a call when he's taken it in. He has your details. They have a lot of questions.'

So do we.

CHAPTER FORTY-TWO

Cal's shopping in the village a couple of days later when he gets the call. He can see from the area code that it's an international number, so he abandons his basket in the aisle, waving to the cashier that he'll come back, and heads outside, his fingers scrabbling to swipe to accept the call.

There's a pause so long he thinks he's missed it, then a rich, deep voice that fills his head.

'Is that Cal Lovett? The podcaster?'

'Yes. Ian? Violet's son?'

'That's right.'

'Thank you for calling me. I'm so sorry for your loss. It must be a terrible shock.'

The man sighs. He sounds tired. 'It is, but also, we've waited a long time for answers. We've searched the bush for years in places we thought she might have gone. And now we finally know.'

'I understand.' Cal knows this feeling all too well. 'It's strange when there's sadness and relief.'

'We're all just so confused, to be honest. We spent years traipsing round the outback, looking for her, and she was in Scotland all along. Part of me is a bit pissed with her. But then to be told she was most likely murdered... How can I be mad? It's such a shock.'

Cal has drifted over to a bench in a welcome patch of shade while he listens.

'You must have a lot of questions. Maybe I can help with some of them.'

'I really hope so.'

'Was it your daughter who did the test?'

'It was my niece. Leia's always been into family history. She had kids a few years back and I think she wanted to know more about where she came from. We've had all sorts of cousins on my dad's side pop up but nothing for mum, not until now.'

Cal explains how he came to be involved in the case. The call stretches on as he details all the elements he knows, even the fact that they've found other bodies and the plane while investigating. Ian wants to hear all about Lucie, too.

'What was your mum like?' he asks when the man seems to run out of questions.

'To tell you the truth, I really don't know if I knew her at all. Not after this.'

'Your memories still count,' Cal tells him. 'They're still real.'

'She had an edge, I guess. Always did. Dad loved her to bits and they were both great parents, don't get me wrong. I just think as kids we were all closer to Dad because he was an open book, you know? She used to disappear sometimes. Not physically, not till the end, but you'd be talking to her and she wouldn't have heard a word. Just staring out the window.'

'That must have been tough.'

'I guess it was what it was. After Dad died, she got a lot worse, though, grumpy at times, wouldn't accept much help. We thought it was grief. Maybe it was. I'm seventy-one now. Older than she was then. I suppose I understand the tiredness, but it felt like there was something else.'

'Do you think it's possible your mum had some sort of confusion or dementia?'

Ian considers the question.

'I never saw any sign of it. And there's no record of her coming to the UK – the police checked all travel manifests at the time under Violet Martin and Violet Reed. So how did she manage that? Nah. Mum was always pretty sharp, far as I could see.'

'You were born not long after she reached Australia?'

'Yeah. She was seventeen when she had me. Dad always said they couldn't wait to get started. They left it a while before they had my two sisters, though. They're five and seven years younger than me.'

'So when did your parents meet?'

'When Mum was fresh off the boat from Scotland.'

'Do you know what year it was? It might help us track down people here who knew her when she was growing up. We're going to try.'

'It was 1952, cos I was born the year after. She was a ten-pound pom, came over for a better life. Dad found her on the beach her first day, stopped her getting burned in the sun. He told me once that it was love at first sight. Soppy old git.'

'Did she talk about her life in Scotland? Did you ever come over for a visit?'

'No way. She wouldn't talk about it. Ever. Dad would always shut us down if we tried to ask. That was something we never talked about.'

Cal can sense Ian is flagging. His words are slowing as he speaks from the other side of the globe where night is falling. 'It must be late there with you?'

'Yeah, pretty late.'

'Maybe we could talk some more tomorrow? I've got a lot of questions and I don't want to bombard you with them now.'

Ian clears his throat and Cal thinks the gruff Aussie has been crying.

'You know. I was actually thinking that I'd like to come to Scotland. This whole thing's got me in a spin. I didn't sleep a wink last night. My sisters can't get away but I've got no one who needs me around. I'm divorced and my kids are grown. Just have a dog that the girls will take for me.'

'If you think you could, then I'd be happy to show you where she was found, take you through everything we know.'

'That would be good. I need to see where Mum went. I feel pretty helpless here and I think Dad would want one of us to be there.'

They talk for another moment and then Cal says goodbye to Ian, promising that they'll catch up the next day, once he's made his travel plans. Despite the warmth in the air, he looks up at the mountains and shivers. There's something so strange about the story, the way Violet took off without saying goodbye.

There's also something else nagging at him, but he needs to think it through and broach it carefully. If he's right, then it changes things for Ian.

—

As he collects his shopping and walks back to the cabin, Cal muses over the ways he could harness the memory of the older people in the local community – they're unlikely to stumble on the social media posts Lucie has been preparing. Perhaps a community meeting or an appeal to younger people to show their parents and grandparents the picture they have of Violet.

Almost back at the lodge, he is desperate for a cool shower, planning to call Shona to update her on his chat with Ian. But, when he arrives, he finds Chrissie waiting for him, her face grave, fingers twisting together as she paces at the front door.

'What's wrong?'

He sets the shopping down, foreboding shooting into him.

'Dad, it's been on the news. They're saying they found bloodstains in Naomi's house. They've arrested Jason Barr.'

CHAPTER FORTY-THREE

Shona drives down that evening after work. The three of them sit glued to the news, as Jason is questioned in a Birmingham police station. Cal thought he'd feel elated, but he doesn't. Just tired and sad and unbelievably guilty. Eventually, Shona insists they all go to bed, though he can hardly sleep, obsessing over the calls and the mistakes he made with Naomi.

When he wakes in the morning, it is to a text message from Foulds.

> We're releasing him. Not enough evidence to charge at the moment.

Into those stark words, he reads everything. He knows her frustration and fury, because he feels them too.

There's nothing to do but carry on. Ian will be arriving in the country in two days, and he owes it to the family to try and find answers for them. Cal's hoping they'll have more to tell him by the time he lands, and they've agreed to save further discussion for then.

'I'm not sure I can get my head round this,' Ian tells him as they make plans for Cal to pick him up in Edinburgh.

'It'll take time,' Cal says, though he's not sure how true that is. How do you ever square this mystery with the woman who gave birth to you and brought you up?

Shona takes a couple of days off work and it's a relief to have her beside him, her calm and sensible approach needed more than ever. He's acutely aware that he must not take it for granted.

With Sean's help, they secure the use of the village hall for the following evening and run off a load of flyers on the library photocopier. Chrissie and Sean leaflet as many houses and people as they can in the villages at both ends of the loch. They add posters to pub and cafe notice-boards, while Lucie alerts the community Facebook pages she's been joining from the Cotswolds, and the grapevine swings into action.

The village hall is both sweltering and buzzing at six o'clock the following evening. DS Matthews is in attendance to answer any police questions but tells Cal she'd rather observe so has tucked herself away at the side. From there, she scans the room with a hawk-like focus.

Extra seats are set out; others stand at the back with their arms folded. It's overwhelming to see all these faces. Cal isn't the best public speaker and his stomach is churning at the thought of addressing this crowd. When Tavish the minister arrives, rushing in almost last and smiling at Cal from the back, it is good to see another familiar face. He sees Shona greeting the man and finding him a seat.

When it's time to start, he forces a smile to banish the nerves and clears his throat. Some of the faces in front of him are interested and sympathetic, others more suspicious, but it's too late to back out of this now.

'Thanks for coming,' he shouts, waiting a moment for the last of the chatter to die back. 'I'm Cal Lovett, from the *Finding Justice* podcast.'

'Aye, we know...' someone calls from the back and there's a ripple of laughter.

Cal smiles and dips his head in acknowledgement. 'We've called this meeting to ask for your help. As many of you know, we've been working with Police Scotland to try and identify the woman known as Jane who was found on the hill twenty years ago.'

The room is silent now. Waiting. They know this. They want the news. Cal takes a breath and ploughs on.

'I realise some of you have already heard this development, but I can confirm that we have identified Jane. Her real name was Violet Martin, née Reed.'

Cal clicks the button on his laptop and the picture of Violet appears on the screen behind him, cropped so that it shows only her face and not the family around her. There's a shocked murmur in the room at the sight. Hillside Jane is gone. A mythical figure has been made real, given flesh and life before them. He scans the room and finds emotion on many faces.

'When I say that's her real name,' he explains to an audience quiet enough to hear pins dropping, 'I'm not sure that's true. We can find no trace of a Violet Reed in UK records from that time. It's likely that if Violet boarded a boat to Australia from here, she did so under an assumed name. She may even have been a stowaway.'

There's a total hush in the room.

'What we have also discovered,' he adds, 'is that Violet travelled back here from Australia just before she died. She'd been living there for most of her life but her family say she was born in Scotland and lived here until she was around seventeen. She had told them her mother died when she was a child, but she never revealed any more details about her old life. As far as we know, she had no contact with anyone in Scotland after she left.'

He pauses and scans the room, making eye contact with as many people as he can. Some shift in their seats, others stay perfectly still. 'Someone attacked Violet on the hillside twenty years ago and left her dead or dying. Violet leaves behind three grown children and six grandchildren who have lots of questions about what she was doing so far from her adopted home when she died. The facts of this case are extremely painful to them.'

A woman in the front row presses a tissue to her eyes.

'We're hoping we can piece together details of Violet's life here, and for that we need your help. She must have had a connection to this area. But we're going way back. She would most likely have been born in the mid-1930s, between the wars, and she left the area in the 1950s, so we're talking seventy years ago. It's a long shot but we're hoping some of the older members of the community might remember her.'

Cal clicks the button on his laptop again and another picture appears on the screen. A black-and-white photograph of a woman sitting on the beach, her hair flying in the breeze. Her face is slightly turned away, as if she doesn't want to be known. It's the best early image Ian could find of his mother. *She didn't like having her picture taken*, his email said. *Sorry.*

'This is Violet in her early twenties. Perhaps this will help those who might have known her. We're asking you to talk to older family members and see if they can help. Please feel free to take a flyer as you leave – they have both of these pictures and information about how to contact us. Anything you share can be anonymous if preferred.'

Cal looks at Shona and Chrissie for confirmation that there isn't anything else to say. Then he opens the meeting to questions.

A hand shoots up in the middle. A grey-haired woman in a navy dress and blazer, who must be sweltering in this heat. 'What will happen to her grave? Will you change the stone?'

'That will be up to her family,' Cal says. 'It's early days for them, as they had no idea Violet had travelled to Scotland. They'll be visiting her grave soon.'

'What about the aeroplane?' someone else calls out. 'Who do the bodies belong to? How is that connected to all this?' Others around the speaker murmur their approval of the question. Cal searches the crowd and locates the man at the back. He thinks he recognises him from the outdoor-equipment shop.

'I'm not sure,' Cal tells them. 'One set of bones was in the water and one in the cockpit of the aircraft. The latter is due to be recovered and analysed but all we know is that the first set belonged to an adult male. The police and AAIB are working to establish the exact reason the plane went down and when. It's possible that it isn't linked to Violet, at all. I'm sorry I can't tell you more at this stage.'

The meeting wraps up with grumbles of dissatisfaction, but Cal is pleased to see most people do take flyers with them. One woman even hugs Chrissie as she leaves.

'That was good, Dad, well done,' Chrissie says. 'Shall we go to the pub? People might be talking about it.' He sees Sean waiting for her at the doorway.

He catches Shona's eye.

'You go ahead, love. We'll finish up and follow you down.'

He says goodbye to the remaining people and they stack the chairs, though they've been told it's fine to leave them. There isn't really anything to do and he could have suggested they go with Chrissie, but in truth, he wants to be alone with Shona for a moment. Things are coalescing in his mind, pieces moving around like a slider puzzle, the image changing and distorting as he tries to get things in the right place. He has a slight headache, probably just the stress of public speaking, not his favourite pastime.

Outside the hall, he wraps her in his arms. She tilts her face for a kiss.

'Thank you,' he says. 'For being here.'

'How do you think it went?'

'Well, I think, apart from the questions about the plane – I wasn't much use there, but that's to be expected.'

They walk slowly through the village, drained by the heat and the event.

'The plane does seem to be a very big coincidence. I don't understand what the connection could be.'

'Me neither. Maybe it's staring me in the face and I can't see it.'

'Maybe there really is a curse on that valley.' She laughs.

'That would be just my luck.'

She glances at him, slipping her hand into his as they stroll.

'Is something else worrying you?'

'We think Violet emigrated from here in 1952. That's the year she married Ian, so it makes sense, especially if that happened right off the boat, as we believe. I've been looking at voyages that fit those dates. A lot of people emigrated then so it's certainly plausible. The Australian government was incentivising people to go.'

'Okay. So let's assume that's right, what's the issue?'

He rounds the bend in front of the bridge and the pub. From here, he can see the small figures of Chrissie and Sean at one of the outside tables, chatting to a group of people their age.

'The name of the boat that Ian says she was on doesn't match when he said she arrived. He said it docked in September but in fact it was mid-October.'

'It's a long time ago… People get things wrong, especially if there's no documentation and she didn't like to talk about it.'

'True. But Ian was born in April the following year.'

'Oh. That's quick.'

'A bit too quick if the ship actually docked in mid-October.'

'You're thinking Violet was pregnant before she got on the boat?'

'Maybe. That could be why she left. But I'm not sure if I should raise this with her son when he arrives. He speaks very affectionately about his father.'

'Oh God, that's a tough one.'

Cal groans. 'I know.'

'Isn't he supposed to be doing confirmatory DNA tests?'

'Yes, that's the plan. The sample we have currently is from his niece. She's the one who used the ancestry site. One of the sisters has also given her DNA, apparently.'

'So, if it's true, it will come out anyway?'

'Looks like it.'

'Then I think maybe you have to tell him soon.'

He sighs. 'I thought you might say that.'

CHAPTER FORTY-FOUR

Cal feels oddly nervous as he stands at the arrivals gate in Edinburgh Airport, scanning the emerging passengers. He turns his back on the newspaper display, sickened by the headlines.

> Barr falsely accused again?
>
> Ex-con released.
>
> Police target unlucky Jason.

Ian has changed planes in London and confirmed he was on the flight, but he has a bag to collect so is among the final few to appear. Shona has stayed at Loch Tay to give him time to talk to Ian alone. Sean is hopeful they can track down more information now that they have a name, so he and Chrissie have set out to question as many of the older generation as they can.

Cal recognises the tall grey-haired man immediately. There is something of his mother in him, or maybe that's fancy. He waves so Ian sees him and the two shake hands in greeting.

'Let me take that,' Cal says, but Ian refuses to relinquish his case.

'It's on wheels,' he says. 'I'll be right.'

Cal leads him to the car, watching as Ian drinks in all the details around him. He seems fascinated by the

Scottish voices and the people they pass, and this interest extends to the countryside as they leave the outskirts of the city and head along the scenic route to the great loch, past the dramatic mound of Stirling with the castle atop.

'It's impressive, isn't it?' Cal says when Ian whistles.

'My first time in Scotland,' Ian says. 'It's green.'

'It's usually even more so. The drought has really dried things out.'

'We're used to that at home. This is nothing.'

'So,' Cal ventures. 'Your mum and dad never travelled back here.'

Ian shakes his head. 'No. Not for want of trying on Dad's part. It kind of backfired on him to be honest.'

'Really?'

'Yeah. After he retired, he was going to bring Mum here for a trip. He'd even booked the flights as a surprise, but she freaked out when he told her about it so she could get a passport. The next we heard, the trip was off and that was that. Neither of them would talk about it.'

'Was that like them?'

'It was like Mum,' Ian says. 'She was always hard to read. But Dad was the opposite so it struck me as odd. I thought maybe they'd had an argument about it, which was unheard of.' He chuckles but there's a sadness to the sound. 'They never fought.'

'What? Even after being married for fifty years?'

'I know, right? Mum could be tricky but Dad never really went up against her. He always found a way round and she didn't fight him. They had their way and it worked.'

'She must have been devastated when he passed away.'

'Yeah. That was 2002. He was only seventy-five. Had a crook heart, it turned out.'

'So your mum didn't have a passport, as far as you know?'

'I never saw one.'

They fall silent for a while. Ian's head nods a couple of times and Cal can see how tired he is so doesn't push any more questions. When they reach the loch, Ian jerks awake.

'Is this it?' His voice betrays grief.

Cal stops the car and they get out to look at the view. He points to the valley and hillside where the lochan and the site of his mother's discovery lie.

'It's over there.'

'Mum walked up that?'

'Yes.'

'She was always pretty fit. Lots of bushwalking and she liked time on her own, which is why we believed the story that that's where she was going. When we complained about walking uphill as kids, she would tell us it was nothing.' He tilts his head. 'I can see why she said that now.'

Cal doesn't know what to say. He watches Ian – adrift in exhaustion and jet lag, the folds of a new country and his mother's death unfurling in front of him. The fitness must run in the family – Ian moves like a man ten years his junior – but he's clearly flagging now.

'Her grave is in the churchyard there.' Cal points. 'But maybe that's best left for another day?'

Ian nods. 'I wouldn't mind a rest.'

'The lodge isn't far.'

Cal drives Ian to the door of his lodge, which is ready for him with the key in the door. Chrissie has stocked the fridge with some essentials, so he shows Ian in and brings the case from the car. There is no objection to him carrying it now – done in, the man eases himself down onto the sofa.

'Rest as long as you need,' Cal tells him. 'We're on the site too and will go for a meal later if you fancy it. No pressure, just text me when you're ready, or we can see you tomorrow.'

'Thanks,' Ian says. As Cal shuts the door, his eyes are already closing.

CHAPTER FORTY-FIVE

Ian calls them at seven, just as they are wondering what to do for dinner. Showered and refreshed, he's keen to eat and to see some more of the area, so they agree to drive down to the pub together.

Chrissie is champing at the bit to meet Ian and is ready before Shona and Cal, so she walks down to introduce herself. By the time they drive round, the two of them are chatting like old friends and Cal is relieved to see there is colour in the man's face, after he looked so washed-out earlier.

When they arrive at the pub, Sean has saved them an outdoor table in the corner. Most of the other punters appear to be tourists and hikers, mercifully oblivious about Ian's identity. Cal's breathing slows as the Aussie takes photographs of the waterfall before they sit down. He seems in awe of the landscape, transported here by an unknown connection with his mother.

'I feel like I'm trying to understand her, but we don't even know if this is where she lived, or what her real name was,' he says as they head over to the table. The lightness of his words belies the sadness beneath.

'Maybe her real name was the one she chose to have with you,' Chrissie says.

Ian wipes his eyes and they all busy themselves with the menus.

Once they've ordered food, they talk about the place where Violet was found, how isolated it is above the small, deep lochan. Cal has brought an OS map and some photographs so he can show Ian the route they think she took.

'Do you think I could make it up there?' Ian asks, his fingers tracing the line on the map.

Though he's nervous about taking the older man up the hills in this heat, Cal's seen enough to believe Ian has the strength his mother must have had. 'I think so,' he says. 'We can take it slow and turn back if you feel it's too much.'

Their food arrives so he refolds the map.

After dinner, Shona raises the subject of Ian loading his DNA onto an ancestry site in the UK to see if there are any hits that could help.

'If we can find some cousins or distant relations, it might help us pin down where your mother came from and what her birth name was.'

'I think we should give it a try. The Aussie site doesn't link with all the same data, then?'

'Not all of it,' she says. 'You never know, she might even have had a sibling here. Lots of people have given older relatives DNA kits for Christmas in recent years, not realising some of them would open cans of worms they didn't know existed.'

'I'm game,' Ian says, draining his pint. 'Our worms are kind of out there already.'

Cal shifts in his seat. This isn't necessarily true. Is it unfair to continue down this track when he suspects Ian might also find other details that he's not expecting? What if the man he was named for and clearly adored isn't his biological father? What is that going to do to him?

They've set something in motion that may have all sorts of unintended consequences. He stares at a group of tourists taking pictures by the waterfall, collecting himself for a moment.

Ultimately, it can't be concealed, but he won't raise this now, in front of the others. It will have to be done in private. He makes himself smile and listen, trying not to feel the meal he's eating curdle inside him at the thought of what is next.

Shona and Chrissie decide to walk back while Cal takes Ian to look at Finlarig Castle. As they drive there, Ian studies the landscape around them. The castle near the edge of the loch looks ethereal in the soft evening light, surrounded by trees. The older man is keen to stop and look at it, rejuvenated by the food and with his body clock skewed. He peers at the ruins of the ancient structure, taking pictures for his family back home.

Afterwards, they walk down to the lochside and look out at the water over the reeds, standing in front of trees with exposed roots that look like clawed hands in the sand.

'You've been quiet,' Ian says, startling Cal out of his reverie. 'You going to spit it out?'

Cal laughs, taken aback by his Aussie directness, but grateful for it.

'I do have a concern that I wanted to mention, but I don't want to upset you.'

'Okay...'

'It's to do with the DNA test you're planning.'

Now it is Ian's turn to be silent.

'I think I might know where you're going with this one,' he says eventually, sighing.

Cal winces at the heaviness in his tone. Occasionally, his work leads him down these paths where he feels like the bad guy.

'I noticed your date of birth is quite soon after your mum arrived in Australia, that's all. I don't want to stir anything up, but the date of the ship docking doesn't really add up.'

'You know, when we were growing up, it never really occurred to me. My parents were always very vague about when they got together. If we asked about it, it was all "we don't live in the past, we look to the future" and we never really questioned that. If anything, we used to have a laugh at how coy they were about getting it on before they were married. Like it would matter these days. But when Dad died and Mum went missing, I had to go through their stuff and I found their wedding certificate, and it was only five months before I was born and it brought that all up. My uncle said something funny once when he was pissed at a barbie but, you know... I didn't want to think about it.'

The lines in Ian's face seem to deepen in the gathering darkness. Cal sees the pain in the jovial man's expression, though his gaze is distant, like he's staring into the memory. 'What did he say?'

'I don't quite remember, but it was something about Mum and it wasn't very nice. Everyone looked at me – I can only have been about ten. I do remember Dad, though. He was such a mild bloke but he went absolutely bloody mental. He grabbed Den and took him outside. I thought he was going to punch his lights out. We'd never seen him like that, ever. Never did again.'

'We don't have to carry on,' Cal says carefully. He can almost hear Sarah's fury as he offers to stop looking and close the door on this. Does he mean it, really?

But it doesn't matter. Ian looks up at the hulking hills to the left, thick with secrets.

'No, mate. I think this genie is coming out of the bottle. Let's rip the plaster off.'

CHAPTER FORTY-SIX

MORNA, 1952

Ian falls for her, hard. She knows it and encourages him, though she cannot feel the same simple joy he does. It's not that Morna doesn't like him. She likes him a lot, but every time they meet, there is a heaviness inside her that comes from the secrets she is keeping. They feel like stones in her gut.

She doesn't have long. Every day that passes makes it harder to conceal the truth.

'You're quiet tonight.'

They're walking along the beach, hand in hand. The sand is so perfect – Morna thinks of a trip her friend Betty once took to the west coast of Scotland. She said the sand was like snow but here it is spun gold. She has learned to wear a hat everywhere she goes here, but is permanently hot and bothered, longing for the chill of a Scottish afternoon.

'Sorry,' she says. 'I'm tired, I guess.'

'You must miss home.'

'No.' She halts abruptly and her hand slips from his. 'I don't.' Apart from the cool weather.

'You don't?'

'Things weren't… good back there. I needed to get away.'

His face clears of the clouds that had swept in. 'So you'll be staying, then?'

'I guess so.'

'Good.' Ian turns to her suddenly, with a rush of courage. 'Because I've never met anyone like you, Violet.'

Her fingers shake and so she clasps them tightly to stop the movement. She tries to look him in the eyes but she can't, so she fixes somewhere between them.

'I'm really hoping you'll stay,' he says.

'What do you mean?'

'I mean...' He takes her hand. 'I know this is fast, but I'm twenty-five and I want to settle down and have some kids.' Her heart thunders. 'And I was hoping you'd do that with me.'

One small word. *Yes*. That's all she needs to say and her problems are solved. Well, almost.

But, just when she thought quiet, biddable Morna was buried and gone, leaving ruthless Violet firmly in control, she wavers. Her lip trembles and she turns away from Ian to look at the ocean, trying to stop the tears from blurring her vision. *What is she doing? This is the moment.*

'I'm sorry,' he says. His fingers graze her shoulder, tentative and kind. 'It's way too soon, I know, I shouldn't have said anything. I'm sorry, Violet, I hope I haven't ruined anything between us. You're younger than me. I've jumped the gun.'

He's so good, so decent. She can't do this to him.

'No,' she says. 'That's not it, Ian. You really haven't done anything wrong.'

'Then why are you crying?'

He leans down to try and see her face, but her chin is tucked into her chest.

'Something happened, back in Scotland,' she says.

And then she finds the courage to look up into his eyes. They are filled with concern. It's on the tip of her tongue, really it is. Pictures of the hill and the lochan and the man are flashing through her mind, and she wants to tell him all of it, the whole truth. A great unburdening. But the goodness in him undoes her. So she can only find the strength to tell him the most relevant part of it.

She touches her stomach and tears run down her cheeks. Because she has no other options.

'I'm going to have a baby, Ian. And I'm alone and I don't know what to do.'

There's a moment of silence and understanding between them. He drops her hand, steps back from her. He pushes his hair off his forehead and she can see the recalibration on his face. *She's done it now.*

Morna drinks in his simple good looks and his gentleness, because this is the last she'll see of them.

But then something miraculous happens. He swallows and he steps forward and wraps his arms around her, taking her weight, holding her steady.

'No,' he says. 'You're not alone. If you'll have me.'

CHAPTER FORTY-SEVEN

The next day, while he waits for Ian to wake up, Cal sits outside the cabin with a pot of coffee, unnerved at having little to do, for once. He's heard from Bobby but the voicemail he received was cryptic, referring only to 'progress' and telling Cal he'll be in touch as soon as possible. He has the strange sense that the investigation has taken on a life of its own. As if he's lost control of the reins and the horses are running down the hill.

Whenever there is a vacuum, Naomi sweeps into his thoughts. The shock is passing into sadness. He decides to try Foulds, though she may still be mad at him. She's one of the few people who understand and he hates that they're at odds.

'Cal.'

Her tone is softer than the last time they spoke and she sounds tired.

'How are you?'

'I've been better. There's nothing I can tell you, I'm afraid.'

'I know. I'm not calling to ask. I just wanted to check in. I'm sorry this happened. I'm sorry I didn't warn you.'

They're both quiet for a moment. Cal closes his eyes and listens to the birds.

Abruptly, Foulds drops her professional detachment.

'I don't understand,' she says. 'It seems so obvious and yet he slips out of things every single time.'

'One day he won't.'

'I used to believe that,' she says.

'I have to.'

'We're going to have to stand down the search, unless something else comes up.'

Cal thinks of a body, lying under the ground, wrapped in a blue tarpaulin. If Naomi's fate matches that of Margot's, she won't stay hidden forever. She'll rise to the surface and he'll be waiting.

—

Making things right with Foulds lifts a weight from him. By the time the others are up, he and Rocket have been down to the village for supplies. The smell of cooked bacon fills the cabin and – not sure what Ian will prefer – he has set out soft rolls, butter, jam, fresh fruit and juice. He's relieved to see the man tucking into almost everything.

'I guess this heat doesn't bother you,' Chrissie says. Already it's stifling.

'It's pretty familiar,' Ian says. 'We have better air conditioning at home, though. I really wasn't expecting this in Scotland.'

Their focus today is the graveyard. After they've cleared up, Shona has to work, but the rest of them drive along the loch and park near the church. The village is beautiful and dramatic, with an old stone arch that Cal loves, but Ian barely seems to notice it. His mood is sombre.

'Is there somewhere I can buy flowers?' he asks Cal, suddenly. 'I don't have anything.'

'Yes. We'll stop in the village shop. Don't worry. And then Chrissie and I can show you where your mum is and leave you for a bit if you like.'

Ian nods. His hand goes to his phone in his pocket.

'I promised my sisters I'd send them pictures. Don't let me forget.'

'Of course not,' Chrissie says. 'Don't worry. And we can come back again if you need.'

'One of them isn't well,' he says. 'That's why they haven't come with me. She's had breast cancer.' His voice cracks. 'She couldn't even ask Mum if there was a history of it in the family. I just don't understand why someone would want to kill Mum. None of this makes any sense.'

Chrissie hugs Ian and they wait until he's ready to move forward.

The woman at the till in the shop looks at Cal in recognition. She was in the front row at the community meeting. He smiles and braces for a conversation about the case, but when she sees Ian and the armful of flowers he carries, her eyes soften and she simply comments on the weather and how it's shaping up to be another hot one.

As they walk in the direction of the graveyard, Ian's step slows and becomes heavier. His hand grips the bunch of lilies, the heads of which are already drooping in the heat. Her face creased in worry, Chrissie darts a look at Cal. He tries to telegraph his reassurance, knowing she wants to do something but that this is a part of this work – you can't fix the pain or even reduce it; you just have to stand and bear witness.

They lead Ian to his mother's headstone, but before they reach it, Cal can see something is different. He glimpses flashes of colour through the stones. He frowns, unsure what this means. But, when the path turns, he sees that the area around the grave is laden with tributes. There are pots with flowers in them that someone is clearly watering, and a carved wooden plaque sits against the stone with one word elegantly inscribed across it. *Violet.*

'Wow,' Chrissie says.

'Was this here before?' Ian asks, looking at Cal.

He shakes his head, staring at the grave in wonder. 'No. This has been done since the community meeting.'

The three of them stand before the stone, scanning the tributes. Ian lays his bouquet on the grass and then bends to read the cards and messages that have been left.

'We'll be over there,' Cal says. 'There's a bench beneath some trees.'

Somehow, it doesn't feel right to talk, so he and Chrissie sit in the cool shade of a yew tree in silence, the tiniest hint of a breeze drifting to them from the loch. He closes his eyes for a moment, letting his mind float. Only, it won't be still. He sees Naomi Barr, imagines blood splashes on the walls of her executive home; he sees Jane dying on a hillside and pilots drowning in a lochan that's cold as death.

CHAPTER FORTY-EIGHT

Cal is out for a walk the next morning, when his mobile rings. He answers in time but there is nothing on the other end except some strange rustling sounds. He says hello a few times then hangs up. As he is still staring at the screen, wondering if it's Naomi, it goes again.

'Oh, sorry, these things get me all confused. Is that Cal Lovett?'

The voice is that of an elderly man, croaky and distressed; he almost recognises it but can't quite place him.

'It is. Who's this?' He steps out of the fierceness of the sun into the shade of some parched trees, dried-out leaves crackling under foot.

'It's Alastair Bainzie, Mr Lovett. We spoke about the remains I found on the hillside. Jane. Or Violet.' He sees the old man in his mind's eye now, sitting with his face turned to the hills, the folds of his skin as craggy as the peaks.

'Of course I remember you, sorry – it took a moment to place you. Are you okay? You sound upset.'

'I'm looking at this pamphlet you've been giving out. One of the carers just brought it in…' Cal waits for him to take a breath. 'I know who she was.' He sounds broken-up. 'Her name wasn't Violet when I knew her, though.'

The man is struck by a bout of coughing and Cal listens, his heart clenching as he waits for Alastair to be able to speak. He hears someone in the background and moments later a new voice in his ear. A young-sounding woman.

'I'm afraid Alastair can't speak right now, he's not well.' Before he can reply, he hears Alastair remonstrating in the background, clearly disagreeing. 'I don't know what to suggest. He's insisting you speak but he needs to take his medication now.'

'Would it help if I came down to see him?' Cal starts heading back to the cabin as he speaks, urgency making him move quickly in the dense heat, hardly noticing the pounding sun on his head.

He waits for a brief exchange between the old man and his carer before she comes back on.

'It will have to be a short visit.'

Cal breaks into a jog. 'I'm on my way.'

—

When he arrives at the home, he takes the gentle ramp into the large modern building, signing in at the desk next to the spacious, bright lounge. The doors to the garden are thrown open and there is the sound of birdsong from the trees outside. At the foot of the parched lawn, Cal catches sight of a dry burn with a little bridge arched across it.

Unlike last time he visited, Alastair is not outside with a blanket over his knee, looking up at the hills he loves.

'He's in bed and this will need to be brief, please,' one of the carers tells him. 'His daughter's coming down to see him later on.'

Cal takes the corridors to his room, knocking softly before going in. The man lying on the bed is barely recognisable. Alastair's face has sunk into itself since Cal last saw him, and there's a change in his features and the tone of his skin. Something tells him the old schoolteacher doesn't have many weeks left.

As he moves into the room, Alastair's eyes open and Cal can tell he recognises him. He sits at the chair placed by the head of the bed, trying to hide the urgency he feels, the sense of panic that this man could take the information he needs to his grave. But he needn't have worried – Alastair is desperate to tell him what he knows.

'I knew her when she was a lassie,' he says in disbelief. 'I knew her. I taught her.'

He looks at Cal and grips his wrist with a surprisingly strong hand. 'I helped her get away – why did she come back?'

There are tears in the man's eyes and his chest is rising and caving. Cal looks around for help, rising to call someone. But Alastair grips his arm again and motions for Cal to help him sit up and pass a glass of water. When he has the old man propped up on pillows, he sinks back into the chair.

'Stay calm, Alastair. Tell me slowly. We've got time. Breathe.'

Alastair nods. When he starts again, his voice is steadier, and he sounds more like himself.

'Morna,' he says. 'Her name was Morna Duff.'

Cal sits while Alastair recounts his memories of the girl he taught – quiet and unhappy, ill-used at home. Her father working for the blacksmith before he turned to drink, her mother dead when she was just a girl. He tells him how Morna came to him late one night, desperate for help, needing to get away.

'She was in trouble,' he says. 'My Beth was furious with me for getting involved, but I couldn't leave her to suffer, could I?'

He peers at Cal, seeking reassurance, and Cal nods, unable to speak as he thinks of Naomi.

'I took her to Glasgow, to her friend Betty. And then I never heard from her again. Betty came back once for a holiday. She came to see me and said Morna had gone away, that she had a new name and a new identity, and she was well. I've thought of her through the years. The father died a few years after she left in an accident with some machinery up at one of the farms and there wasn't any family. Never in a million years did I think Jane could be her. Never.'

Tears run down the old man's cheeks as he tells the story.

Cal picks up the pamphlet with her picture from the bedside table and sees anew the woman on the beach with her face turned away from him, defying identification or explanation. Not Jane. Not Violet. Morna.

'When was this? Do you remember?'

The man rubs his face with a shaking hand. 'I've been thinking on it and it must have been 1952 at the end of the summer, maybe early autumn. We only had one of the bairns at the time.'

'That would fit the timeline we have for her emigration. This is so helpful,' he tells him. 'Do you remember how she was that night she left?'

'She was frightened,' he says, eyes distant with memory. 'She wouldn't say much but I assumed she needed to get away from her father and his drinking. I felt so sorry for the lassie and so bad that no one had stepped in to help. It didn't seem strange that she'd need to escape that house.'

Alastair's eyes are closing with the effort of the conversation. Cal whispers his thanks and sits for a moment, digesting the new information, waiting for the old man to fall asleep. There are bubbles inside him at the thought of the new lead and the slow easing of information from the community: pieces stitched together across time to build a picture. This is the way people fall through the gaps and are forgotten, until the collective memory wrenches them up again.

CHAPTER FORTY-NINE

MORNA, 1958

Morna lays the table. Her back is aching and she stops every few moments to put her hand to the bottom of her spine in a futile attempt to relieve the pressure. Her mother-in-law, Glenda, watches her with distaste. Doesn't get up to help. She's never liked her son's choice of wife, and these small, petty moments are common even now.

Outside, Ian is playing in the pool with their son, skimming a ball across the surface, sending arcs of spray into the sunlight. Morna smiles, though her happiness is never full, always tempered by the past. The laughter is like music, her husband and son so close you can barely get a piece of paper between them. Ian's mother may be suspicious, but no one knows that Ian Junior is biologically different to the child she now carries, and no one is going to know. They made their pact that evening on the beach when he asked her to marry him. They've lied to his family about which boat she was on, about when they met.

It helped that the baby came a bit late and was small, perhaps the legacy of those tortured weeks on the ship when she was too sick to eat properly. So far, she cannot see any trace of his biological father; she is not sure how she will cope if that starts to emerge.

'He'll have my name,' Ian said, firmly, when the infant slid into the world, a rushed labour that left Morna shocked and drained. He was telling her, yet again, that this child would be his son.

'Little Ian! He'll be sick,' Glenda exclaims now, watching her son and grandson dunking each other repeatedly. She rises to her feet and strides outside, bangles tinkling on her arms. Exhausted, Morna watches. There is no danger; this is simply Glenda's excuse to be away from her, for the two of them have never been comfortable.

'Why are you marrying so quickly?' was the first thing Glenda said when they met, her eyes narrowed, scraping over Morna's figure. It felt like the woman had X-ray vision to go with her astute suspicions.

'We're in love,' Ian had said, simply, stepping between them to protect Morna from her gaze. 'It's taken me ages to persuade her, don't you go talking her out of it.' He'd leaned in and kissed Glenda, and Morna heard the whisper: 'Be happy for me, Mum, please.'

Weeks later, they were married, moving into a little apartment near the beach and then into this house last year. Life has moved at a whip-crack pace. There has been no time to stop and consider.

She's grown to love her husband, she thinks now, as she watches. The only comparison she has is from the past, and that was an inappropriate obsession, one that consumed her waking hours. She would never wish for that strength of feeling again. No one knows who she was. Not even Ian. She has hidden her passport, her old name barely a memory.

Morna waddles to the stove and checks the casserole she is cooking, turning down the heat. She has two months left, but already she thinks this baby will be early, ready to burst into the world.

Meat and potatoes bob in the stew's thick juices. Another thing her mother-in-law likes to criticise: Morna's Scottish recipes, designed for warmth in a cold climate. Ian claims to love them. He sees that Morna closes her eyes and inhales when she takes the first bite. He has noticed the sense of dislocation when she opens them and realises she is far from home. Far away and never going back.

CHAPTER FIFTY

Chrissie has been busy. She's waiting for him in the lodge, papers spread across the table.

'How is he?' she asks as Cal appears alone after checking on Ian.

'Overwhelmed, I think. He needs to sleep.'

Seeing his mother's grave yesterday has taken it out of the man.

'Did you ask him about the name?'

Cal shakes his head. 'It seemed a bit much. Until we're sure.'

'I think...' she says, indicating that he should sit. 'We might be.'

She shows Cal some printouts of birth and death certificates. 'There was a Morna Duff born here in 1936. See: father Donald Duff, mother Joan Duff. This,' she slides a piece of paper on top of the pile, 'is the death certificate for Joan, who died seven years after she was born. Her father lived until 1960. Sean and I had a chat with a couple of the older folk in the village and they remember him.'

'Really? That's amazing.'

'Well, sort of. He was a horrible drunk by all accounts.'

'That tallies with what Alastair told me.'

'We think we found the house they lived in,' Chrissie puts in. 'It's at the end of the village – look.'

She shows Cal an image on screen, in black and white, of a small whitewashed building.

'It's bigger now. There's an extension and a conservatory. When Donald died, it seems to have been reclaimed by the bank and then sold on. The woman in the house next door said she didn't remember the man, but her mum had told her that the old neighbour had a daughter. Her mum's passed on unfortunately, so we can't ask.'

Cal looks at her in surprise, amazed by the work she's put into this.

'And no death certificate?'

'None,' Chrissie says. 'Most likely because she was thousands of miles away, alive and well in Australia.'

'The other thing Alastair mentioned was a school friend who might have been close to her. Betty. Does that ring any bells?'

'I can ask around.'

Chrissie writes the name carefully in her notebook. Cal feels a shot of happiness at how immersed she is. He knows how good it feels to be in the flow of an investigation.

At that moment, his phone rings and Cal pulls it from his pocket, distracted and trying to assimilate the new information Chrissie has provided. After decades of nothing, the dam has been pierced and it's all pouring out so fast that he can't hold it in his mind.

'Bobby,' he says. 'How are you?'

'Aye, well and I've good news,' the man says, his voice filled with a boyish excitement. 'Sandy's come through for us and I've done some checking. We've got it.'

'Got what?' Cal asks, dumbly, still thinking about Morna and her difficult start in life.

'The plane,' Bobby exclaims. 'We know which one it was, where it came from and who was behind the controls.'

When Bobby tells him the details, Cal can't help but leap to his feet from where he's been sitting. Chrissie looks over in amusement.

'None of those people are connected to your lassie, are they?' Bobby asks.

'I don't think so. But the date – you're sure that's the right date?'

'Positive.'

They finish speaking, then Cal ends the call and stares at the handset in shock. Surely...

'Dad!' Chrissie's voice breaks through the reverie and he looks up to see her face, half-amused, half-exasperated. 'What's going on?'

'The plane,' he says faintly. 'It went down in August 1952.'

'I don't understand.' Chrissie's forehead wrinkles with concentration.

'It could be nothing, but that feels like a very big coincidence.'

'What is?' Chrissie exclaims.

Cal rubs his head, blown away by the news.

'The plane went down,' he says, 'right before Morna caught the boat to Australia.'

CHAPTER FIFTY-ONE

EPISODE SIX: FLIGHT TO NOWHERE

On 7 August 1952, an aircraft vanished from Dalcross airfield in Inverness. So did two of the men working there. It's not known for sure why a nineteen-year-old local boy who was desperate to learn to fly and a savvy World War Two veteran with a drinking problem took the plane that day, but at the time the older man was suspected of using the airfield for smuggling.

Kevin Fraser had been obsessed with planes since he was small. Sadly, his eyesight wasn't good enough to become a pilot and he spent his national service on the ground as a mechanic in Cyprus, before returning to Scotland and securing work at the airfield that today is the site of Inverness Airport. Paul Irvine was older, reportedly unfriendly and certainly not normally the type to take a plane-mad mechanic on a joy flight.

For days, the crews and staff at the airfield waited for the inevitable news that the plane had gone down somewhere in the Highlands. It wasn't uncommon for there to be crashes in those days and it seemed clear that the missing plane was the result of an adventure or a whim gone awry.

Jackie Urquhart is now ninety-five years old and living on the north Moray coast with his daughter and her family, close to Lossiemouth. He can't get as far as he used to, but he still manages to walk the few hundred yards to a bench overlooking the North Sea on fine days, where he likes to watch the jets from the nearby RAF base.

'I remember it was a big fuss at the time,' Jackie tells us. 'All over the papers. The bosses hung Paulie out to dry – that was the pilot. He was a funny one. He'd served in the war and something had gone a bit wrong with his heid, like. He turned mean. That's what was such a surprise to us – that he'd taken Kev with him. It happened in those days: we all wanted a shot in a plane and some of the pilots would take you up. But not Paulie. Never.'

'So what did they think happened?'

'Can't explain it. Never could. We guessed they'd gone down over the sea, like. That was the only thing we could think. After a time, they were declared dead. Lots of people were in trouble over it. Things were tightened up after that. No more free shotties. The airfield closed to all except gliding a couple of years later.'

'Is there any other detail you can remember?'

'Well, I always thought Paulie was up to something on the side.'

'What sort of thing?'

'There would be boxes loaded onto planes sometimes. Money changing hands, people looking the other way… Definitely cigarettes, but I think other things too. Don't ask me who he was working with, though. It's hard to remember. My memory isn't what it once was.'

Neither the men nor the aircraft have ever been located. They seemed to vanish into thin air.

Until now, that is.

Since a plane was found deep in the waters of a mountain lochan in the Ben Lawers range, aviation expert Bobby Grant has been piecing together details of the aircraft and he is certain it's the plane taken by Paulie and Kev.

'We dinnae hae the tail with the flight number on, or a closeup of the cockpit, but from the picture, we can identify the aircraft

and it fits the description of the one that went missing all those years ago. A mystery solved, though we may never ken whit they were daeing there.'

Meanwhile, divers have recovered the second set of remains from inside the plane in the lochan. Cliff Baker is part of the team that has been examining them. 'These are the bones of a young male. Assuming this is the flight we suspect, then they would belong to Kevin Fraser. However, this is unconfirmed until we can locate his closest living relatives to test their DNA.'

Sadly, the find has come too late for most of the people who knew and loved Paul and Kev. Their families died without answers. Sitting gazing out at the brilliant blue of the North Sea, Jackie is glad to be able to put to rest the questions he previously had, but conscious that he's the last of his colleagues from those days.

'Kev was a real joker. He used to leap out at you from the most unexpected places and make you jump. I've always wondered what happened to him. All this time, I thought I was looking out from this bench to where Kev must be buried at sea. But surprise! It turns out he's behind me. He'd have liked that.'

CHAPTER FIFTY-TWO

MORNA, 2003

There just wasn't anything in life to look forward to. That's what she tried to remind herself of in later years, when the nightmares sent churning water and the taste of vomit to haunt her. She would wake dripping with self-recrimination. Why? Why had she been so stupid as to fall for the lies? Blood and cold words have long reverberated in her dreams.

The answer is that there was nothing else for her. She saw that over and over, as she watched her children grow up with a kind of privilege that made her mouth taste of ash. When they whinged or moaned, rage swelled inside her, making her skin hot and her fingers curl. *You are loved*, she wanted to scream at them. *Fed and cared for. Do you have any idea how lucky you are?* Ian had such patience with them but she could rarely summon it.

That's only one of the things that made her different, sullied. She never opened herself up fully to anyone after she left Scotland. Ian had to be content with the parts she could bring herself to share with him. The rest, she locked away.

Still, the defiled parts leaked through in the small hours of the morning, when she would wake with a thumping heart, back on the edge of that lochan with the realisation of what she had done. To save him. What he said about her was true. She didn't deserve the life she'd hewn.

Others might have thought later that there was a higher purpose in her saving. Not Morna. God had deserted her abruptly on a hillside, revealing in an instant the lack of His own existence. There was no higher purpose, no purpose at all. Just terrifying culpability.

On a couple of occasions, Ian tried to get close to the truth. Easing his way back to her past and gently fishing the waters for something.

'You know,' he said once. 'There is nothing you could tell me that could make me love you less.'

And she had looked at him and known that was true. For him. 'I *will* tell you if you ask me again. But there are things I would tell you that would change everything,' she said, softly. 'For me.' He'd stared at her, seeing the meaning. That she needed him not to know. Then he heeded the warning and backed away.

Their children and his family thought she didn't love him enough, she knows that. No one ever said anything explicitly, but she smelled the disapproval in the air like the factory smoke from the next town over, faint but pervasive. The truth that she wasn't going to share with any of them was that she loved Ian as deeply as it was possible for someone like her, with her past, to love. He knew that. The demonstration of his love came when he allowed her to bury her secrets. And in the end, isn't that all that mattered?

Only many years later did she stop to wonder if there might have been others back in Scotland. That she wasn't unique in her vulnerability, and he was too practised and smooth. That he had done it before. Would do it again. More thoughts to haunt her in the hot Australian nights.

The kids loved Ian more and she understood that. He was a lot of things that she wasn't. And he'd never killed anyone. Something inside you changes when you do that. Something that can never go back.

CHAPTER FIFTY-THREE

Back in Aberdeen, Shona calls to tell Cal they have the results of Ian's DNA comparison with Jane's sample and his sister's.

'You should be there with him when he opens it,' she says. 'At least, someone should.'

'Oh.'

'Yeah. I'm afraid so. We're emailing them through now. The good news is that his grandfather was not his father. Morna was pregnant by someone else. A small mercy.'

'He's out for a walk. I'll let him know as soon as he gets back. Thanks, love, for giving me the heads-up.'

'We've sent his profile to Police Scotland as well, as Ian gave us permission to share the information. We got someone to fast-track and the initial check shows they haven't got his father on their system.'

'I suppose finding he was a known and violent offender would have been too easy.'

Shona lets out a dry laugh. 'You're definitely not that lucky.'

Cal waits for Ian on a rock outside his lodge. He watches the man walk up the pathway at a good pace. He's fit and strong. Now that the jet leg has gone, he has taken to the undulating paths and tracks across the hills with little problem. He walks into the village each morning for a paper and a coffee, and has already made friends with many of the local people. There's sympathy for him, but he also has an ease about him that instantly endears him to others.

'Everything all right, mate?'

'Yes. But your DNA results came in.' He holds the laptop up.

'And? What do they say?'

'I haven't looked yet. I thought you might want to do it alone.'

Ian heaves in a breath and shakes his head.

'Nah, don't reckon I do.'

Inside, Cal sits down at the table and waits for Ian to get a glass of water and join him. He slides the laptop over so the older man can open the email himself.

Ian stares at the screen for a moment. His fingers twitch and lift, then set back down. 'You look,' he says, standing and moving away from the laptop. 'I can't do it.'

'It doesn't change anything,' he says, knowing this is only partly true. 'Your dad raised you and loved you.' Cal's hand feels heavy as he lifts it to click on the attachment to the email. He scans the document, already knowing what it will say.

'Well?'

'You and your sister have different fathers. Ian wasn't your biological father.' Silence. 'I'm sorry.' He looks round and sees that the man's face is pale. 'Here, sit down for a moment.'

'I sort of knew it,' Ian says. 'Deep down.'

'It's still a shock.'

The older man's hands are trembling, his eyes watery. 'Yeah. I think this might be time for one of those cups of tea you guys are obsessive about.'

Cal smiles, recognising that Ian needs a moment to collect himself. 'I'll get right on that.'

While he's in the kitchenette, he sees Ian move to the table to study the document Cal has left on the screen.

'Do we know who he is?'

Cal shakes his head. 'His DNA isn't on the police database. We can try and find out if you'd like, but you don't have to do that.'

'Would it help us work out what happened to Mum, though? Find out why someone would want her dead?'

'Maybe. Maybe not. But don't put that pressure on yourself. Here.' He hands over a mug of tea. 'I put some sugar in it.'

'And it's possible I have siblings or other relatives here in the UK?'

'Yes. It's even possible your biological father might still be alive.'

'Christ. That's a lot to take in.'

They sit in silence for a while. Ian seems to be lost in thought.

'What do I tell my sisters?' he asks suddenly. 'This is going to be on the podcast, isn't it? Everyone's going to know. Back home.'

'That's completely up to you,' Cal says. 'I won't air it if you don't want me to.' This is the crunch point that's been coming. If Ian is unwilling for them to reveal his parentage and dig into the past, it's going to limit what they can do. But he doesn't want to put that pressure on the man. He's already lost both his parents, and in a way he is losing them again – only, now he's overseas, away from friends and family who would support him, reliant on the kindness of strangers.

'What do you think happened?' Ian asks him.

'I don't know fully,' Cal says. 'I think maybe your mum witnessed the plane crash. I don't know what happened that day and if it's relevant, but I think she went back there because it was significant to her. And maybe that's what got her killed. In 1952, she was pregnant with you, had no supportive family and wanted a new start, far away. She found your dad and he loved her – and you – enough to raise you as his own and keep the secret.'

'I just wish they'd told us. That it wasn't this big, dark secret.' Cal understands the flickers of anger. But the last thing he wants is for Ian's memories of his family to be tarnished.

'People treated these things differently in those days. There would have been a lot of shame attached. It's not like it is now.'

They have another cup of tea together, Cal letting Ian be silent when he needs to. As he leaves him for the evening, the older man follows him to the door. 'I want to know,' he says, suddenly. 'I think I'd like to submit my DNA to that UK site.'

'You should sleep on it.'

'I won't change my mind. That's the only reason we know about Mum – Leia using that site back home. I'm sick of the secrets. I need to know what happened to her. Let's do it tonight. We can just submit the profile we have, right?'

'Maybe we should wait until the morning.'

But Ian is adamant. 'No. Please. I'll sleep better this way.'

So Cal goes back into the lodge and together they go through the steps to submit the profile. When it is done, Ian nods. 'Good. I'm going to call my sister now. The one who's not crook. I'll tell her.'

'Do you want me to stay?'

'Nah, mate. You've done enough. Thank you.'

Cal closes the door to the lodge and pauses on the step. Above him, the sky is thick with cloud, the atmosphere heavy and oppressive. He looks up, desperate for rain but feeling it will once again pass them by.

—

The ancestry website results come into Cal's email overnight. He opens the message, praying that there will be something they can use. They have the plane and the gold, but no idea why Morna was on the hill watching it crash, whose child she was carrying and why she went back there at the end of her life. He can't help but feel they're missing something vital. A connection.

But maybe it's coming. He stares at the screen. There's a hit. Several, in fact, showing distant cousins from other branches of the family. Ordinarily, these would be leads that a genealogist could use to dig deeper. But in this case, that won't be necessary. There's also a closer match. Cal reads it all again, to be sure. It's not definite without further checks but, judging by the age of the profile, they've got a half-sibling hit.

CHAPTER FIFTY-FOUR

Cal stands at the door to the large grey-stoned property, nestled above the shore of the loch, just down from the church and the sanctuary of the graveyard with its ancient stones and cool tranquility. There are roses around the entrance and it is picture perfect.

He raises the elaborate door knocker and raps it three times, hearing the echo inside. After long moments, Tavish answers. Wiping his hands on a tea towel, he looks naked and unprotected without the dog collar he usually wears. It's strange to see the man behind the profession.

Now that Cal knows their relationship, he can spot the similarities between Tavish and Ian. The Australian does not know he is here, does not yet know he has a half-sibling a loch's length away, and Cal wonders if Tavish has already seen the notification from the ancestry company. He's come quickly, hoping to catch him off guard. Whether right or not, Cal felt he had to – he wants to protect Ian from the pain of another difficult revelation and he is not sure what Tavish's reaction will be.

Tavish isn't his only consideration – the minister's mother, Rose, has been on his mind. Her husband fathered another child. Does she know? Then there's the matter of the old minister, Ian's father, being alive, and whether he's capable of understanding and speaking to them. Is death about to cheat them of justice?

'This is a surprise. Would you like to come in?'

'If this is a convenient time? I have some information for you.'

'It's fine. Mother is asleep and I've got some time before I need to be back at the church.'

Tavish motions Cal inside and into a room immediately on the right, before the grand staircase. He sees it is the minister's study, for a large desk sits beneath the window with a view of the loch. It is swimming in paperwork, weighed down with a variety of paperweights, stones, bronze engravings and glass with etched worlds inside. There is a simple crucifix on the wall next to paintings of the hills, as well as photographs of Tavish at his work as a young man, newly ordained, perhaps. A proud parent either side.

Cal peers at the images. 'Where did you work before you took over from your father?'

'I ministered in Glasgow, various churches, and then I was in Kilmarnock for a long time before I was needed here.'

Cal walks along the wall of pictures. There are so many of Tavish surrounded by groups of people, smiling. 'Where was this taken?'

'Tanzania. I was helping to build a school.'

He sounds wistful.

'Did you really want to come back here?'

Tavish shrugs. 'I was needed and I came.'

'Have you always been close to your father?'

The minister laughs once, mirthlessly. 'My father is a difficult man, Mr Lovett. I'm not sure he's close to anyone.'

'This is a delicate question. I'm sorry to ask, but have you had your suspicions about your father's fidelity?'

'I'm sorry?'

'Ian, Jane's… Morna's son submitted his profile to a UK ancestry site to try and find his father.'

'And did he?' The face that turns towards him is partly in shadow, and it looks gaunt and tired in this low light.

'No. He found a brother. A half-brother.'

There's a long and terrible silence that Tavish breaks before Cal does.

'And what does that have to do with me?'

His words are stilted and quiet, waiting for the axe to fall. His expression is pleading.

'He's your half-brother, Tavish. You share a father. I imagine you'll have the notification in your email too.'

The minister takes two steps back and sinks into a wingback chair. When he looks up, Cal feels that he's staring at a ravaged person.

'What do you want? What does he want?'

'I don't know. He doesn't even know about you yet. But I think he may want to meet his father. He'll have questions.'

'My father isn't well.'

'When I first met you, you told me he has lucid days. If he's able to speak and understand, then perhaps it's not too late to find some answers?'

Tavish rises from the chair and paces the floor towards the fireplace.

'I-I don't know what this means.' He spins, suddenly joining the dots. 'Are you saying he had something to do with what happened to her?'

'I don't know, Tavish, honestly. And I want to keep an open mind. But we do know she came back here twenty years ago and I'd like to know if your father saw her,' Cal says gently. 'I'd like to know if she witnessed the plane crash into the lochan. He may be able to help with that.'

'Please. You can't tell my mother. This will kill her.'
'Don't you think she has a right to know?'
'I'd really like to leave her out of this.'
A voice from the doorway cuts in.
'It has never been possible to leave me out of this.'

CHAPTER FIFTY-FIVE

MORNA, 1952

She thinks again that he won't come. Waiting in the shattered ruins, perched on a staircase to nothing, she doesn't bother to watch the pathway where he would emerge. Instead, she wonders if she can drown herself in the loch, if she would sink beneath its cold waters and give in, or if her limbs would disobey and force her to swim. She looks doubtfully at the hanging tree... Could she find rope, courage, strength enough? If he found her there, swinging, would he cry for her? Would he say a prayer?

Lost in her imaginings, she doesn't realise he's upon her until he touches her arm and she almost falls off the steps.

'Come,' he says and she scurries to his side.

Anxious, she studies his face. She expected the same anger and coldness he showed outside the church, not this distant neutrality. Her heart slows and she hurries to keep up with him, relieved that the man she idolises is here, not that cold monster from before. Something tight and twisted in her gut loosens a little. He will help her; together they'll figure out what to do.

He doesn't talk as they take quiet paths through woodland and up onto the hillside. The tightness inside her twists back into a knot. Thirsty, she kneels to drink from a burn that crosses their path and he stands, silent, until she wants to scream from the tension. She wonders if he will bring up the subject, or if she will have to. She'll wait until he turns them back, she decides, then she'll broach it. At the furthest place from home.

And yet on they go, with no suggestion of turning around. Several times, he stops to admire the ribbon of the long loch behind them and loudly exhorts her to drink in the landscape and appreciate the beauty of the country in which they live. 'It is God's country,' he tells her, ever the teacher, breathing deeply, his skin rosy with exertion. She pauses, relieved to stop and rest as she is panting with the exertion of keeping up with his longer legs. There's something different about him today.

He takes her on a new path, nothing more than a little sheep track that then trails into nothing.

'Morna,' he says, stopping suddenly. 'I need to ask for your forgiveness.' It is as if a cloud comes across him. She feels the urge to turn and run.

'Why?'

He doesn't answer. Instead, he leaves the path and begins forging a way across open hillside, meaning she has to use all her concentration not to fall into one of the bogs or holes that pock the landscape if she is to keep pace with him. He appears to have a plan in mind. The introspection is unnerving her.

'Look.' He halts and points below them. She sees they have climbed the side of the steep hill until they are above the lochan. Above them tower the craggy peaks, unfriendly and looming.

'You mustn't be afraid, Morna,' he says, though she wasn't really until he said that. 'We simply need to wash away our sins. To be made new.' There's a fervour to his words, like he's conducting a sermon.

She frowns, confused by the odd detachment in him. But he is already moving on, seemingly needing no reply, his long legs striding across the heather towards a cluster of boulders. Limbs aching and chilled, she staggers behind him. It is late in the afternoon and already the light is fading. Will they still be up here in the darkness? Where is he taking her? Could she find her way back alone?

When she reaches the boulders, she sees that behind them there is a level platform, tucked into the hill and perfectly sheltered, covered with a rich green grass that is soft and inviting.

'Oh,' she says, surprised at the beauty of the hidden place. Let into a secret.

He turns to her. 'This will be our church, Morna. We will confess our sins to each other.'

But how will that help her?

Unsure, she steps forward, surprised to see he has packed food and drink for them, a blanket to lie on. Tears prick the back of her eyes, more from exhaustion than gratitude, and she sinks onto the soft ground, done in not just by the slog uphill, but by the lack of sleep, the endless worry about the movement inside her and the shame she is due.

Below them, the lochan is a dark and watchful presence. She peers at it but cannot see the bottom, just an impenetrable well of water. She shudders to look at it.

He hands her bread, pours her a dark ruby liquid from a bottle.

'Drink,' he says. 'It will warm you.'

The liquid is overwhelming. A fruity, bitter taste that fills her senses so that when he places his lips over hers, she cannot taste him, can only feel his tongue forced inside her mouth. 'Is this wine?' she asks, when he pulls back, panting heavily, a sort of distance in his eyes. She knows that it is, though she has never tasted it before and doesn't want to follow in her father's footsteps. She needs to distract him.

But he is unfocused, pulling at her clothes. 'I am weak,' he mutters. Then: 'We cannot be together after this, Morna.' His eyes are beseeching her as he lifts her skirt, pulls at her underclothes. She didn't expect this. The words do not match the meaning of his actions.

'Please,' she says, for she needs this time to talk to him, to find out what she should do. But he silences her by pushing her backwards, covering her mouth with his. For the first time, it is an unwelcome sensation. His breath is brackish. 'Quiet,' he says into her. It feels like she is struggling for air, a fluttering in her chest fighting upwards. Before she can think, he is pushing inside her, fast and surprising, causing a cry to escape from her lips. She tilts her head to look up at the sky and she does not want to be here. Suddenly, he repels her.

'I know, Morna.' He groans above her, mistaking her cry. 'I. Will. Miss. You.' Her body grinds into the blanket with his words. She looks up at him and she sees the tears in her eyes reflected in his. 'I'm sorry,' he whispers. His hands stray to her throat and tighten till her breath won't come. And it feels like she is looking at someone different. Like this is the first time she has seen the real man behind the mask.

She holds his gaze and watches as he loses himself completely in her, while she is paralysed with fear. It is like staring into nothingness. The sky is darker now, the light closing down around them. She should not be here. This has all been a terrible mistake.

She is too shocked and desperate for escape to register the sound immediately. Through terror, she becomes aware that there is a shadow above them. A stuttering and groaning noise fills the air in the small valley. It could simply be the feelings inside her. But he loosens his fingers and she sucks in air, raising her head and crying out his name, pushing at him, trying to get him to take in the unbelievable sight.

A small aeroplane has streaked into the valley, tilting from side to side, seemingly unable to regain equilibrium. There is smoke pouring from the engine and she can see two figures in the cockpit; she registers panicked movements as it falters and drops, slowing but not quickly enough. He falls back off her and exclaims in bewilderment.

'It's going to crash,' she whispers.

The plane is heading for the side of the mountain. Saliva fills her mouth. All they can do is watch.

CHAPTER FIFTY-SIX

Tavish whips around to see Rose standing there, one hand on the door frame.

'If only your father had thought of me, once or twice. But he only ever thought of himself.'

'Mother. I thought you were sleeping. Where's your walking frame?'

'I heard voices,' she says. 'Hello, Mr Lovett.'

'I'm sorry if I've disturbed you.'

'Not at all. Why don't you come through. I can see that my son hasn't so much as offered you a cup of tea.'

'Oh, I'm fine. Please don't worry.'

'Nonsense. Tavish. Put the kettle on. Mr Lovett will help me to the conservatory.'

Her tone leaves no room for disagreement. She reaches for his arm and leans her bird-like frame on him, feather-light. Together, they take the mosaic-tiled hallway through to a living room at the back of the property. They move slowly so he has time to take in the walls lined with photographs, paintings and maps of the area. There are certificates and awards, countless commendations bearing the name Fearghas. A pillar of the community. Just one with a rotten foundation.

They reach a bright conservatory filled with plants, and in among the foliage, there is a cane furniture set, so he settles her into a chair plumped with extra pillows and cushions. It is easy to tell the seat is hers by the table next to it that can swivel over her knee and is stocked with a box of tissues, a water bottle and a well-thumbed Agatha Christie novel. She sees him looking.

'Old comforts, these days. Old comforts for an old woman.'

'It's a good one.'

'What would Agatha have made of this mess?' she asks him, shrewdly.

He sits down opposite her.

'Did you know that your husband had had some kind of relationship with a young parishioner by the name of Morna Duff?'

Rose sighs and shakes her head. 'I did not. Though I confess it does not surprise me. Fearghas had a roving eye.'

'Mother!' Tavish has halted with a clinking tray of tea things at the doorway. 'What are you saying?'

'It's time to stop lying to each other,' she says irritably. 'I've known about your father's "dalliances" from shortly after I married him. She was not the first, I would guess, and she wasn't the last. You saw it too. You've just never let yourself believe it, Tavish. Though you must have had an inkling if you were using those websites. They were always so young and starry-eyed over him.'

Tavish looks lost and Cal almost feels sorry for him – now he will no longer be able to maintain the illusions built over a lifetime.

'I saw it,' he mutters. 'But I was trying to protect you.'

'Here.' Cal rises and takes the tray from him. 'Let me.'

He pours the tea while they sit in a heavy silence. There is no breeze from the open door to the garden. He can see it backs on to the graveyard; stones on the rising ground peek above the mossy wall at the rear. Above it all, the church dominates. When he sits down, he turns to Rose.

'I'm sorry to have to bring all this up for you.'

She glances at Tavish. 'I'm not going to protect Fearghas anymore. These days I'd have left him. But back then we didn't really do that and I was a slave to convention, I'm afraid. So we were stuck with each other. I made a mistake in marrying him and I had to live with it.'

Cal thinks of Naomi, of how mistakes can be difficult to undo.

'I need to tell Ian who his father is when I go back,' he says. 'I don't know what his reaction is going to be. He was incredibly close to the man who raised him so he may not wish to meet Fearghas.'

'Well, that is his decision. But he must be allowed to see Fearghas if he wants to. He should have that chance.'

'Mother! Father is an old man. Sick.'

'All the more reason,' she says. 'There isn't much time for him to ask his questions.'

'I really don't know if we should agree to this.' He glances at Cal. 'I'm sorry, I don't mean to be obstructive.'

Rose looks at Cal. 'I'm his next of kin. I will agree to it if Ian wants. I caught sight of him, you know. When he came to the graveyard. I almost knew then. He has the look of Fearghas about him. My son has it, too.'

'The last thing I want to do is make things difficult for you both or to put Fearghas's health at risk,' Cal says. 'But it's possible he may have information that can help us.'

'Fearghas is not a faultless man, but I do not believe he had anything to do with that woman's death,' Rose says. 'There must be another explanation. This way he can rule himself out. We have nothing to hide.'

'There's a lot that's confusing about this case,' Cal says. 'Anything that throws any light on it is helpful.'

'How sad that no one knew there was an aeroplane in that lochan all this time,' Tavish says. He helps himself to some tea, seeming calmer and less shocked. 'We saw the police van at the foot of the hill the other day.'

'There were some items of value recovered from the wreckage. The police were here securing them,' Cal says without thinking.

'What items?' Rose leans forward, her rheumy eyes bright and interested beneath heavy lids.

What harm can it do? They now have permission to release the episode that details the find so it will soon be public knowledge.

'It's going to sound fantastical, but... the divers we took up there found a case of gold bars.'

'What?' Rose sits bolt upright.

'I know.' He smiles. 'Treasure in a lochan in the hills. It sounds like something out of your Agatha Christie novel.'

'What did it look like?'

'There were three bars in a metal case. Quite an unexpected discovery. We think perhaps they'd been looted or lost in the war. One of the men in the plane may have been smuggling them.'

'Mother? Are you all right?' The blood has drained from Rose's face and her hands grip the arms of the chair. 'Mother?'

Cal sees Rose is trying to find him. He kneels in front of her. 'I'm here. Take some deep breaths.' To Tavish, he adds: 'Does she have any medication?'

'An inhaler. It's just there.'

Cal grabs it and offers it to Rose. She takes it with a trembling hand and holds it to her lips, the shaky movements painful to watch. 'I think you should call a doctor,' Cal says. But when she hears this, Rose shakes her head and reaches out to Cal, bony fingers gripping his wrist in a vice.

'No,' she breathes. 'One… minute.'

It's excruciating watching her as the sounds of the children playing on the water filter in through the open door. But gradually, the colour returns to her face, though she is still gripping Cal's wrist.

'Come with me,' she says. 'I need to show you something.'

CHAPTER FIFTY-SEVEN

MORNA, 1952

Morna leaps to her feet, pulling her clothes back into place as, at the last minute, the plane turns down and glides onto the lochan, water spraying up into the air around it. Waves barrel towards shore, crashing up over the stones and washing back, before slowing to a stop in the middle. Everything around is silent, save for the steam rising from the water and a horrible shifting and groaning of metal. The elegant tail is ripped. A small figure jumps from the body of the plane into the water.

'We need to help.' She scrambles over the lip of the platform, grabbing onto thick bristly heather as she goes, trying to avoid tumbling down the slope to the shore.

'It's too late,' he calls. 'Wait.'

'One of them got out.' Why isn't he following her?

'It's deep,' he calls after her. 'Too deep to swim out for him.'

Belatedly, he follows her to the shore and they stand transfixed, watching the plane.

'Look!' She points. 'He's swimming.'

The small figure is striking towards the shore, clumsily, lumbering in clothes. As the man approaches, she rushes forward, wading into the freezing lochan to meet him, calling to him. His face is a rictus mask of adrenaline and pain. He seems to be dragging something behind him. Could it be another person? As she reaches for him, she's surprised that he looks up and almost snarls at her, pushing her arm away so she falls back into the water, instantly shockingly cold. There is a bleeding gash on his forehead.

Gasping, she rights herself, watching as the man crawls onto the shore with a box, not a body. He collapses, panting in a heap on the stones, clutching it while she watches.

She looks to Fearghas for help, but he looks small against this onslaught. Behind her there is a rending, bubbling sound. The craft is sinking, the shorn tail rising to the sky as the nose tilts downwards. 'Where's the other person? Is he still on the plane?' she shrieks.

The man on the shore says nothing, heaving air into his lungs.

Finally, Fearghas takes up her call, crouching beside the man and the box.

'Is the other man alive? Can you hear me? What's this?'

He puts his hand on the box that the man has struggled to shore with, and it is then that the airman reacts, launching himself upwards in a snarling, animal attack.

She screams as the airman punches in a frenzy, the two men down and rolling on the rocks together. Wading from the lochan, she sees scarlet blood on the stones, feels the same liquid pulsing inside her. She tumbles, but wrenches herself back up, clothes sodden and heavy.

'Stop.' But her voice is a hoarse whisper. 'Stop. We're trying to help you.'

She cannot make them. She cannot make men do anything. The airman has the upper hand, seeming to find a fierce and desperate energy from somewhere inside; he has his hands around Fearghas's neck. For a moment she wants to leave them there, but the bug-eyed purpling face brings her back to reality and she rushes forward, throwing herself on the airman's back, trying to wrench him away.

He's strong, far too strong for her to overpower. She is thrust back and sprawling, striking her head on the ground, dazed and dizzied and cold. Her lover's legs thrash beside her, heels grinding into the peaty earth. Moaning, she pushes onto her hands and knees, grasping for purchase – something, anything. Her fingers close around a rock – hard, solid and dependable, like nothing else in her life has ever been.

Without thinking, she staggers to her feet and the rock leaves the ground in her grip. Cold and heavy. She looks down on the men, one drifting from consciousness, the other still gripping his neck, thick oil-stained fingers squeezing and throttling.

She raises the rock above her head and as she brings it down, she is conscious of everything around her: the simple stunning green and the movement of the stream below, the undulating surface of the loch, the high and grey peaks, the bubbles rising from the sinking plane.

The feel of the rock striking the back of his head makes bile rise from her stomach and she tastes the acrid wine in her mouth. The airman slumps forward, the back of his skull a gaping wound seeping red. She stumbles to the side and is sick in the lurid moss.

CHAPTER FIFTY-EIGHT

The journey to the church could be walked in two minutes, but with Rose it takes more like twenty, step by painful step.

'Mother. This isn't sensible,' Tavish protests. Cal is in complete agreement. The sun is burning a hole in the back of his head and he's worried Rose is going to keel over.

'We can do this another day,' he says. 'I think you need to rest.'

But she will not be deterred, and restraining her doesn't feel like an option. 'Who knows how many more days we have?' There seems to be no way to turn her back. 'I've seen him,' she keeps muttering. 'When did I see them?'

Gradually, they make it up the rise to the churchyard, where the new stones glitter in the sunlight and the older ones bow, mossy-coated, towards the earth, their inscriptions barely legible, their long-lost inhabitants forgotten. He can see slivers of Morna's grave through the crowd. Then they are up on the gravel path around the church and Tavish is pushing open the door so they can step into cool relief.

It's perfectly quiet inside the vestibule, the outdoors muffled and the smell of polish, dust and centuries of devotion drifting around them. Cal can't help but wonder what the church might be like in the depths of winter, with the wind battering the stained glass and the waves pounding the shore outside.

'Down there,' Rose directs the men. They help her down the aisle and she sinks into the front pew, breathing heavily. 'They're right here,' she mutters. 'I've seen them. I wondered what he was doing.' She gestures to the step up to the altar, under which a grill is fitted for ventilation. 'In there.'

Cal and Tavish exchange a look.

'Mother, this is ridiculous. You've had a funny turn. It's time to get you into bed for a rest.' He looks at Cal and the dread is visible on his face. 'You should go.'

But Cal crosses the floor and kneels in front of the grill.

'Always so devout,' Rose mumbles, though there is disgust in her voice.

Curious, Cal slides his fingers between the slats and tugs gently. With a grinding sound, the grate front pops out, spewing dust onto the immaculate floor.

Tavish makes a noise in the back of this throat. 'There's nothing in there. It's ventilation.'

'Hang on.' Cal lies on the floor, reaching for his phone in his pocket and putting on the light. 'I think there is something at the back.'

Rose makes a humming noise of approval. 'Church treasures.'

Cal reaches in, shuddering a little at the feel of cobwebs on his fingers. But then they close around something and he pulls, gently. The item moves forward and he tugs more until it slides out into the light. Surprised, he sits back. A metal case. Heavy for its size. He's seen a case like this before.

He looks at Rose and there's a sad sort of knowing in her eyes.

'Open it,' she says.

'Mother, what on earth is—'

But Tavish is silenced when Cal opens the lid. Two gold bars nestled together. A gap where a third should be. A perfect hiding place. A perfect match for the box lifted from the plane. These must have been in Fearghas's possession for more than seventy years.

'What is that?' Tavish whispers. 'Not gold?'

'I saw it once,' Rose whispers. 'I'd almost forgotten. It was so long ago. He said it was church property and I should leave it be.'

'I've seen an identical case to this. Either Morna or your father took it from the wreck of the plane,' Cal says. 'But there were three bars in there.' He touches the empty space.

'He used to pray here,' Tavish says, slowly. 'Right at this spot, on his knees. I thought it was because he was so devout.' The minister seems to be almost in tears.

'He was keeping an eye on his secret,' Rose says.

'That's not possible.' Tavish sounds faint. 'The plane is at the bottom of the lochan.'

'It is now,' Cal says. 'But it wasn't when it crashed.'

Pieces falling into place. A narrative that fits.

'It will have floated for a time. Or... the airman who was found apart from the wreckage,' Cal says. 'He could have brought it ashore. Swum for safety.'

'But then what happened to him?'

Cal looks back to where Rose is sitting. Her words ring in his head. What did happen to the airman? Was he swimming back to rescue the other pilot when he drowned? And how did Fearghas come to have this gold? There's only one man who can tell them the truth. But he's been keeping this secret for a very long time.

He clicks the case shut and stands, dusting off his hands.

'We need to take this to the police, I have to call them,' he says. Then he crosses to Rose. 'And then we're going to have to speak to your husband.'

She looks up at him, weary-eyed. 'Yes,' she says. 'I think he has some explaining to do.'

CHAPTER FIFTY-NINE

MORNA, 1952

Sobbing, Morna approaches the men, who are still and slumped in position. Hand shaking, she reaches for the airman and pulls at his shoulder, using all her strength to roll him off. Fearghas is still and pale beneath. Nothing moves for a moment. And then he jerks upwards, sucking air noisily, his eyes rolling, the whites huge as he comes back to life.

He reaches up for her, but she cannot touch him. She stands above, arms wrapped tight around her shaking body.

He must roll himself to the side, pushing into a kneeling position.

There's a terrible sound from the lochan. They both turn to see the plane on its end now, water streaming into the hole where the tail should be. Only a tiny piece left above the water, sinking, sinking, gone. Bubbles, and a sucking sort of whirlpool for a moment. Then nothing. Just the settling of old water over old scores.

She lets out one sob that wracks her whole body, then turns towards the men, beseeching. He's looking at her now. There is not the gratitude and attraction she was expecting. The look he gives her is calculating and damning.

'You've killed him,' he says in wonder. 'You're a murderer, Morna.'

Her mouth opens wide in a scream that won't come. She staggers backwards from him, repelled. But then, in an instant, he is upon her. Stroking her, cajoling, drawing her to his warm chest.

'Shhhh, shhhh. I understand. It's okay. I'll help you.'

She tilts her head in question. Help. That's why she's here. That's all she wanted.

'We need to hide his body. Hide it where it will never be found.'

'But... he was attacking you. I didn't have any choice. The plane...'

'I know that.' He soothes. 'But they won't.'

'Who's they?' She spins on the spot, searching for faces, figures. There is nothing. Just them and the empty hillside.

'There is no plane,' he says. 'Look.'

Everything is concealed in the fathomless depths. It is like the crash never happened. She can't think straight. Surely, they need to tell someone what they saw? But he would always do the right thing, wouldn't he?

Numb, she complies as he directs her to gather stones and fill the airman's flying suit with the rocks. It is slightly too big for him so they use up every space and drag him into the lochan. He helps her, but only to the water's edge.

She is almost blue with cold now, unable to feel her skin. He is dry.

'Take him out,' he directs. 'He needs to be near the plane.'

'I can't.' She sobs.

'You have to. It's not far. Just there, look... where the edge drops away.' She can see it now. A place where the clear water darkens to black and nothing is visible below.

But she will have to wade out twenty feet at least to reach that point.

'Hurry,' he urges. She must do as she is told.

The body is heavy, dragging under as she pushes it further, up to her knees, her waist, her shoulders. Water washes over his face. Daggers of cold inside her. When she is far enough to reach the edge of the deepest parts, she loses her footing and is cast over, treading water and terrified, her head dipping briefly under in a shock of cold.

'There,' he calls, unnecessarily. 'Let him go.'

She rolls the heavy weight of the man onto his front, away from her. As she does, she senses movement. Is she imagining it? She lets go and for a moment he floats, then slowly he is pulled down by the weight of stone and water. She is also yanked under for a moment, a sucking feeling at her legs like the lochan wants to take her too. Her eyes jerk open in the cold water and it's almost possible to forget which way is up and let it take you.

But she feels her legs fighting for life even if her mind will not. Kicking upwards, powering to the surface, breaking free.

It takes every ounce of willpower she has to get to shore.

He hasn't waited for her. He has returned to the grassy platform, where he is crouched, gathering their things, scraping them into his bag, only bothered with concealment now. He keeps clearing his throat, putting his hands to his neck where there are livid red marks. He has not thanked her for saving him. She looks back at the water. Something else is wrong, nagging at her through shock.

She looks down and sees the rock at her feet, stained with blood. She picks it up and casts it into the water, desperate to be free of it and to wash away the stain. Teeth chattering, she slowly clambers back up to the flattened grasses above the lochan, no longer physically afraid of him. He is too weak to hurt her now, barely able to walk after what happened.

He is gulping the wine, and she reaches out and takes the cup for her share. She can see, next to his bag, the box the airman was clutching. Without asking, she strips off her dress and drops it on top of the box, taking his coat and wrapping it around her, caring for herself as he will not. He makes a noise of disagreement but she stares into his demon eyes and he is silenced. She knows now. He is not going to help her.

As they trudge back the way they came, she turns and takes a last look at the water behind. It is flat and still. There is no sign of what happened here. Only when they reach the foot of the hill and he staggers away from her, does she dare to reach into her pocket and wrap her fingers around the cold gleaming metal. If he will not save her, she will save herself.

CHAPTER SIXTY

EPISODE SEVEN: BREAKING FREE

The case of Hillside Jane has been far from the simple experiment in new scientific procedure that we at Finding Justice *had planned when we began this series of the podcast. But then, maybe that's to be expected when you add the messiness of human beings into the equation. The truth is that we couldn't have made vital connections without the science, but human endeavour has driven us through.*

Someone always knows something, and when you join those pieces together, a picture forms.

What we now know, from piecing together information, is that Jane was born Morna Duff in the village of Killin in Perthshire. Her mother died when she was only seven years old, leaving her under the care of her father. Care is, however, the wrong word. A violent drunk, he abused and neglected his daughter, leaving her hungry and unprotected.

Elsie Comrie once worked at the village shop, which was run by her aunt. 'Morna was always bruised and stick-thin. She didn't really have enough to eat and her da was a real piece of work. A'body was scared of him.'

Given her upbringing, it's not surprising that Morna, starved of affection, was vulnerable to anyone who gave her the kindness she must have craved. The local minister, Fearghas Dewar, was relatively new in his post. Young, good-looking and single, he was nevertheless in a position of power and authority.

We don't yet know a great deal about the year between his arrival in the village and Morna's departure to Australia. We do know that, at some point, Morna, aged sixteen, entered into a sexual relationship with the minister. Her eldest son, Ian, allowed us to submit his DNA profile to an ancestry site as part of the investigation. Discovering that the Australian man who raised him was not, in fact, his biological father has been a huge shock for him.

'Dad was the best. He really was. He and Mum had a strange relationship to outside eyes. She always seemed pretty shut-off, compared to him, but they had fifty years together and he never once let on that I wasn't his. Never once treated me any differently to my sisters.'

The DNA search we conducted resulted in Ian locating a Scottish half-sibling and, through him, the knowledge of who Ian's biological father was.

Today, Ian is meeting that man for the first time. Fearghas is now in his nineties and resident in a local nursing home. His health is failing and we have been asked not to put him under too much pressure with our questions. We reach the home just after lunch, as we've been told early afternoon is the best time to catch him.

'How are you feeling, Ian?'

'I don't know. Nervous, I guess. This is all a bit overwhelming. I can't quite believe I'm meeting the man who is technically my father when I didn't know about him a few days ago.'

'What are you hoping will happen today?'

'I'm not looking for an emotional reunion. My dad was the man who taught me to ride a bike, who looked after me and my

sisters and Mum all those years. I need to know what happened to her at the end.'

'And you think Fearghas can tell you?'

'It feels wrong to be relying on him, that he's the only one who can tell us, but that's where we are. At this stage in his life, he doesn't have much left to lose. I want to know what Mum was doing on that hill and I want to know who killed her.'

CHAPTER SIXTY-ONE

MORNA, 2003

The anger has been building inside her like a volcano. Every news story she sees, every crime, seems to feature male violence towards women. So much of it, all the time. It's like a light has turned on and she can see what's been there all along, foul and dirty. The sense of injustice and fury keeps stoking and the pressure is building.

With the anger come the memories she's suppressed. They bubble up through the lava of her incandescent rage. Without her husband of fifty years to anchor her, she's been floating adrift from the rest of her family. She could confront it all. She could go back.

But leaving isn't quite as easy as she intends it to be. She unearths her long-expired British passport from its hiding place and sets about replacing it. As soon as she does, it is as if they sense that she is pulling away. All of a sudden, the invitations to barbecues and afternoons by the pool watching her grandchildren jump in are flowing more freely than they have for a year. The sheer volume of them exhausts her.

'Grandma! Look at me!' Evan, seven years old, waits until he sees he has her attention before cannonballing into the water at the deep end. It's the fifteenth time, easily.

She pulls her muscles into a smile. The twang of his broad accent seems foreign to her, so mystical and strange.

Lying on a sunbed in the shade to escape the fierceness of the heat, she eventually manages to ignore their demands, closing her eyes against the harsh light and allowing herself to sink back into memories, to start to make a plan. It's been there, all this time, and it's heavy.

When Ian was alive, he acted as a buffer against these thoughts and, if she's honest, these people she forged. He saved her, when she was fresh off the boat and looking for a new life. It would have been disloyal to linger on the past and he wasn't one for looking back. But now he's gone, there is no check on her mind lurching into the past and she's looking at it all with different eyes.

'Quiet, Evan.' She hears the hissed tone of her daughter, Ruth. 'Grandma's sleeping.'

'She's not,' she protests, opening her eyes and shading them, more irritated by the solicitous tone than by her grandson's constant desire for attention.

'Oh, Mum, I'm pretty sure you were dozing off,' Kathleen tells her. When did this happen? When did someone tell her daughters that their roles had been reversed and they should speak to their mother like she's a child? And why didn't she get the memo? Because she'd like to send it back. *No thank you*, she wants to say. *Not today*.

If only they knew what she's been through, what she's done. How would they look at her then? One thing is clear: they wouldn't understand her plan, her need to visit the past, to seek retribution. They live in a different world. She will have to do this without them – to start with, at least. So that she has the courage. When she returns, she will have to find a way to tell them.

'I'm going to head home,' she says, standing and stretching.

Faces turn to her in consternation.

'What? Why?'

'Are you tired, Mum?' *Christ.* Don't blaspheme.

It's easier to acquiesce to their view of her.

'Maybe I've had too much sun,' she says.

'Do you want some water? Do you want to lie down?'

'No, no.' She bats away the insects of questions buzzing at her.

'Well, you can't walk home. Chris will take you, won't you, Chris? Mum's going home. She's tired. She can't walk home…'

'It's only a few blocks,' she says, though no one is really listening to her. 'It will do me good.' If they don't understand her desire to walk a few streets away, what will they say if she tells them her plan to return to the Highlands?

'Chris! Chris!'

'Coming, let me just get the keys…'

'Mum, I really think you should have some water.'

On and on it goes, round and round in her brain. Building until the pitch is intolerable.

'No!' She doesn't mean to shout. A shocked silence falls. Faces all turn to her. Her cheeks boil. 'Stop fussing. I am going to walk home, and I will be fine.'

There's an awkward silence while she gathers her things. She's sure she hears: 'Way to go, Grandma,' muttered by her usually sullen granddaughter Leia, but she's too fizzed up to stop and look.

'Thank you,' she says, feeling bad as she leaves. 'I'll see you soon.'

Her son-in-law, Chris, follows her to the side gate.

'Are you sure you don't want a ride?' At least he manages to say it in a way that lets her know he's only checking – he expects a no, away from the fussing.

'No, thank you, though,' she says more gently, glad to be treated like a grown-up.

'No worries.'

Out on the street, away from the hushed silence and conspicuous hurt of her family, she can breathe again. She sets off along the sweltering road, focused on the cool silence of her empty house. It's too damn hot, a lifetime of too damn hot.

Once home, she can lie in the garden and sink into the better part of her memories for a while. Scotland. A childhood in the drizzle, fog and cold that she now longs for. She stares at her sandalled feet on the hot pavement slabs and remembers long white socks in sturdy boots, skirts and woollen jumpers that weighed so much when they got damp.

Those early memories are preferable to her life here. She'd like to sink into them. But then other thoughts follow, pushing the benign ones aside. These have been buried so long, done with. But they are all coming back now. A flash of bubbles and a voice shouting at her. She comes to a halt in the sun. Sways and swallows bile. *Yes. Come on. I remember. You thought I'd gone forever.* Well, maybe it's time to go back and face the music. She needs to let the burden go. She needs to return to Scotland.

CHAPTER SIXTY-TWO

In the modern room, Fearghas is a different man from the one Cal's seen in pictures. In his prime he was tall, strong and good-looking, with dark hair and bushy eyebrows. Now, propped up on several pillows, he is shrunken into the bed, what little hair he has snow-white, his skin sensitive and translucent. He may be failing, but his eyes are sharp. He knows who they are and why they're here. His gaze fixes on Ian immediately.

Rose makes the introductions and then a terrible silence falls. The old man beckons Ian to the side of the bed and he sits next to him.

'She kept you.'

Ian's lip curls.

'Yes. She did.'

'I always wondered where she'd run to.'

'Australia.'

Fearghas closes his eyes and nods, putting his oxygen mask briefly to his face.

'What happened? How did you two come to be together?' Ian's voice wobbles.

'She used to sit in the Sunday service. I noticed her and she seemed like she needed help. I took her under my wing.'

Cal can see the Aussie trying hard to keep his cool.

'What do you mean?'

'She was very persuasive. I was a red-blooded young man, who took what was offered to me. It lasted a few months. I ended it...' He looks at his wife. 'Before we got married.'

'She was just a kid.' Ian's voice cracks. Fearghas breathes heavily but doesn't reply. 'And she got pregnant.'

'That was regrettable.'

Cold words said to his eldest son.

'Did you offer to help her?'

Fearghas is consumed by hacking coughs. Ian looks at Cal in alarm.

'Maybe we should take a break?' he asks, but Fearghas gestures they should continue.

'Did you see Mum again? When she came back here twenty years ago?'

Fearghas shakes his head, his eyes on his wife, not the son he has never met.

'No. I never saw her again.'

'Why did she go up to the lochan?'

Another silence broken only by the wheeze of machinery and old lungs.

'I don't know.'

'Fearghas, enough,' Rose says, her voice sharp. 'We found the gold. In the church.'

His eyes fly open. He looks more concerned with this than what happened to Morna or the long-lost son sitting next to him.

'I just want to know what happened to her. We don't want there to be secrets anymore.' Ian's voice is strained but calm. 'You owe me a bit more than this, mate. You're supposed to be a man of God.'

His words make the pale man fade back into his pillow. There's a long pause. Fearghas clasps the mask to his face and closes his eyes, breathing for several minutes while they all wait to see if he will speak again.

'You saw the plane go down, didn't you?' Cal says softly.

'Who are you?'

'I'm Cal Lovett. I'm helping Ian find some answers for his family. Since you have the gold, you must have been there when it crashed.'

'I need you to go now. This is too much for me.'

'Fearghas. The truth, please,' Rose says. 'Were you there with Morna?'

Fearghas doesn't reply. He closes his eyes and lets go of his wife's hand. But he does nod, once.

They wait, but he seems to have drifted off.

It's an answer but not an answer.

Rose shakes her head. 'I think that's all we're going to get. I can let you know if he says anything more.'

—

They leave the nursing home and emerge gasping into the fresh air. Ian looks relieved to be out of the building.

'Christ,' he says. 'What a piece of work.'

'I'm sorry,' Cal tells him. 'That can't have been easy.'

'It underlines the fact that I haven't been missing anything.'

He can tell Ian is rattled, despite the levity.

'He was adamant he didn't see her twenty years ago, but it might be possible to challenge him again, another day.'

'I feel like we were so close to an answer,' Ian says, rubbing his face. 'And it just slipped away.'

'We know he was there the day the plane crashed. Something happened that affected your mum so badly, she travelled halfway round the world fifty years later to go back there.'

They walk to the car as they talk, both tired out by the interaction with the dying man. It feels to Cal that he still has the taste of the place on his tongue, something of the sickroom atmosphere sticking to his skin.

'We can ask Rose to facilitate another conversation, without the recording side of things.' Cal watches Ian for his reaction. The man looks up at the building and scratches his head.

'I've had a gutful of him,' he says. 'He's not my family. But... if it helps get some more answers, then maybe.'

As they open the car doors and Ian gets in, Cal sees Tavish watching them from the corner of the building, tucked out of sight. His eyes are fixed on Ian, a stricken look on his face. Cal waves, hoping he might come over, but the minister shakes his head and ducks into the lobby of the home. Ian hasn't noticed the interaction and maybe it's just as well. The man has his head back and his eyes closed, clearly overwhelmed by the experience.

The journey back is quiet. When they reach Loch Tay, Ian stares out at the glistening water flashing through the trees. At the lodges he pleads tiredness and a need to be alone. Cal watches him leave the car with a feeling of heavy responsibility.

'Will you be okay?'

Ian's eyes are heavy and dull as he turns back. His shoulders droop.

'Would you speak to him again? I don't think I can do it.'

'Of course,' Cal tells him.

'I wonder if we're getting close to the end, for me. I'd like to go home for a bit, see my family. I was thinking I might book my return flight.'

'That's a good idea.' It is obvious that Ian needs a break. 'You have time to think about what you want to happen with your mum's grave. All of that can wait.'

'I came for answers but maybe it's too much to hope that we'll know the full truth. Maybe I need to be satisfied.'

Cal watches Ian walk to the lodge. He wishes he could say that it's possible.

CHAPTER SIXTY-THREE

Cal drives down to the village, needing to take a moment to think. He buys a coffee and walks to the falls, finding a quiet rock to sit on, away from the tourists and the bustle. The day has been exhausting, and seeing the truth about Rose's marriage has shaken him. He should know by now that no one really knows what happens behind closed doors. Lucie and Tyson, Naomi and Jason, Rose and Fearghas. All toxic connections in their own way. At least Morna broke free and found someone who genuinely loved her. If only she'd stayed in Australia and lived out the rest of her life.

He's still sitting there when Detective Matthews finally calls back. She sounds like she might burst with shock when she hears about their discovery in the church and the conversation with Fearghas.

'That gold is hard evidence. Where is it now?'

'I've got it,' Cal says, glancing over at the car park. 'Rose didn't want it left in the church so it's hidden in the back of my car. I'd appreciate it if someone could come and get it, though.'

'Don't let it out of your sight. I'll send someone now. You'll need to make a statement as well.'

They agree that Cal will go back to the lodge to meet the police. He forces himself to his feet, realising how tired he is. After driving back, he pulls up at the side of the property, a hidden spot where he can leave the car until the police arrive. No one, except Tavish and Rose, knows he has the gold, but its presence makes him a little nervous. He doesn't believe in curses, only bad human beings, so he's not sure why his neck is prickling quite so badly.

From his vantage point, he can see Chrissie and Shona drinking coffee outside in the shade. Neither of them sees him as he sits for a moment – it's quickly going to become stifling in the car with the engine off, but he feels so tired he thinks he'll just close his eyes for a second.

In his half-sleeping state, Cal hears the rear car door open, and feels a waft of slightly fresher air. His cue to get moving.

'I'm coming—'

But before he can say more, there's a cold, sharp point pressing into his neck. He is immediately clammy with sweat, jolted awake but frozen in place while his daughter and Shona laugh in the distance. It's not one of them in the car. His thoughts fly to the gold, Morna's abandoned body.

The back door closes and he's trapped. A knife at his throat.

'Where is she? Don't move. Put your hands on the wheel.'

What's happening? He knows that voice but staying in denial would be preferable. Its presence here makes him shake. Body pressed back against the seat, unable to turn his head, he flicks his eyes to the rear-view mirror for confirmation and finds it. The face he sees there turns the sweat cold. His ears are ringing so he can barely hear the words. His sister's killer is in the car with him.

'What are you doing here, Jason?'

His voice sounds calm, though his hands are trembling.

'Where's my wife? I know you're hiding her. She's here, isn't she?'

'She isn't here, Jason.'

'Let's go and ask that pretty young woman over there, shall we?' He spits the words into Cal's ear. 'Looks very like her aunt.'

The cold sweat on Cal turns to boiling anger. If Barr makes one move towards his daughter he'll kill him with his bare hands, knife or not. His voice comes out different: low and guttural.

'You stay away from her.'

Cal's heart is thumping and his mind running fast, looking for a way out. From the brief glance he took in the mirror, Barr seemed frenzied, his eyes wide and his face gaunt.

'I just want my wife!'

His voice cracks and the sharp point presses harder; Cal feels the smarting sting like a razor cut. There's no way he can move – the man will split his throat. Terror at what could happen to Chrissie and Shona floods him. He has to get Barr away from here.

'Wait,' he says. 'Okay, okay. She isn't here, Jason… but I can take you to her.'

'Where is she?!'

'Not far. I'll drive you there now, Jason, just ease up so I can reach properly.'

The man moans and his lack of control makes Cal cold. Taking short sips of air to quell the nausea, he starts the car and reverses slowly out of his hiding place. As he glides backwards over the bumps, the sharp point nicks at his neck and his blood trickles into his T-shirt.

He focuses on the retreating sight of his daughter and Shona, laughing at something, Chrissie leaning over to pour more coffee, red hair tousled and striking against the trees behind, and then they are gone. Tears come to his eyes. He has a terrible sense of doom, a feeling he will never see them again. Something inside him is paralysed. He cannot fight back, he cannot resist, he can only comply.

As long as Chrissie and Shona are safe, he thinks, as he pauses the car at the main road. That's all that matters.

'What are you doing? Where is she?!'

'She's close by. We just needed somewhere quiet.'

Cal's mind fumbles over places he could go. The area is packed with tourists, always busy.

'Hurry up.'

'Okay, I'm moving, hang on.' Sucking in a tight breath, he indicates and turns onto the road towards the village.

CHAPTER SIXTY-FOUR

It's like he's seeing everything around him for the last time. The world looks brighter and sweeter than ever, technicolour real.

'How far is it? Where's my wife?'

'Not far. Just a few minutes, I promise.'

'Why did she come here?'

'She just wanted a little break.' Cal swallows. 'She loves you, Jason.'

'Don't fucking lie to me.' The man leans in and jabs the point of the knife back into Cal's neck. His shouting fills the car, battering Cal's senses so he almost misses the road to the ruin. 'Where are you taking us? Stop the car! Is this a trap? Stop right fucking now.'

Blood is dripping down Cal's neck and over his collarbone. But they are passing a house where two small children are playing in a sprinkler on the front lawn, squealing as they jump through the cold water. There is no way he is stopping here, no way at all.

'Calm down,' he says, as much to himself as to Barr. 'We're almost there. She'll be there waiting for you, I promise.'

'You better not be lying to me.'

'I'm not.'

The chubby-limbed children vanish in the rear view and Cal exhales a shaky breath.

They drive in uneasy silence until they reach the lay-by near the ruin. Mercifully, it is empty. People have been flocking to the little inlets and beaches on Loch Tay, desperate for the cooling water to dip in. They are alone.

'Wait.'

Barr gets out of the car first and Cal keeps his hands on the wheel. The other man pulls open his door and orders him out. He'd forgotten how huge Jason Barr is – taller and twice as wide as Cal; he clearly hasn't given up the bodybuilding. 'Face forward.' He feels the tip of the knife on his spine. His phone is in his pocket, but there's no way he can reach for it at the moment. He thinks of the gold in the car, of the police coming to the cabin to collect it, too late. They will have missed him by minutes.

Slowly, Cal leads Barr into the thicket of trees that conceal the ruined castle, his mind desperately seeking an escape. It only occurs to him now he has a moment to think that this means Barr really doesn't know where Naomi is. As unbelievable as it seems, unless his delusions have reached another level, he hasn't killed her.

When they're standing in the clearing, he stops.

'Where is she?'

Cal braces, sensing Barr's frantic confusion. A rough hand spins him around so he almost falls, caught by surprise. For the first time, he sees the size of the blade – it looks like a hunting knife. He can't take his eyes from the shining length of it. Barr jabs it at him.

'Where is she?'

'I don't know.'

'You said she was here. You're lying.'

Barr is breathing heavily. His eyes are crazed and rolling, like a frightened horse.

'She wouldn't come to me, Jason. She's not here.'

'You've been talking to her. Turning her against me.'

'*She* called *me*.'

'That's a lie.'

Barr is advancing towards him, the point getting closer, so Cal is forced to back away, moving into the ruin until he feels the cold, uneven stone of the castle wall behind him.

'It's true. Why would I want to speak to her?'

'You're trying to destroy my life. You've taken her from me.'

'God, I fucking wish I could destroy your life,' Cal spits, suddenly far too angry to worry about the blade. 'You killed my sister.'

'I got off for that.' Barr's eyes are close together and would be piggy on his wide face were it not for the lack of light in them. They look like shark eyes, utterly devoid of humanity.

'We both know that's bullshit. Maybe Naomi—'

'Don't you fucking say her name.'

Something wild is raging in Cal. A sense that if he obeys this man, he is going to die. It's insane and illogical but there is no time to question it.

'Maybe *Naomi* finally realised who she'd married. What you've done.'

'I'm different now. That's all in the past.'

Cal holds his breath, wishing he dared press record on his phone. His hand moves towards his pocket as a test, but Barr comes closer and there's no way to reach it without being seen.

'Not for the families, it isn't,' he says, instead.

Barr's fist meets the side of his face unexpectedly quickly. His head whips round and smashes against the stone. He is stunned, disoriented, falling into the wall and feeling it wobble behind him. This ruin is not safe. There are signs everywhere telling visitors not to climb on it.

Barr punches him again. Through the pain and the confusion, Cal pictures Chrissie drinking coffee with Shona; he thinks of the gold in the car that Barr completely missed and wants to laugh. But he doesn't have time to think more, because Barr has him by the collar of his T-shirt, hauling him up as Cal writhes and tries to get away.

Then Barr is slamming him against the castle wall and he can barely see, his skull rattling in his head and starbursts appearing like fireworks across his vision. He closes his eyes and all he can hear is Barr's heaving breath and growling anger. The stone behind him wobbles, dust rains down.

He opens his eyes and sees two figures running across the green of the clearing. They're moving fast, but stealthily. He has blood in his eyes from a cut in his head, but he recognises Detective Matthews and a uniformed officer. The PC is carrying a Taser. Barr transfers the knife to his right hand and grabs Cal's hair.

'Tell me where she is,' he screams into Cal's face, pulling him round.

The officers halt, ten metres away, just as Barr sees them out of the corner of his eye. He reacts like lightning, whipping round and yanking Cal in front of him, knife held to his throat. Cal is lifted like he's weightless. He closes his eyes. There is now no clear path for the Taser.

'Put the knife down,' Matthews yells. 'Put the knife down and your hands above your head.' She's making a valiant attempt but Cal can see that the uniformed officer's hand is shaking on the Taser and he doesn't have a lot of faith that Barr can even hear their words, never mind listen to reason.

'Get back!' Barr waves the knife in their direction, gripping Cal tighter.

'Jason,' he mumbles through the pain. 'You're making everything worse for yourself.'

'Shut up,' he screams in Cal's ear. 'I want my wife.'

But Cal can't shut up. 'It hurts, doesn't it,' he says. 'When someone you love is missing and you can't see them, can't touch them, don't know if they're lying hurt somewhere… what someone might have done to them.'

'Shut up!' Barr wails.

'You lie awake, picturing them. Thinking about their last moments. How much pain they were in, what he did to them. How someone you love so much could mean so little.'

'Stop!' He almost feels Barr break.

As the man moves the knife towards Cal's throat, he sees a flash of red. For an insane second, he thinks it is his sister, watching with the ghosts of this place, so real is she in his memory and thoughts. But then his vision clears.

Chrissie is at the back of the clearing with Shona. She steps out from under a tree and he sees the tears pouring down her cheeks, the stricken look on her face as Shona holds her arm, stopping her from running forward to him.

Everything stills. He looks into his daughter's eyes and sees her pain, her mouth opening wide in a scream as Barr raises the knife and Detective Matthews starts to run towards them, everything in slow motion. Cal smells the dry grass, the mossy decay of the castle, the ancient stone.

This is not happening. They will not watch him die.

Taking a deep breath, he closes his eyes and rams Barr backwards into the ruin. Unbalanced by the unexpected force, the huge weight of the man slams into the wall, his hand flying out to the side. At the same moment, Cal dives forward, away from Barr and the unstable structure, hitting the ground with a burst of pain that almost knocks him unconscious.

He can hear the grinding of rocks, the animal cry of frustration and anger from Barr, and the scream from his daughter's throat – and he braces as he rolls and rolls and rolls. He lies winded, turning his head in time to see Barr scrambling to right himself. As he does, a huge piece of masonry tumbles from above, hitting Barr's shoulder so he once more falls back on the wall and the whole thing starts to crumble, pieces dropping around him like rain.

The wall teeters above them.

Barr covers his head and cowers against it.

'Move,' Cal yells, despite himself. 'Move out of the way!'

But Barr is taking so long to sense the true danger. Detective Matthews has reached Cal and she pulls him up by his arm. Both of them are shouting at the killer to get out of the way. With an exasperated noise, the detective moves forward to help the man, just as the stone grinds apart above and Barr seems to come to his senses, a look of panic crossing his face. Cal looks up and sees sky and death above him.

Karma. Just desserts. But Matthews is in the firing line.

He isn't thinking, he can't be thinking. There is no time to tell the detective that it's not worth saving this animal. Instead, he dashes forward with her and between them they grab Barr and pull, the three of them staggering then falling out onto the grass, as the entire back wall comes down in a thunderous roar of rock and destruction.

CHAPTER SIXTY-FIVE

Cal lies perfectly still for a moment. Jason Barr is half on top of him. Matthews is the first to move, leaping to her feet and reaching for handcuffs. Cal crawls away from them, meeting Chrissie and Shona as they run across the clearing, sobbing. Dropping to their knees, they both wrap their arms around him. Though everything hurts, Cal holds on tight.

'How did you find me?' he croaks.

'Matthews saw you driving away. She showed up at the lodge and said you were supposed to be there,' Shona says. 'We realised something was wrong.'

Chrissie half-laughs, half-sobs. 'We used Find My Phone.'

Cal smiles. 'Invasion of privacy,' he says, wincing as his face cracks with pain. 'Ow.'

The instinct to turn and face the predator is strong. Afraid to look, he is nevertheless compelled to seek out Barr, to make sure he's contained. That he isn't either running away or crushed beneath the fallen masonry. He could be dead now. Cal ignores the twang inside him that wishes he was.

Barr is lying on the ground, his cheek mashed into the earth while Detective Matthews cuffs his beefy hands behind him. The other officer is on his radio, calling for backup, while centuries-old dust hovers in the air above the castle, and Jason Barr stares at Cal with hatred as he is manhandled into a sitting position to be read his rights.

Two more officers sprint into the clearing and take in the sight.

'He's refusing to give his name,' Detective Matthews approaches Cal.

'That's the murderer Jason Barr,' he says. 'I'll give you the number of someone who can help. She's going to think Christmas has come early.' The thought of Foulds' reaction is amusing. Maybe this will make up for Cal's secrecy around Naomi Barr's calls.

'That's two statements we're going to need from you, but you should get some medical treatment first,' Matthews says. 'Maybe try not to get into any more trouble for an hour or two?'

Cal grins at her, then casts one last look at the thunderous Barr as he is frogmarched past them by three officers.

'Come on.' Chrissie tugs his arm. 'We should go...'

'Oh. Wait.' DS Matthews swivels, a panicked look on her face. 'The gold bars.' She looks over at the tumbled ruin. 'They're not...'

'No.' Cal shakes his head. 'They're in the back of my car. I think Barr was sitting on them.'

-

The rest of the afternoon passes in a blur of statement-taking and phone calls. Chrissie keeps hugging Cal, tearful every time she thinks about Barr, and she won't let him out of her sight. Shona is pale and quiet.

Foulds insists on speaking to Cal herself. He takes the call on the sofa in the lodge, gauze stuck over the cut from Barr's knife. He's been cleared by the doctor and has maxed out on paracetamol and ibuprofen.

'Sometimes I think you have nine lives,' she tells him.

'Is that your way of saying you're wishing an historic castle had fallen on my head?'

She sighs. 'No. You did a stupid thing, but I think you've probably been punished enough.' Cal can hear the smile in her voice. 'We got him. Kidnapping, assault, attempted murder if we can make it stick. Whichever way you cut it, he's back in jail for some time.'

He exhales and they are silent for a moment together, both taking in the events of the day. But, when she speaks again, Foulds' tone is grave.

'Did he say anything about her? About where she is or what he did with her?'

'Naomi? No. I know this is going to sound mad, but I don't think he knows. He thought she was here.'

'You don't know where she is, do you?' The sternness in her voice makes him feel guilty even though he hasn't done anything.

'I promise I would tell you if I did. Lesson learned.'

'How can she just vanish?' Foulds says.

'I wish I knew.'

As he says goodbye to her, he can see Ian walking up towards their lodge. He points him out to Chrissie and she goes to meet him. The older man looks heavy to Cal, tired. This investigation, the truth, has taken its toll. Matthews has told him that Fearghas is too old to pursue through the courts, even if they could prove he did murder Morna on the hillside. He's going to have to break it to Ian.

But when the older man enters the lodge, Cal can see immediately that something is wrong.

'What's happened?'

'You've had a hell of a day, mate, I don't want to burden you…'

'I'm fine, Ian, totally fine. Sit.'

Ian slumps onto the sofa and Cal waits for him to catch his breath.

'I got a call from Rose,' he says. 'She couldn't reach you. Fearghas passed away ten minutes ago.'

The three of them stare at each other. Ian lets out a bitter laugh. 'You couldn't make this up, could you?'

'I'm so sorry,' Chrissie says to Ian, her voice faltering.

He puts his hand on her shoulder. 'Thank you, we were just a little bit too late. At least I got to look the bastard in the eye.'

As well as frustration over the secrets Fearghas takes to his grave, Cal feels a beat of sorrow for Rose and Tavish. The man was a powerful force in their lives and has left turmoil at the end for them to deal with. Despair pulses inside him. How much damage has the podcast done? Is any of it worth it?

Ian is watching his face as if he knows what Cal is thinking. 'If it wasn't for you, I wouldn't know what happened to my mother,' he says. 'We have more information now than I thought we would ever have. It's going to give all of us some peace.'

'I just wish we could have filled in the blanks for you,' Cal tells him.

He feels the hills at his back, wrapping themselves back around dark secrets. He sighs. It is as it is. Podcasts have messy endings because lives do.

CHAPTER SIXTY-SIX

Coffee fuels the morning start and when he's dropped a weary Ian at the airport, Cal drives back, stopping at the village north of the loch. The sun is shining across the water, turning it a deep glittery blue, but he thinks there's a coolness to the air that wasn't there before, more of a breeze. Sure enough, there's a small sailing boat tacking a line away from him, its sail puffed and full.

He's parking outside the lodge when Chrissie runs out to him.

'Dad! How did it go? I've been waiting for you to get back.'

'It was okay... why? What's happened?' His mind flies to bad news. She looks worried and it sends chills through his veins.

'There was a man here. He knocked on the door and said he'd seen the leaflet, and they were just leaving for home but he's been holidaying here for years and he recognised Morna.'

'What?'

'Yes. The grown-up version. He said he once gave a woman a lift to the start of the track up the hill. He thinks it was approximately twenty years ago.'

'You're kidding?'

'No. He remembered her when he saw the picture. He hadn't seen the previous appeals or the news coverage until this week. He wasn't going to say anything but his family said he should before he left. Someone in the village told him where to find us.'

'And where is he?'

'That's the thing. He had to drive back to Devon and I knew I couldn't reach you, so I recorded an interview with him. I'm sorry. I didn't know what to do. What he said complicates things.'

Her forehead is creased and she looks so like the small child who hand-painted the hallway at home while his back was turned that he wants to laugh.

'And you think that's going to make me mad?'

'Yes, no, maybe?' She squints at him.

'I'm not mad, Chrissie. I'm thrilled. Are you going to get out of the doorway so I can come in and have a listen to your maiden voyage into podcasting?'

'Yes. Quickly.'

He sits down at the table while she pulls up the recording on his laptop.

'I used the proper mics.'

He presses play and immediately the clear bell of her voice sounds, introducing Derek Knowles and taking him through his history with the area, the fact that he and his wife used to holiday here with their children and are now reliving the memories with their grandchildren after a fifteen-year hiatus. She effortlessly makes him comfortable and guides him through the important questions skilfully, making Cal puff with pride. He pauses to tell her.

'You're really good at this, love. It's enjoyable listening to you.'

'Dad!' She's biting her nails, anxiety in her eyes. 'Keep listening… You haven't got to the important bit yet.'

The nervous impatience hits home and he restarts the recording.

'Thank you for coming forward. Can you tell me what you remember about giving Morna a lift?'

'Well, a woman stuck out her thumb as I was passing and I know you're not supposed to pick people up these days, but back then it was a bit different and she really didn't look like your stereotypical dangerous hitchhiker, if you know what I mean?'

'She wasn't very threatening.'

'No.' [He chuckles] 'She was silver-haired and stern but I didn't think she was going to rob me.'

'What was she wearing?'

'I don't really remember. I think she was dressed for hill-walking. She asked me if I was going along the loch and if I could drop her at Lawers, about halfway along. I'd been doing some shopping in Aberfeldy and we were staying at the far end of the loch, so there didn't seem any harm. We left at the end of the week and I never knew she'd died up there. I feel awful.'

'It really wasn't your fault.'

'Maybe not, but I keep wondering if there's something I should have spotted, you know?'

'That's just natural. I don't think there's anything you could have done in this case. What did she seem like in the car?'

'She wasn't chatty, but we did speak. Now that I think of it, she only asked me questions. Didn't volunteer any information herself, as far as I can remember. When I dropped her off, I asked if she'd be okay and she gave me a thumbs up. I drove off and hadn't thought about it until I saw that picture they were handing out in the village the other day. Even then, it didn't hit me until the middle of the night that it could be her. I went back and checked the photo, and I'm sure it was. I don't know how useful this is, though.'

'It helps us work out the details. It's good of you to take the time. Where did you pick her up?'

'Outside the church at the north end of the loch.'

'I know where you mean. It's not near the bus stop so she must have walked through the village. Had she been to a church service, do you think?'

'I've no idea. That's odd, though. I'd totally forgotten until now...'

'Forgotten what?'

'No, maybe it's nothing.'

'Honestly, anything could help us build up a picture of her state of mind and movements.'

'Well, as we started to drive away, a man came sprinting through the churchyard. I don't think I've ever seen someone move that fast. It looked like he wanted to speak to her. I asked if she wanted to stop and she said no.'

'That's odd.'

'I thought so at the time, but I had ice cream in the shopping and I didn't really think about it. When she told me to just go, I went.'

'Do you remember anything about the man?'

'Well, yes. He was wearing robes. He was the minister.'

'You said he was sprinting? Wasn't he a bit old for that, even then?'

'I don't understand what you mean?'

'It's just... The old minister would have been in his seventies.'

'This man wasn't old. He was barely forties, I'd say.'

Chrissie leans over and clicks off the recording.

'Holy shit.' Cal stares at his daughter. The cabin is silent apart from the thrumming of the fridge and the fan on the laptop as it desperately tries to cool itself.

'I know. Right? It wasn't Fearghas running down the path after Morna.'

'It was Tavish.'

Cal rubs his face with his hands, trying to wake his addled mind.

'He met her, and he never said a word.'

CHAPTER SIXTY-SEVEN

Cal drives to the village at the head of the loch, alone. In the car, beside him, he has a sympathy card that Chrissie sketched for Rose and Tavish, the first time he's seen his daughter pick up art materials for a long while. It's an elegant pen sketch of the loch with the church rising on its mound at the end. They both added their condolences. But it's just an excuse.

He strolls through the village towards the church, white and gleaming as it was on the day they arrived, but concealing far more than he had ever imagined. Sweat trickles down his back in the close heat. Rumour has it there will be rain soon. Much needed, something to wash away the dust and the past.

Cal lifts the heavy door knocker and brings it down twice. He waits a long time, disappointed that it looks like no one is in, but then the door swings back and Rose stands there, wrestling with her walker and the heavy door. Her features are etched with worry.

'Oh, I'm sorry,' he says, brimming with guilt. 'I didn't want to disturb you, I was just dropping off a card. I'm so sorry for your loss, Rose.'

He hates these words; they always seem so inadequate. Even when they're not said under false pretences.

She looks up at him, her previously clear blue eyes now troubled water.

'I think you'd better come in.'

She beckons Cal into the hallway and closes the door behind them, casting them into a muted, stale kind of quiet. The house feels like it needs a good airing. It can't be damp in this weather, but it smells musty, feels like a museum of artefacts, not a living, breathing home.

'It's Tavish,' Rose says. 'I'm worried about him. I need your help.'

Cal isn't here to help.

'Grief can be such a personal—'

But Rose shakes her head. 'It isn't that. We've been grieving for Fearghas for months now, waiting for the end. This is more.'

Without waiting for an answer, she shuffles forward and presses a hand to the study door. 'Tavish,' she says. 'Cal Lovett has come to see you.'

There is no sound from within. Rose looks at Cal. 'Please,' she says. 'Talk to him.'

He clears his throat, wishing desperately that he didn't have to do this. But he owes Ian and Morna, Violet, Jane. 'I'll try,' he says, pushing the door open.

The state of the room shocks him. The office has been ransacked: drawers lie open, papers spill onto the floor and precious knick-knacks are scattered. Cal leans down and picks up a glass paperweight that lies at his feet, setting it on the bookshelf to one side.

At the desk, Tavish sits, motionless and slumped forward. He hasn't stirred at Cal's entrance or his mother's words and Cal would think he was asleep were it not for the wide staring eyes, unfocused and red-rimmed. Tavish's gaze rests on a photograph on the desk. Cal steps closer.

'Tavish,' he says. 'It's Cal Lovett. I've come to pay my respects.'

The man remains still, so Cal moves closer, craning his neck to see what Tavish is staring at so intently. He imagined that it would be a picture of his father, but in fact Tavish is looking at himself in his minister's robes as a younger man, fresh-faced and grinning, surrounded by a group of smiling children.

'That's a nice picture,' he says, wondering if he should stay or leave Tavish to his sadness. No matter what Rose says, Cal doesn't think you can prepare yourself for the loss of a parent, even one as tyrannical and flawed as Fearghas seems to have been. Perhaps it's even harder in those cases – too many regrets and uncertainties, too many 'what ifs'.

Tavish picks up the framed image and holds it on his lap.

'It was a trip to the beach with a group of city kids,' he says. 'Most of them had never seen the sea. It was bloody freezing but they paddled and we bought them ice cream anyway. On the way back, one of the boys told me it was the best day of his life.' A tear drips onto the picture and Tavish wipes it away. 'I think it was probably the best day of mine, too.'

Cal's heart twists despite himself. He perches on the window seat a couple of feet away so he can be on the same level.

'It's going to take time,' he says. 'Grief can floor you, and your father was a huge influence in your life.'

At this, Tavish looks up and meets Cal's eyes for the first time. There's something raw and stripped away that almost frightens him. It's like looking into the bleak darkness of Lochan Nan Cat.

'I think we both know this isn't about him,' Tavish says, quietly. He stares at Cal, his dark eyes challenging him to make the next move.

Cal swallows. He is watching a man boil over in front of him. In the end it is easier to be blunt. 'You saw Violet when she came here twenty years ago.'

Tavish closes his eyes and it is a momentary relief to be out of the vortex-like gaze, a break from the man's despair.

'I should never have come back here,' Tavish says. 'I was happy. Making my own life, away from him. But then he got sick and needed to retire, and it seemed the obvious thing. My calling.' He touches the picture. 'Now I see that it pulled me away from my path and it led to...' He shakes his head as if trying to dislodge water from his ears, then buries his face in his hands. 'I keep trying to forget,' he says. 'I had almost forgotten. But then you came here. Asking questions, bringing everything back up again.'

'Did you already know you had a brother, or did she tell you?'

Tavish moans at the thought of Ian. 'How could I look him in the eye, knowing what I know, what I've done?'

'And what is that?'

There's a long silence, Tavish shaking his head back and forth. Cal takes advantage of his distraction and reaches into his pocket to start recording. He feels hot and guilty as he does, but Ian and his family need answers, and this could be their only chance to hear them directly.

'She was looking for him, not me.'

'She came to the church to see Fearghas?'

'I don't think she had planned it. She kept saying she had to go back there, that she knew he'd hidden it, that she was going to finally tell the truth. I didn't understand what she meant.'

'You thought she was going to tell the truth about their affair? Tell everyone that Fearghas had fathered her child.'

'She couldn't,' he whispers. 'My mother. She didn't deserve the humiliation.'

'Had you known about her before then? Did you know you had a brother?'

'No.' His eyes fill and his face contorts. 'But I knew it was a possibility. I don't know if she was the first, but she wasn't the last woman my father "helped" a bit too much. He always did it under cover of good deeds, which made it even worse.'

'Is that why you submitted your DNA to the ancestry site?'

'I never should have done that. If I hadn't...' Tavish rubs his face. 'I was a teenager when I first saw him with someone. It changed everything for me. I'd idealised him before then. I've never really been able to forgive him – though I've tried. I've prayed on it. It felt like I was colluding with him after that, to protect my mother. She couldn't know...'

'But she did know.'

'I know that now,' he roars. 'I was trying to protect her and all along she knew!'

'But when Morna came here, you were trying to make sure your mother wasn't upset. I can understand that, anyone would.'

Tavish just stares at Cal pleadingly. As if he can change it all.

Cal's senses are tingling.

'We spoke to someone who gave Morna a lift to the path to the lochan,' he says, gently. 'He remembers seeing you running out of the church in a hurry, trying to catch up with her.'

'I just needed to talk to her,' he says. 'That's all.'

'So what happened next?'

'I drove after them. I knew the road so I was able to catch up, but the driver dropped her at the path and by the time I'd found a safe place to park, she'd vanished, up into the woods.'

'So what did you do?'

'I should have gone home, left it.'

'You followed her.'

'I was so upset and so angry with my father, with her. I just wanted to talk to her properly, to ask her not to expose him. To tell her that it wouldn't do any good, he was retired, no longer serving as a minister. It was done. But in the church she kept talking about a crash. She said he had to pay, they both had to pay... I didn't understand. She was raving. And then when we were interrupted by a parishoner, she left. I almost caught up with her but that man had given her a lift.'

The room is still, as if the house is listening as well. Cal sits motionless, not wanting to stop Tavish's stream of confession and the filling of the gaps in the narrative.

'And where did you catch up with her on the hill?'

'I lost her a couple of times but then I saw the green coat, high above me, near the lochan. I'd thought she was going for one of the peaks, as they're the better travelled pathways. That's where everyone goes. But she wasn't.'

'What were you hoping to achieve?'

'I don't know.' He wails the words, striking his forehead once with the heel of his hand. 'I was so worked up, I just got more and more upset as I climbed. She was so strong. By the time I reached the lochan, she'd vanished. I was going to turn around and come back. It was like I was bewitched, following a wisp across the bogs. It's such an ungodly place, I can't explain it.'

'I know,' Cal says.

He remembers the feeling of watchfulness at the lochan, the claustrophobia of the crowding peaks. Lying there with Lucie, waiting.

'Then I saw her,' he says. 'Above, climbing towards some rocks.'

Cal can picture the climb so easily – the great drifts of black peat and tufted grasses, springy heather.

'I just wanted to talk to her,' Tavish says. 'That's all. I just wanted to ask her not to say anything that would hurt my mother.'

Like the clouds parting at the peak to show the landscape laid out below, Cal can suddenly see it all.

'That wasn't what she was planning to expose,' he says. 'Was it?'

CHAPTER SIXTY-EIGHT

MORNA, 2003

She's both fleeing and coming home. As Morna walks, her muscles scream and her memory stutters. One moment, she is an old woman with aches and creaks in her limbs, the next she's little more than a child, trailing after a powerful man, taking the crumbs of affection he offers, not realising that he's taking payment and that the price she's paying is far too high. She ploughs on, trying to outwalk the torrent of realisations.

Quickening her pace, she presses her thighs with her hands for support, up through the trees and over a stile onto the windswept hill. Now progress is slightly easier, following little more than a sheep track on the edge of a steep gorge. At the bottom, the river tumbles over stones in a series of falls and pools.

She pauses a moment and drinks the last drops from her bottle. No matter – there is a wee bridge across the stream just a little further, when the path takes you down into the gorge with the roaming sheep. She can refill her bottle there.

Stupid, so stupid to go to the church. But after not being recognised in the pub, she'd decided to risk it. Just to see. Just to look the devil in the eyes. It had never really occurred to her that he wouldn't be there, in all his arrogant superiority and his sexual deviance. She came here to punish herself, but somewhere along the journey she looked again. Looked again with new eyes. Saw the past as an adult, not a child.

Only a child. Turning to her minister seemed such a natural thing to do. The right thing to do when at home there was cold and the bottle and a quick temper that blamed her for the loss of her mother. If only she'd talked to Ian all those years ago when he tried to get her to speak. He would have helped her to see. Wouldn't he? Or would he have been so disgusted that he'd have turned away?

Up she goes, her eyes fixed on the horizon, simultaneously fleeing and coming home. Her soul throbs with the pain of being here. Her eyes cannot take in all of this beauty, it's too much. She could stare at the river for days as it makes its dance from the hill, down to the vastness of the great loch below. The bogs and hillsides are covered with a thousand plants and textures: the dark, soft earth and the squelching green mosses, the safety of the hard tufts of grass which signpost the places where you will not sink. Her body sings out that she's home from exile.

Is this a betrayal of her family, her adopted country? She cannot square the circle. All she knows is that she's crying properly for the first time since she left all those years ago, as if she has been unstoppered and her grief is pouring out.

Morna doesn't know why she's here, what she hopes to achieve, but she has to see where they were to believe it, to reassure herself that she did not imagine it all. Then, she will tell the truth. She'll reveal what lies beneath the water.

Suddenly, there it is, arresting her thoughts and bringing her to a halt. The lochan, impenetrable and still, nestled in the crook of the mountains. Nothing moves before her, save the lone elegant drift of a heron, unsettled by her movement and taking itself further down the lochan for peace. After resting a moment, she fills her bottle at the rushing stream and turns her eyes to the grassy platform above. Not far now. Almost there.

She is intent on her journey: moving without pause, her thoughts and memories racing and colliding, limbs burning with exertion. When she reaches that place, she collapses onto the green platform with relief, sweat cooling on her as she presses her forehead to the earth.

It is there, as she lies prone, sucking in air, that he finds her.

Morna cries out as he steps over the lip of the rise onto the platform. For a second, it is him: clerical collar, those dark eyes and bushy eyebrows, the unhappy expression a blast of ice from the past. But that image dissolves. It is the son, that is all, the slight traces of her own child in his face.

'What are you doing here?' She scrambles to her feet and the wind whips the words out into the sky.

'You just left,' he shouts. 'You tell me my father is a monster, that I have a brother I've never met and that you're going to destroy my mother's peace of mind, and then you just walk away? He's an old man. What good are you planning to do with this?'

'It's about doing what's right!' She feels dizzy up here. The lochan is mocking her distress so she will mock him too, this child of her tormentor. 'You're supposed to be a man of the church – are you just like him? A hypocrite beneath that public image?'

She sees she's hit home. His face clouds. 'I'm trying to protect my mother. You're going to destroy her happiness with this talk of an affair, a child. It was over fifty years ago!'

Morna stares at him a moment and then tosses her head back and laughs, wildly, wickedly. Tears stream down her face. 'Is that what you think this is about? I don't care about that! It happened. I have a son and he's a gift – all the more so for keeping him well away from your father. He's like his real father, thank God, and he's miles from here.'

'Then why are you here?'

Morna stills. Her hands are shaking. She steadies herself and steps towards him.

'Your father had me kill a man,' she says. 'I'm here to confess. To tell the truth.'

The minister shakes his head. 'I don't believe you.'

But Morna's crying hard now. 'He did! I tried to save him and I hit that man over the head for him. And the thanks I got? He told me he was dead. He called me a murderer! I wasn't.' She sobs. 'Not then, I wasn't.'

'What are you talking about?' But she can't speak for a moment and the man steps forward and puts his hands on her shoulders and shakes her hard. 'Tell me!' And he is Fearghas again, looming and awful. Morna cries out, tries to escape, pushing against him so he's off balance, but then he recovers enough to lash out and push her back, and she's on the edge and then she's falling…

It's going to hurt, she thinks, as she tumbles down the rich and beautiful slope, the lochan rising up to meet her. She doesn't see the rock in her path, though she feels the crack on the back of her head for a second as she hits it. Everything flashes through her in that instant. Hands around Fearghas's neck, throttling. Striking the airman, stunning him. The grief and guilt she felt as she weighted him down and sent him to a watery grave. Fearghas taking the gold while she buried the man in the lochan. She saw it, God help her, took just one shining bar. Her ticket out of here, selling her soul to the devil forever.

Some of it was self-defence – she had to stop him hurting Fearghas. But what came after that… It took her so long to understand. The bubbles. Spiralling upwards, peppering the surface. It came to her later, what they meant. A dawning of horror as she's lived her life. The man wasn't dead when she sank him. He was still alive.

CHAPTER SIXTY-NINE

Cal is frozen on the window seat, his eyes fixed on Tavish, though the man is twenty years away now and can't see him. Instead, he is on a windswept hillside, watching the woman he has pushed tumbling to her death. His chin trembles. If they weren't pressed between his knees, his hands would be doing the same.

'I carried her back,' he says. 'To the platform. I didn't know what to do.' His eyes are swollen, his voice cracked from his story. 'I was going to come down and get help.' Cal says nothing. 'I was.'

'So what happened?'

'She stopped breathing. I didn't know what to do. When I reached my car, it all seemed so far away. Like a dream. A terrible nightmare. As if maybe it never happened at all.'

'But her family. When she was found, you could have told the authorities who she was, that you'd met her in the church. Then at least they could have buried her.'

He's shaking his head again, over and over. 'But there would have been questions. I couldn't.' Tavish raises his head to Cal again, then his eyes slide to the window. 'I buried her. I've been watching over her. She's safe.'

He thinks of the damage to Morna's skull. He thinks Tavish is lying. Telling the story he can almost live with.

'What happened to her bag?'

'What do you mean?'

'She had a bag with her. You must have gone back?'

Tavish's eyes glaze.

'I threw it in the rubbish. I'm so sorry.'

Cal feels a wave of exhaustion swooping over him.

He knows now. Ian will know too. And the rest of his family. And the police.

'You need to tell your mother,' he says as he stands. 'She's worried about you.'

Tavish looks up at him like he's a child desperate for approval.

'I didn't mean to hurt her.'

Cal can't give him the absolution he wants.

When the police arrive, he plays the recording for Matthews while Tavish waits in the kitchen with his mother. As he slips from the house, he breathes more easily in the clean air. He stands at the gate, filling his lungs, as the first drops of rain start to fall. From the hotel opposite, streams of people emerge, their hands to the sky. When they feel the drops and smell the petrichor, they whoop and shriek until he smiles despite himself. They stand in the downpour and he watches them dance.

CHAPTER SEVENTY

EPISODE EIGHT: SINS OF THE FATHERS

People who kill are different to the rest of us, aren't they? We aren't like them. We couldn't take life, lash out and cause that sort of pain. They must be evil or different. It's too frightening to think otherwise. And yet. Tavish Dewar was a minister in church. For years he did nothing but good, helping his parishioners, devoting his free time to charitable causes, taking orphaned children on holiday. Arguably, he wasn't just like you or me – he was even better.

But now he's on bail awaiting trial, having been charged with the manslaughter of Violet Martin, the name Morna Duff went by when she died in 2003. For twenty years, Tavish kept secret what happened on the hill that day, but now the story has come bursting out, like the torrential rains that have caused mayhem and mudslides in the aftermath of the heatwave.

While he waits to go before the court, Tavish is spending all the time he can with his mother, Rose. Together they often sit by the shore of Loch Tay and look out at the waves created by the wind, talking and waiting. Now they have shared their secrets, they can understand the past a little better.

His mother finds it hard to hold the two images of her son together.

'He never should have been in this position. It was all down to Fearhgas.'

Her denial is understandable – he is all she has left. But Tavish made his own decisions back then and now he has to pay for them.

Rose will not be alone during the trial. As well as the people in the village who drop gifts of food on the doorstep of her home, support has come from an unlikely quarter. Tavish's half-brother Ian has returned to the Highlands. They've met briefly and will do again.

'My real father was the best man you'd ever hope to meet. He didn't hold grudges or have any place for hate, and I know this is what he would want me to do.'

Ian and his sisters have already made a pilgrimage to the place where their mother died. A plaque is mounted in that secret place if you know where to look. They were joined by Lucie Barnes, the hiker and social media star whose accident in the hills led to developments in Morna's case. Lucie's broken ankle has healed and she now works as an advocate for survivors of domestic abuse.

'It changed a lot for me, going back there. I'd built it up in my mind to be a terrifying landscape, full of menace and evil, but it isn't like that. The water doesn't frighten me anymore and my nightmares have stopped. It just had secrets to share, that's all. No one was listening.'

We say goodbye to Ian and his sisters in the churchyard on the day Morna's new stone is lifted into place. The family have decided that her remains have been disturbed enough and that she will rest here. They have brought some of their father's ashes to inter with her. As the stone is set in position, a cold breeze blows off the loch and misty rain touches its hand to our skin.

The inscription is simple.

Violet Morna Jane. Beloved wife and mother.

Born 1936, died 2003.

If there's another world, she lives in bliss.

EPILOGUE

With Shona needed back in Aberdeen, Cal and Chrissie stay to tie up loose ends. They hunker in the cabin and watch the ground pool with water. The crevice of the burn fills and overflows, singing with rain running over hard earth, flooding down to the loch. It smells so fresh and new.

His daughter makes him a cup of tea.

'Here. Are you okay?'

Cal nods. 'Just getting my head around it all.'

'Have you heard from Foulds? Is she still in Edinburgh?'

'Barr's not talking. It doesn't matter. They have enough to charge him and he won't be bailed.'

'But still no news of Naomi?'

'None.' Cal stares at the flooded ground outside, unable to absorb this volume of water.

'Do you believe that he didn't hurt her?'

'If he did, then he'd blanked it out. He's not that good an actor – I saw his eyes and he really wanted me to tell him where she is.'

Chrissie sighs. The two of them sip their tea.

'I've made a decision,' she says after a while. 'About what I want to do next year.'

'You have?'

She looks shy for a moment.

'I want to switch to journalism.'

Cal feels a smile breaking across his face. He tries to contain it, to ask the right sort of responsible parental question.

'Are you sure?'

But it's an unnecessary question. He can see the resolve on her face, a sort of glow of certainty and excitement around her that hasn't been there for a while.

'I love connecting with people, Dad. I want to be out meeting them, talking to them, making a difference. Journalism is the right thing for me. Doing that interview and making the link about Tavish mattered. I've loved this summer. And don't worry, I'm not doing it to please you or anything stupid.'

Cal laughs.

'Sometimes it can take a while to find these things out about ourselves,' he says. 'At the start of this summer, I thought I was done with this. Podcasting, investigating. It's so messy and painful sometimes, but then when it all comes together...'

'It's a rush,' she finishes.

'It really is.'

'You're good at this, Dad. You make a difference.'

He holds out an arm and Chrissie snuggles next to him.

'For what it's worth, I know you'll be amazing at it. You have a way with people, you always have.'

He plants a kiss on her tangled curls.

—

When they go to bed, it is still raining.

Something wakes Cal. He lies there in the dark for a moment before he realises what it is. His phone is ringing.

Rolling to the side of the bed, he reaches for the handset and raises it to his ear, knowing without looking at the display who it will be.

'Hello?'

There's a silence and a stillness at the other end of the line. Then he hears a woman crying, her breath hitching and ragged. His heart skips a beat.

'It's okay,' he says. 'They have him in custody. He isn't getting out. Not for a while. It's safe now.'

'I've caused such a mess.'

'Where have you been? What happened?'

'We had a fight. He hit me and I just ran. I've been staying in one of my ex-husband's holiday properties. I broke in. At first I wanted to punish him, but then everything got out of control and... I just couldn't tell anyone. I'm so ashamed. If I hadn't run, then Jason wouldn't have attacked you. It's all my fault.'

The sobs increase in tempo and volume.

'No,' he says, firmly. 'Nothing he does is your fault. He is one hundred per cent responsible for his own actions.'

'I'm sorry,' she says. 'I've been so stupid. He made me feel wanted and protected until...'

'Until he didn't.'

'He could have killed you,' she whispers.

'It'll take more than that,' he says, trying to tamp down his own fears – the fact that his daughter almost watched her father die. Barr's wife needs help, not censure. This is his chance to get it right.

'Naomi,' he says, half out of bed already, reaching for his clothes, mentally preparing to rouse Foulds and tell her the news, grabbing his keys. 'Tell me where you are. I'm coming to get you.'

Acknowledgements

Unknown is set in the Loch Tay area of the Scottish Highlands, where the villages of Kenmore and Killin sit at either end of its deep waters. The geography and the setting in the book are a blend of fact and fiction, so are inspired by rather than faithful to the reality, which I highly recommend you visit if you ever have the chance.

At Killin, you will find the ruins of Finlarig Castle and the Falls of Dochart, while a picturesque church stands at the Kenmore end of the loch in a graveyard filled with mossy, tilting stones. The lochan in the story is inspired by Lochan Nan Cat, a beautiful rather than sinister spot beneath the peaks of the Lawers range. The lochan is nowhere near as deep as my fictional version and, as far as I know, there is no secret platform on the hillside above it. The destructive heatwave that hits Scotland in the story is also thankfully entirely a product of my imagination.

As ever, huge thanks to my editor Louise Cullen, whose suggestions on the first draft helped me reshape the story in crucial ways, alongside the structural edit provided by the brilliant Miranda Ward. Thank you to Daniela Nava for her copyediting wisdom and gifs and to Vicki Vrint for proofreading. The whole process simply wouldn't work without Alicia Pountney, who keeps everything running and patiently reviews every messy version. Thank you to Andrew Smith for the gorgeous cover and to Kate Shepherd, Kim Yudelowitz and the wider Canelo team for everything you do to put my books in the hands of readers.

It's such a blessing to have the wonderful Charlotte Seymour in my corner. Your calm and supportive approach is the ideal backdrop to creativity. Thank you also to Anna Dawson, Ed Wilson and Hélène Butler at Johnson & Alcock for generally fabulous agenting and advice.

Graham Barlett and Jim Smith helped with police procedure and technical details in *Unknown* – thank you both. Anything less than true to life is totally my fault and down to my habit of willfully straying from the trodden path. Thanks also to my (not so little) brother Daniel Greig-Smith for patiently fielding my questions on 1950s aircraft and airspace, and to Sam Holland for sharing her extensive expertise on decomposition.

Rachel Wolf and Sam Holland read early versions of the manuscript and provided invaluable feedback – I am so lucky to have such generous and talented friends. Thank you. Likewise, the incredible Tammye Huf, Gillian Anton and Chris May all read and commented on the full manuscript – it's thanks to them there are no teabags in the 1950s scenes.

Pincers up to the Criminal Minds who provide both daily support and hefty doses of nonsense to make the writing hours so much more enjoyable. I learn so much from you all. I'm also incredibly grateful to the authors who've taken the time to read and blurb this book and others. Writing may be a solitary pursuit but the crime fiction world is one packed with colleagues and friends.

To my wonderful friends and family, a million thanks for the ongoing support and for keeping me sane when I decide to rewrite huge sections of the book at the eleventh hour. I'll try to avoid that next time. Will – thank you for the tech, plotting and emotional support, and for holding everything together while I disappear on book shop tours, research trips and writing retreats. Rachel and Adam, thank you for cheerfully trailing up Ben Lawers in the mist and rain and then for happily returning two days later to hike to Lochan Nan Cat. You deserve all the jelly babies. Murphy – thanks for diving into the lochan and conducting water-based research.

To the readers, bloggers and booksellers – none of this would be possible without you. It's a dream to be published and have you reading my stories. Thank you for reading, commenting on and recommending them. If you'd like to get in touch, I'd love to hear from you. You can find me on Instagram at heather.critchlow or join my VIP Reader's Club at www.heathercritchlow.com for news and book giveaways.

Do you love crime fiction and are always on the lookout for brilliant authors?

Canelo Crime is home to some of the most exciting novels around. Thousands of readers are already enjoying our compulsive stories. Are you ready to find your new favourite writer?

Find out more and sign up to our newsletter at canelocrime.com